HARD WINTER

HARD WINTER

ED HUTCHISON

bluebullseye press

Ascend and descend;

descend with Nephthys,

sink into darkness with the Night-bark.

Ascend and descend;

ascend with Isis,

rise with the Day-bark.

Pyramid Text Utterance 222 line 210

Wintering Over

They had only one redeemer come into their lives, but he died before he could save them, or he gave up (and then died anyway) before saving them—if they were capable of being saved at all. The potential was there, but the action didn't follow, at any rate. This family is of no significance. Theirs is an insignificant story, and it shouldn't be mistaken for anything other than the fact, the plainness of the fact, that it is inconsequential. It isn't a story of love, although there are significant moments of love, left mostly unexpressed: a wasted potential for love. Minor, they are beaten, pushed to the sidelines, made insignificant. This family takes little notice of others, except in the capacity of labeling haves—when they are, in comparison, self-labeled and equally self-demonstrated have-nots. Paralyzed by the perceptions of others, they fail to act.

Others, determined to be more significant, and events too, edge slowly past and, finally, firmly beyond their grasp, like muddy Ohio River waters pushing at a quicker pace, moving forward, while they stand motionless, rocking until they cease to rock. Before their collective, before the unit is snuffed out, they mire in internalized and externalized and perpetually unresolved squabbles and baser intrigues, the lowest common denominator, waiting for something imperative to happen to change these engulfing low circumstances. This something does not need to transpire within the context of the collective, to the family, but preferably to an individual within the collective—a greedy something of luck and good fortune for a change, changing everything, showing the others that they have been bested. They do not admit this, but know it is true. These are individuals who, by some sad luck of the draw, enter into domicile together in such a way that they are surprised by their tethering: a family wondering what they have in common, and how being common (in the basest sense) brings them into such close proximity with these others—surrounding, always surrounding, on top of, under, next to—whom they love and then unlove in the same measure.

This history begins with a downfall of the most moral kind, brought about in desperation, by consequences that remain the reverberations of any typical downfall. The mother resents them. Not for anything her children have done, but what they have done to her, what they have cost. She mixes resentment with the ferocity of love a mother has for her children. She does not tell why. She does not tell that she loves them. She cannot cede that, not to anyone. Through her, this collective is compelled to exist with the consequences of marching futilely on, without direction, or even perception that the results of their individual and collective actions could conclude in any other way. Her children resent her too—the poverty, the un-normalness—and, as a result of this lacking, they are unkind to each other. It is a desire to inflict defeat, but only as they perceive winning, inside the four shabby walls of a hovel. They are perversely, proportionally kind to strangers and friends, overly courteous as an apology for want. This they do in pantomime of what others do, what abstract families do, although it is somehow less lustrous and therefore more deceitful.

In contrast, this family parcels out jagged-edged affections to each other—hard-to-swallow, hard-to-embrace flinty shards that are not mineral-based, but a chink in the armor they erect against each other, managing survival. Overcome by some small, intimate victory or kindling of emotion, an uncontrolled welling-up of sentiment before it can be suppressed or forced down, they recoil as if struck. Her children are aware of the cost of the slip. They are not sincerely happy for the successes of others, as it makes apparent their own inability to succeed. In an attempt to control their surroundings, her children are compelled to be stingy with allowances of affection toward one another, as if giving them is a sort of wresting of a prize from a champion for a game with which they are unfamiliar. Reduced, they become a reluctant family, short on the affection afforded to others because that is the only thing left to withhold, to make into a rare thing, the one thing left that is of any value. It is a pricey commodity. Affections, once given, leave behind little resentments of loss, of having been cheated. This family does not fathom the embarrassment of mischance.

This Mother: hers is a convolution of unfortunate events. Her children are her history, the open equation. This is an attempt to tell her story, to capture the lives of a family fallen from social grace, living in the background, living without thriving, dying without mourning, except in the way individuals mourn, coddling the forced emotional affliction of death; that branded bit that does not sear the flesh but still leaves indelible traces; the loss that infiltrates a singular entity and not a collective—it does not happen to a family. It is the microcosm of loss. Death does come, but not yet. Not before the story is told.

Etta, Symsonia, KY 1900

It isn't her fault really, how Jeannie becomes a woman. It comes early, because she is obsessed with death. Gloating on it, twelve years old, the girl-child, one of four daughters to Marjorie and Marvin, granddaughter to Etta and Jesse, she can't be faulted for how she is reduced. Jeannie descends into a family that is borne on tradition. Jeannie gives witness to her mother unloving her father, an irrelevant fact in the dictating ministrations of Etta and Jesse's matchmaking. The stoic union of Marjorie and Marvin results in Jeannie being born of a respectable, community-approved liaison, somewhere between one brother and four sisters. There are no objections.

Three generations live in the large, white, turn-of-the-century farmhouse just past the hard bend in Oaks Road in Symsonia, outside of Paducah, in the last vestige of Kentucky before heading southwest through Missouri or Arkansas. It is an American-style Gothic horror family: stern and built by the religious zealots that overtook this country in its infancy, without affectations of fondness, but with plenty of discipline and labor. Each child is required to pull his weight, to make himself useful, to contribute to the overall common good. Theirs is a family clinging to remnants of a Southern American Dream that long ago faded, but nobody notices its lack of luster, or perhaps they posit that it is all still great despite fact and lack of contrarians. It is easier to pretend, after the Depression and two world wars and generations of consequences, recovering from that kind of want. Living respectably in a general less-than environment is a way of life for those around them, and eventually for them too. It is a step back that everyone in Symsonia collectively takes but pretends they haven't for the sake of appearances.

In the depressing 1930s, in Jesse and Etta's time, Kentucky and the states surrounding it are like the rest of the world. Everybody is poor, some poorer than others, and everyone scrambles to make up for it. The so-called Great Flood in Paducah and its surrounds leaves the working-poor destitute, living on cardboard boxes in the street, and those who still have a little something are little better off. As a fact of life, Symsonia families need male offspring to make up for the lack, perpetuate the family name, take over family businesses, and make money to sustain children who are not yet useful, or elders who outlive their usefulness.

Jesse, the patriarch, is sick, an invalid for most of his potentially lucrative years, exacerbating the want of males to bring in cash. The need is urgent. Etta sells assets as a counterfeit income for a while, thus leaving no assets, no income, and no sons to compensate for the loss. No amount of parsimony alleviates the fact that money is required to maintain a household. This is the family Jeannie is born into.

Limited by her sex, Jeannie watches Marjorie, her mother, demonstrate that her purpose is to become a woman quickly, to ease the lives of parents on the way to making a family of her own, and to care for grandparents who no longer serve a purpose. Jeannie also learns another unfortunate fact: girls cost money to keep and should marry off quickly. A union produces laboring sons that bring food to the table and money to the jar. There is no room for a love story in this kind of determination.

Symsonia has eyes for other people's trouble as a pastime, an intimate stage of performers, a tabloid of the insignificant. The Gothic farmhouse is most prominent as one sees it first, just after the hard bend in Oaks Road, and that's how everybody knows them, knows all about them, and keeps tabs on them, and everybody else, in a neighborly and kindly way—unless you deviate. Your neighbors correct you, put you in your place for your own good. Scandals are sought after by folks with little to do. Drinkers and suspicion of drinking is the lowest tread of gossip. Sex scandals are at the top and last a generation or longer. Culprits are run out of town by an onslaught of sermons and public shaming. Seemingly casual conversation passes the day: those connections, those little knowing's that everybody has about everybody else in that kind of town. It is comfortable. Jeannie's family is no different from the rest.

Marjorie falls victim to the town's base discourse. Her death arrives suddenly, violently, and with egregious consequences for her actions; her death is spectacular. The last survivor of

Etta and Jesse's three children, in her death she abandons her children to a widowed father and two grandparents, removing the familial core, but the debris orbits the void. Marvin, too, Marjorie's husband, drifts away from them all after her death, leaving only his body behind. With Marjorie's absence, he becomes a phantom, a speechless specter.

It takes only one anomalous sputtering out of morality to choke up the family, that incident with Etta's only daughter, Marjorie, that the family no longer mentions, and suddenly left-behind grandparents become guardians to Marjorie's children. Etta makes up for the moral slip by harsher, rigid management. The damage done, the old woman tolerates smaller margins of error, demonstrating moral management. Lists of labor grow longer for everyone, trumping the slip of public opinion.

A small solace lingers from Jesse's extended, languorous death by cancer, the bouts of pneumonia grinding slowly against him, reducing him, extinguishing him. He rarely ventures out of his relegated, cooler back room, doted upon, treated like the invalid he is, with an endless parade of untouched sustenance. His death chamber is out of sight. It beatifies him and luckily balances out what eventually becomes of Marjorie, a daughter missing the strong hand of a healthy father. It keeps the talk down, sparing the harsher communal lashes usually doled out in similar circumstances.

It is particularly egregious that Marjorie does not give the community the chance to posture, rejects demurring to the fold. She wounds Etta particularly by her lack of prodigality.

As in many families clutching at a crumbling security, Death unstitches the catalyst that propels the family forward by excising first Marjorie and then Jesse, and the performance of pressing on then leeches itself onto Etta's back and shoulders. Staggered by the weight, the stern old woman takes up the slack. She did it after the Depression and the war and the '37 flood, and now she does it once more because the name is about all the family has left. Old women are gifted with an awareness, a rare facet exposed in the slicing away of what is precious but not necessary; one not afforded younger women and never found in men, a habitual loosening of, a shakeout, and the ability to go on with dignity. What is left? A house, a little property, some trinkets of a languid prideful heritage sputtering slowly to a halt exactly one generation before anyone tells them, and the name: this is what remains with the fierce pugilist memories. It is hard to be proud with that kind of legacy, but Etta manages.

"Cover it and make sure you get the meat in quick so it don't go cold, Donnie! Cover it with a plate, now." Etta calls it out behind her grandson, wiping her dish-soaped hands on her smock. "I washed up and laid out the big meat platters. Put all that on there and then carry them both to the big dining room. And don't spill juice on the tablecloth as I just pressed it special for dinner!"

Boundless meals parade to the house and into the proper service dishes and then into the dining room all summer and into the fall, "So as not to heat up the house," Etta says, which has an element of truth in a structure built before air conditioning or ceiling fans – luxuries of the rich and idle, and not for the descendants of English workingmen.

Her home persists in its original form, from when electricity was a relative novelty. Hot copper wires still run unlined over porcelain spools through the attic, and the electricity still isn't trusted not to burn your house to the ground, which therefore gives the added excuse for why she uses it sparingly.

Entertainment in Etta's house is the process of cooking. Insurmountable detail whittles out the hours before Marjorie and the granddaughters set out the good Coalport china and Waterford crystal on the long table, luxurious left-over fragments of a previous generation that Etta recalls with precision, along with the guest list of semi-mediocrity, recounting it whether you listen or not. Incessant culinary instructions serve the multiple purposes of sharing the bounty, bringing family together, providing an outlet for gossip, and teaching young girls how to behave like the women they are expected to become. Etta, Marjorie, Jeannie, and her three sisters leave the roasting meat to the men outdoors, attending to them frequently with pitchers of ice water with lemon. Meanwhile, they lay out the side dishes in the pantry galley to set. After, women join the men in the gazebo before serving dinner, cooling off from the kitchen inferno of boiling pots and simmering vegetables and baking cornbread. With windows thrown open to the screen in the shade of bunched sycamore trees, the formula never changes.

Serving up a roast doesn't include a roasted bride: "Powder your nose for an appetizing meal," as Mabel Claire points out. Once the house screen-cools and the afternoon heat grudgingly relents, after the sweat on the women evaporates to an acceptable level, the aprons fall away, dresses are smoothed, hair is refreshed, and the food is consumed at the formal dining table, lined with one of the hand-embroidered trousseau tablecloths set with the china and silver and crystal. It is a tradition meant to match the plates, outliving slighter luxuries that Etta singularly carries on well after the opportunities and venues for fine dining pass, and before her daughters cease to be indoctrinated. Etta refuses to part with it to compensate for lack of income, or when neighbors stop seeing her socially. It is more meaningful than selling off land and the car and all the other trivialities for making ends meet that come from having no income. This cannot be sold. Her daughters keep it up for her, for a while, and her granddaughters, too. Dinner is a ritual that requires the entire family's presence and participation.

Before Marjorie, the mother of six, the wife of promise, dies unexpectedly (and in a death that Etta sees as no small mercy and the only acceptable outcome to her dishonor), Marjorie and Etta relentlessly converse over the chores, an oral tradition of handing down through the generations. The two join in open dialogue about preparing dishes: how much Mazola salad oil goes into the sunburst chiffon cake or corned beef fritters, how celery is chopped and when to add it to soup or roast, and how homity pie is manipulated just so to cut the heaviness. Incantations to daughters making creamed cabbage and chestnut soup and peach chutney without recipe cards, sincere dissertations on the benefices of enamel roasting pans versus cast iron, and crusts, both savory and sweet, are an obsession. Cakes are another matter altogether, slick and shiny concoctions sweating in the heat, that are reserved for such occasions as births and deaths and church gatherings, where such prowess is actually important and gets noticed: the grand finale of homemaking.

"Just a pinch of salt in the batter cuts the sweetness. It also helps it set up. First, cup it in the palm, like this, then pinch it in like so. Otherwise you get too much and you cain't cut the taste of salt with nothin' after. Except potatoes in beans, then it draws out the salt. Especially if it's from the meat added."

Etta and Marjorie dole out chores to the girls, preparing them for work they soon perform daily. A plate's praise dictates its excellence and reappearance. It is in this way that jellied chicken, creamed codfish on toast, and tomato aspic disappear from the table, and veal loaf and potato Jane replace them. The four girls also receive the unspoken lesson that their future contains nothing other than this. Grown, the four daughters will bring their own girls to be versed in women's work.

On days with no meat to cook, Jesse, Marvin-called-Charlie, and Marvin's boy, Donnie – the only male heir to survive for a time – sit in the living room, oblivious to the din of the kitchen chatter, making small talk about the rain or the drought that had not been predicted in the Farmer's Almanac, or reading the Kentucky Gazette or the Christian Observer newspaper out of Louisville (if the newsstand has it that far south), or the Paducah Sun Democrat if it doesn't.

"Did you hear up in Louisville they got women working over at Kane Manufacturing? Started with the war and they just never left off. Now they got a lady pumping gas at the filling station right outside Paducah. Women'll be working jobs that don't need a man 'fore long, mark my words. I don't know what the world's coming to." Jesse says it without looking up from the paper. The men drink coffee in silence, calling out for more as needed, as if it is none of their business to know how dinner is transformed from the raw state and ends up on the stately plates on which they eat.

Afterward a change occurs in that stalwart Gothic home, happens in the death of Marjorie. It is only one change, but it creates the imperceptible shift in perception that moves orphans from a point of innocence, from the earnest education received in kitchens and in sawmills and in outhouses and turns this white Gothic farmhouse after the hard bend in Oaks Road into something sinister. It begins about that time, just before Marjorie dies.

In the fallout of scandal, the familial decline after is inevitable. The disgrace devours her generation and those after, offers up that lesson, too, of taking it in from the shadows, without instruction, without knowing exactly what one learns from being a witness, from the scandalous talk and the equally appalling recoil in Etta. That's what does it, moves her children into the slender gap between innocence and something carnal, changes everything, leads them astray, leads to awareness of the capabilities that are sometimes found in women when pressed hard enough to bring recklessness to the surface.

It is Marjorie who shatters tradition. She doesn't mean to, couldn't know it in her selfishness, but it happens that way. And on a day just like that, but years later, her only boy, Donnie, the only uncle, takes it upon himself to shatter something too – not tradition, but in other ways. This is how it happens. After Marjorie dies, in the trickling out of those remnant and intermittent family gatherings without her, the sixteen-year-old half-orphan Donnie, Jeannie's brother, takes into his hand the five-year-old hand of Jeannie's only boy and leads his nephew away from the women's work, into the yard behind the house that stretches past the manicured lawn. Donnie takes the boy to where the disheveled order of the yard stops and turns to the in-between stretch of property, property that once had a purpose, just before the wilderness and just after the shrunken functionality of the house. He takes his nephew to the open field and tells him about the time his family owned horses, and how much his sisters enjoyed mounting their backs and riding. The uncle tells the boy that, without saddle, the girls put hand to mane, swung themselves onto the palomino, or the pinto, or the fearsome Arabian, and rode away.

"Sometimes your aunts and your mother rode a horse at the same time, when they all was little, all reined in, in their white dresses after church. Granddaddy Jesse was so careful and watched over 'em as they trotted around this fenced place here. If you squint, you can still see the horses trod in the neat paths, goin' round and round and round just there. See how they cut a circle in the hard-packed dirt? You can still see it if you look close enough."

The child imagines all of this as he glints into the not-quite-silver, not-quite-gold of the now overgrown meadow, heavy with bobwhite and sparrows, with the sun buttering the stretch of fenced-in neglect. Brambles and blackberries encrust the perimeter, with the now occasional sapling growing up through the fine hay that perpetually reseeds itself.

The uncle, Donnie, then takes the boy to the fence post, a left-over sawed-off utility pole from the sawmill, anchored deep in the black dirt and covered over in Cherokee roses, and shows him the 16-penny nail gone black that still protrudes at a 30-degree angle.

"See here? A gate was latched to this here nail, so's the horses couldn't wander. Once, your aunt Melody rode this big Arabian, 14 hands tall, when Daddy told her not to. It's right about here that horse stopped short and jest threw her off his back. Well. That horse flips her over his neck and she throwed off here, on this nail right here. That horse crucified her. Jest impaled her inside thigh to this stuck-out nail head." The uncle slaps the post hard for impact and stares at the boy to see if it thrills him.

The uncle explains that where her thigh caught, it poked deep in the flesh, the weight of her body ripping out just as mercilessly, gutting out muscle and fat.

The uncle tells how his grandmother Etta, without time to spare, sent the kids into the outbuildings to gather cobwebs. She blended these with oak ash and honey and dried-out coffee grounds and packed the mixture into the ripped-out fissure. So old women know these things, and this is one of those recipes lost for want of use. For weeks after, the matriarch watched for the fever to break, dressing and redressing the red and purple, mangled flesh.

"When it's over anyways, that 16-penny nail branded her with a thick, healed-up scar. She still carries the shape of a M – like lookin' in the mouth of a big ol' catfish."

After, Melody discovered that the horses were sold.

Donnie himself is in transition; no longer a child, but yet not regarded as an adult because everyone has seen him as a child, and what's once seen cannot be let go.

"Now you gotta see the old outhouse." The boy uncle has a story about that place, too. The building, now devoid of any purpose, served as bathroom in the years before county water ran to the house. The outbuilding is one of those spaces you take no notice of. As the two approach, the uncle slats his eyes and asks the boy, "You sure you wanna go in? Black widow and brown recluse and water moccasin and diamondback like forgot-about places."

It is a tiny box of a building sitting near the post. It is difficult to mow close to, so weeds creep through the door and boards of the small building that forgot which color it was painted. It teems with under-life creatures making use of abandonment. The boy, terrorized, thrills to such danger with his uncle, this between-adult. The building agonizes and twists in the heat and elements, from innumerable snows weighing on the corrugated tin roof. It bloats and parches in the slow melt and long damp of spring, and fall rains soften rafters and beams. The heat now scorches the box straddling the small real estate between the tame landscape and the wilderness it backs itself into, smelling of hot wood under a white sun and of spaces no longer occupied. The scent of neglect is thrilling: a vacant space, a forgotten space, discovered.

Inside, they find that it is surprisingly cool and instantly conspiratorial, there where dust floats through the cracks and incising light penetrates just enough to see your way around, giving it the orange glow of sacristy candles, white hot at the point of entry reflecting back to them the washed out slivers of the main house far in the distance, then fading into golden softness soon after. The light is at ease, easy, and rubs up against them. Nailed flush to the back wall and floor is a makeshift box with a cut-out hole covered with a hinged lid. Scraps of paper discolor in the corners and crumble into chalky floorboards the color of graying linens. Bits of history reflect Truman and Johnson vignettes, orderly columns of war propaganda still plastered over the boards. The uncle takes out a shiny dime and lets the light catch President Roosevelt's head, lets it flash across the boy's face and dance on the interior.

"Would you like to have it?"

"I don't know. I never had a dime before, Donnie," replies the nephew, but his eyes falter with the shine, suddenly greedy for it, and his uncle knows it.

The uncle peers intently through the boards toward the house, then fishes into the front of his trousers like he is just deciding what a dime is worth.

"Here. Put your hand out. Now pull on it slow. Like that."

The nephew does what he is told as he stares at how big his uncle's now lengthening pee-pee gets, much bigger than his own five-year-old penis. The boy marvels at this new game and wonders where his uncle, now a man, learned it from. "Now, you ain't gonna trick me and not give me my dime, are ya?"

The uncle puts the dime in his nephew's hand. "Now you cain't tell nobody about this, you hear? You gotta swear to me that you won't say nothin' or else we'll both be in big trouble and I'll take back my dime. You got that?" His eyes remain locked on the house and his forehead beads up.

The boy puts the dime in his pocket and places his hand back on his uncle's now rigid shaft and yanks inquisitively, not understanding this absurd action's relation to receiving a dime.

The uncle grimaces. "Wait. You're not doing it right."

The boy tries again, incorrectly, and the uncle panics, quickly depositing himself into his pants again.

"Jest forget the whole thing! I'm warning you; you better not tell nobody." He shoves the door forward into the bright light, leaving the boy standing there in the filtered light now carving back the dark.

The child too, bewildered, exits the box, pushing closed the door as best he can with his small body, and awkwardly shuffles back to the front porch. Pleased with himself, but unsure of what happened, the nephew pulls out the dime to make sure he still has it, just as he reaches the creaking boards of the front porch. Before, the kid had no money, nor the desire to possess money. In his marveling about it, the dime falls, perfectly perpendicular, through a crack in the porch boards and into the shadows below. Exasperated and unable to reach his dime, the boy sheepishly finds his uncle and explains what happened and asks if he could he have another dime.

The uncle hoarse-whispers through the distortion that is his face, "NOYOUCAN'T and you better shut up about it!" By his desperate searching to see if anyone overheard, the nephew sees that this must remain undiscussed, like many of the other secrets they do not discuss, like what happened to his uncle's and his momma's momma, Marjorie, so he goes back to the front porch to see if he can see his lost prize through the boards.

After dinner, after the good dishes are polished and the water spots on the crystal rubbed clear, after all is put away, tidied, and the floor is clean, the women sit at the kitchen table and prattle about the impossibly small and uneventful lives that nobody is living in that town. After dusk, the matriarch puts up a cold plate for supper. Etta's granddaughters lovingly finish the small refinements of cleaning as they talk and return the relics to the back-porch pantry to stand sentinel over the once socially ranking family, exactly seven more days. It goes on like this for this family, the putting into place, the keeping one in one's place. Etta's efforts uphold tradition, maintaining civility, and she is the last to do so.

Marjorie, Symsonia, KY 1926

Marjorie is the one who first breaks orbit, who first goes astray. She does everything the way she is required to do for as long as she remembers. Marjorie watches as Etta instructs. The daughter absorbs the correct and expected way; she does the acceptable. She is groomed, toils in the kitchen since she is eight, learning to be an adept cook with whatever is available, what is left from good times with fat meat and lean times with vegetables and leftover bacon fat and gelatin molds, growing and putting up row after row of Liberty Garden vegetables and the fruits of languid summer for the hard winters coming. These to be tucked away in darker regions of the dim and even-temperatured root cellar, dug out of the cool side of the house, its thick Symd unbending planed oak shelves weighted down with bounty, preparing for, foreseeing the needs of the family, and meeting them before being asked or facing want or, worse, imposing want on others. All of this Etta shares like dripping wax, one small layer that warms and then melds to the thin layer already secured to its foundation, spreads out, bonds, and prepares to receive the next.

Marjorie scrubs baseboards and hard wood floors and oils them down and rubs sheen on the handmade furniture her father, Jesse, constructed in his good years, the years before his illness, a trade from his father before him. Generations of handmade heirlooms stand as tangible proof of the respectability of a family made by labor and skill, stand as evidence in that poor white farmhouse with the fine oak floors that Jesse hand-planed and lathed and put into place from the very trees cleared to build the farmhouse, and let those objects announce the grandness that family had when everybody else had less. He built it for Etta, but he built it big for a family. A house needs boys to make the fruit come from the branch. Finally, they have two sons and one girl but the final tally comes in much lower after the jolt of death claims both male heirs. The younger boy dies of childhood pleurisy and the firstborn son dies at 19 from illness of the heart, one prized male youth after the other before any fruition of their toil, resulting in the one leftover girl – after it is too late to do anything about it.

Marjorie compensates for her family's want, an apology of sorts for being left behind, for not being a male, a breadwinner, for not carrying on the family name, for not supplying namesakes. After his boys die the saplings and not the oak, both lost in their youth, Jesse also compensates for his daughter, Marjorie. She raises her family in his house.

As the lone sibling survivor, as a woman, she takes up the yoke pressed upon her by the molding hands of Etta, slowly putting into revolution all that makes a house and its folks, if not happy, then at least satisfied and without want. Etta supervises the feminine burdens, parceling out the work to Marjorie as she demonstrates proficiency.

The young woman labors and, just as methodically, Marjorie's four daughters join in while her one son learns to beat against the brow of hard labor in his father's sawmill. The immediacy of need overshadows the luxury of school. This, too, is the legacy of a daughter's misfortune and of a family with no sons.

This female, Etta's one last child of a family that sputters out, should have died without sons; she learns the thin border between managing a house with too severe a hand and the damage it leaves on delicate things. Without proper force, the ever-present dirt and stains linger on in the house; they have to be scrubbed out and removed with vigor on discovery. Etta demonstrates beating out the rag rug that winds around itself into neat coils and tight braids. Marjorie leans into the balance of thrashing it so that the stitching and bindings of the twisted fabric do not tear, while still flogging it sufficiently so that any sign of its having been sullied is removed. This works on clothing and sheets in the wash and is applicable to dislodging dust from the drapes. It works on children, too.

Marjorie achieves this balance just as she learns to make carpets from old clothes and bed linens and household items that cannot be handed-down any longer, learns to repurpose instead of discard, to find pride in thrift and lack of deficiency. The mark of a good woman is this: that although she is unable to work for money, she can still save it, which is almost as important.

"Looks like a wind's coming up. I'm gonna go ahead and open up the house a little early," she calls absentmindedly to Etta, who is boiling out the potatoes for dinner and for the ironing starch in the kitchen.

Marjorie knows the best time of day for opening doors and latching the breezeway screens that run back to front of the house and are constructed to take advantage of the winds that breathe in and cool it. She opens upstairs hall windows and transoms for maximum advantage in cool evenings, just as those who left un-cleared the monumental trees on all sides of the house knew that sheltering shade would collect the cool and push it inside, making it possible to sleep in that big farmhouse at the hard bend in Oaks Road, while wafting out the stench of night chamber pots and the stink of too many working bodies in an aging house.

The forever-swirling dust settles and resettles on every surface, requiring Marjorie to perpetually remove it. She cleans the porcelain so that stains don't set in and empties the relic, left-over dry sinks still in the family bathroom for shaving and daily toiletry needs, and sterilizes those lingering areas of stale air and sweat and the dirt of working bodies. She throws open the windows and throws over the sills the quilts made by Etta's hands and the hands of Etta's mother before her to dry out the dampness of stagnant summer nights and dissipate the smell of fireplace winters that gets in the clothes and furniture and into the bed with you.

Somewhere in the middle of all this girding for the abyss, a short time after the death of her last brother, the urgency reveals itself and the family settles on marrying Marjorie to a man named Marvin, but whom everybody calls Charlie.

"Mamma, not to be disrespectful, but I just don't know him," she speaks it without vigor, knowing it holds no meaning.

"You will soon enough," is Etta's reply. "Besides, what do you need to know about men, anyway? You learn to stay out of their way and they learn to treat you respectfully, nothin' more to it than that. It all takes some gettin' used to, that's all. That's been the bedrock of a solid marriage for your daddy and me. It'll do for you, too. Now, go in there and show him the best side of you."

She is slim and tall with a long jaw and a short under bite and outrageous hair that on the calmest days whips around her in an auburn frenzy that resembles the heat that comes off of choked-out coals. Pensive, with a furtive and darting look that resembles a fox hearing the huntsman, she is also suppliant and commands a clean house, so she talks about that with Charlie/Marvin in the spotless living room, but mostly lets him talk about himself, although he doesn't have much to say in that regard. She doesn't like strangers much.

Marvin works at Carter's sawmill that sits just off the Clarks River, running the 12-cylinder Packard engine for them, and he is from a family that traces its roots back through the War Between the States alongside her family too, wavering on what is morally right and what is socially acceptable and what is God-given rights, on back to the Revolution and to the roots of the country before it is a country, right to the city of New Amsterdam in the 1600s. He has the passionless resolve of Dutch religious heretics in his blood, gone stagnant with so many generations behind him. His immediate family is from Rock Island, and he is tall like her and thin, too, from hard work, and even though he is an inert stranger in perpetual danger of utterly disappearing, his family is a respectable one and he is a provider and it is decided that he is a good match for their equally passive daughter.

They marry. With him being a working bachelor renting a room in a boarding house and she being the only daughter – only child – now left to Etta and Jesse, Marvin whom everyone calls Charlie brings his suitcase with three pair of overalls, two pair of boots, four work shirts, and one white, slightly discolored church shirt with matching dress pants, and he moves in with her folks in the white clapboard farmhouse as is expected. He is acceptable and he blends in with the furniture. The urgency comes to an end and Etta sleeps better at night. Marjorie discovers that she is not in love with him. Matters of the heart have little bearing on the broader subject of companionship and provisioning, which are trump cards. Marjorie is a good wife immediately, as she has trained to be. Not having given it much thought in the first place, she shrugs it off, if she thinks about it at all, and simply adds his laundry to her workload. But he loves her and nobody else for all of his days, as sometimes happens with couples. One loves enough for both of them.

"Your supper's on the table under the fly screen. Fresh zucchini and fried squash and meatloaf. And I made those rolls you like so much," she smiles at him as he knocks the sawdust off of his steel-toed boots on the gray steps leading up to the porch.

"Margie! You sure are a sight for sore eyes after all those wood boards. Come over here so I can steal me some sugar!" Marvin beams at his wife.

Some legacies are not meant to be, and daughter after daughter comes to them, to the dismay of Etta and, therefore, of Marjorie. Finally, a son is born and the child-making slows and then ends the transaction. The marriage is a welcome distraction to any shortcomings she does or does not feel with her lot in life, filling the house with needing children and expanded responsibility to care for the new husband.

Practically nothing, yet everything, changes. Manual labor is harder while pregnant. Children add to the myriad tasks she performs each day. She bears these new responsibilities with the constant oversight of Etta and applies herself doubly to her days that become weeks and months, to her task of doing what is expected: what is proper to a good wife, a good mother, a good daughter. For all of her training, her indoctrination into the sisterhood of womankind, she is indeed good: in action, in deed, in perception of the life around her. She doesn't know any other way to be, because there is no other reference for being another way. Her place, like that of the oxen and dairy cows, is mapped out long before she arrives into a hierarchy of sorts, with a predetermined niche into which she is placed, not by herself but by those who determine the shape she takes to fit. She accepts. She makes herself compliant and complacent to the collective need.

It does not overwhelm because she does not allow the bigger set of duties to engulf the task of the moment. Each chore, each service fits neatly into the next, and a running tally in her head races against the hall clock signaling the end of the day. Daylight begins with her setting out once again to remove the traces of daily living, of housework and cooking stains, of shit and baby sick and farmer sweat and sawmill worker and making her five kids acceptable for public appearance.

Marjorie daydreams about lightening that toil as she sweats

at her labors, her rut, and her minuscule feats that slowly add up to a satisfactory day. Every Saturday begins by rolling out the satin white-enameled aluminum Kenmore Water Witch gyrator/wringer/washer with the gravity drain hose onto the back porch and filling it with hauled-out boiling well water and Ivory Snow soap. It is a model left over from another decade, but they are fortunate to have such a contraption to make the work lighter. She lets it sway back and forth with its *ugg, ugg, ugg,* churning away the filth with its bounty of Ivory Snow and water, agitating the mix into a dull gray, sudsless slop. She does these tasks while with child, and then with children in tow, and often while with child and with children in tow. The Kenmore paper circulars in the newspaper don't discuss how to best maneuver this so she makes do.

Marjorie starts each wash the same way, following the unwritten guidelines with the whites first and then working her way down to the coveralls and over shirts, which are dirtiest. She watches as the thick-black, spongy gravity hose finally pulls out the filthy gray water through the hole that threads out of the opening poked through the screen. She allows the mixture to drain into the backyard, all the while hand-feeding soggy clothes through the wooden hand-turned wringer, crushing out the water and the last of the sweat and grime and letting them drop into the corrugated zinc tub beside her, fat and limp and misshapen, ready for the collective rinse.

The smoke from the gas engine powering the gyrator settles into everything, including the freshly washed clothes, her hair, the house, onto those dishes and onto the children playing on the porch close to her, or settling onto the sleeping child and sometimes children in the bassinet. These fumes no longer bother her as she works, because tolerance for that too had organically affixed itself to her in its weekly repetition.

And she takes the clothes to the wire clothesline crucified to the post that runs away from the house all the way to the dead-end stop at the end of the yard. She drags the cloth bag along the wire as she pins the flattened and lifeless clothes to the line, waiting for the breeze to break down the stiffness and to slowly and relentlessly work them into airy things whipped by sunshine and light, with only the slightest scent of engine oil and kerosene fumes left in them. As she works, she toes along the length of the clothesline, inching her way down, squeezing the fabric from top to bottom, gauging the work of the sun and air, judging if their part of the job is complete, if they have fulfilled their promise. She watches too for those sometimes carefree cardinals, the duller one and the brilliant red one, nervous, fleeting, full of color and vigor, living petulantly, mockingly, somewhere just out of sight, beyond her reach, that sometimes alight on the zinc wire, sometimes on the end product of the chore, just as she finishes, just long enough to soil the sheets and flit away, bringing her to the annoying purpose of redoing the task.

Marjorie takes the laundry out of the white heat of the afternoon that darkens the freckles on her face and hands and arms, and folds and sequesters the supple cottons and wools away into oversized pieces of furniture in the darker corners of rooms. These are chores for after feeding chickens and horses and cows, first and favorite, and then the other animals, then tending the little kitchen Liberty Garden as the clothes dry, but in between cooking breakfast and dinner, and all of this completed prior to starting supper. Her chores cycle on until the cicadas start their repeating script at dusk. And her days renew themselves week after week and year after year until one day, when it is not the same as the week before and the routine descends into an abrupt and unwelcome disorder.

Of course, this Saturday begins just like any other. She is alone with the children on the back porch that also serves as the pantry, with the Coalport china and the Waterford crystal lovingly washed and polished and placed on the shelves waiting for tomorrow's family dinner. The Kenmore is in the middle of the fourth load of gyration, and her mind is running over the pinned-up clothes and rushing down the clothesline that runs away from the house to the point of its dead-end stop at the end of the yard when it happens. A flash of red and then a sudden and inescapable siege forcing itself into her chest that stops her breathing and rips her aorta apart and begins pumping blood into her chest cavity like that gravity drain hose on the Kenmore Water Witch gyrator/wringer/washer, instead of through her blood vessels as it should have. And it does it in silence as she watches the clothesline run away from the house and abruptly dead end at the close of the yard of that old white farmhouse at the hard bend in Oaks Road in Symsonia, and she falls first against the cool enameled surface, then to her knees, and then fading light around her and the dead end closes up her sight and she is slipping to the floor, her dress fluttering up around her in the silence that submerges her. Other than the oddity that she ceases to work, nothing around her changes. The brightness of the sun does not dim. The breeze wafts through the shotgun hallway of the house and over her still body. The gyrator continues to churn murky waters just to the right of her shoulder.

Marjorie lies crumpled to the porch boards with the life wrung out of her. They hear, and by some miracle, they half drag her to the road for a neighbor to provide the ride to the Baptist hospital in Paducah, and in sufficient time to create a crude artery inside her. But the diagnosis doesn't comfort her salvaged life.

Doctors identify this genetic disorder, understand its cause, and offer a repeatable quip for inquisitive and well-meaning neighbors sifting for gossip.

"President Lincoln most probably had what you have, Mrs. Skinner. Had he not been shot, he would have died like you will in the next year or so. You were born in Kentucky. Are you a relation of the late president? Are you aware?"

Simply a medical curiosity to the doctors delivering the news, other than telling her she has that which cannot be repaired, not permanently, that she'd live for maybe a year and then this fickle aorta would give in and the whole terribleness of ripping her chest open reoccur, and even though they fixed up the aorta this time, the next she wouldn't be so lucky and she would die. There is nothing they can do. And of course they are very sorry. The doctors turn their backs on them, leaving the family quietly huddled around Marjorie, abandoned in the bed, engulfed in the buzzing white fluorescence of the white recovery room.

Marjorie goes away sterilized by the medical opinions of the Baptist hospital and the white officials in white coats and returns to her compartment in the little white Gothic farmhouse with the six kids and the laundry, as if nothing is changed, and they tell her about God's will and Marfan Syndrome and a bigger plan and she is expected to listen and to nod and to acquiesce. She meant to submit to her martyrdom as something bigger than her. But in her selfish lament, something else ruptures and splits open; the yellow squash, ripening too long, given too much abundance of sun and rain, swells and bursts. Marjorie is a tangle of emotions and then emotionless in a swinging pendulum with no center of gravity. She sentries the long hall connecting her to the front porch as her husband knocks the sawdust off his steel-toed boots, as she has watched every day of the week for sixteen years straight, when it materializes. Everything changes but nobody notices, or acts as if they have not noticed, which is more horrifying for her.

"All these kids, Charlie, all I've given and this is the payment? And for what? To what end? This is my reward?"

It is a bitter giggle that pushes up and out of her before she contains it. She stares harder at that zinc pole at the end of the yard, just before the wildness found there, where the carefree cardinals sometime appear. She keeps staring, transfixed, until it takes on a new shape and calls to her. The still wet scar she bears pulses.

"I can't anymore. I can't, Charlie," she whispers under her breath. The realization that she says it out loud leaves her breathless, that she gives life to something so abhorrent, unspeakable. "I. CAN'T. ANYMORE," she says, with more conviction, when she has her breath in her again.

In this unbalance, Marjorie suddenly sees past that clothesline that runs away from the house and in a pitiless, emotionless moment she steels herself to follow it. In the flash of sun on the face of a dime, she unexpectedly sees. She grasps and despises all that is around her, which shocks her and excites her all at once.

A calm and cold panic clutches Marjorie, as if she is someone else filling up with desperation to live, to get out, stuffing herself full of the life that is slowly pumping out of her with each cheating heartbeat. That defective heart, that torn heart: it is beyond repair. She is past mending and she will not regain it, cannot overcome it. She walks unsteadily into the kitchen and over to his chair and places her slim fingers onto his sleeve as if its coarse fibers will jolt her back to sanity.

"Charlie," she croons unsteadily. He looks up at her quizzically, because they are not tactile, touching in that friendly and familiar manner, and her voice is too high, almost shrill. She looks jittery, he thinks.

"Can't you and I just slip away for a while? Can't we just ... go...." But she flinches as if half struck by the two distorted images of herself trapped in his eyes, of the woman she has been, could no longer be. Her words choke up, choke off, break up inside Margie, and belie her wish for them to go. She sees in his blankness that her words are preposterous even as they fade from her lips. "Oh, nothing. Go ahead and eat your supper. I'm sorry, hon. This heat is just stifling." She gives him a quivering smile and half a laugh. The nerves of the fox before the huntsmen overtake her again. Marvin goes back to eating his supper.

'I should ask Etta to keep the kids for a bit,' he thinks to himself, while pulling the remnants off the chicken bone. "Maybe I'll take Marjorie to the pictures down in Paducah sometime. She needs a nice dinner at C.C. Cohen's. She's been through the wringer," he reminds himself.

Destiny, her singular purpose, is what overtakes her and changes her, changes everything. That thought becomes her, becomes her heart. That will to live. That moment when she knows that she has to cram a lifetime into every second she has left, into that potential year before it stops beating.

It's funny when you get news like that. You believe it like it's told to somebody else about somebody else. It is one of those shared stories over a Sunday dinner about a body down the road and you just can't believe it happens to somebody like that and what a shame it all is. Try as she might to force the association, the act of connecting the dots, from that somebody else to herself, well, that's harder. It actually *is* a shame because it isn't a conversation taking the place of scandal rags for nobodies: it's you. It's your life with an expiration date. And the family says what a shame it all is too. Emotions aren't part of the equation.

And Etta worries to herself but isn't doing much good to a young woman in a cold panic. In her desperation, that internal and unexpressed mania driving Marjorie's thoughts suddenly and without warning turns her foolhardy. It isn't to anywhere good, not for a respectable woman with six kids in a town where everybody says hello in a polite way, seeing you in church or on the street, but when you pass, rattle off generations of scandals with the cheapness of boredom. You don't escape a town like that. She wants no pity, but her unexpected and expected death is big news. A perfectly polite family presents a united front for the town unfortunates, and she wants no part of that either.

This new Marjorie escapes and what remains, what the pieces look like after, has no consequence. A woman desperate does not map out deals or negotiations because there isn't time for any of that. The diagram she draws for her time left, what they say about her kids, about Etta and Jesse, or Marvin, *tsks* and head shakes, are for somebody else to consider, for the stragglers, those left behind, and for those who have time to outlive their shame. She is not considerate. The fee Marjorie pays is infinite. Deliberation is for those with the sumptuous feast of time to gorge on. She is not among them. Marjorie can't save everybody, just herself now. And not even herself. She defies martyrdom and the sad and pitying stares she would get in the market and church and the sadness that would extend to the children she had always in tow. She retches at the thought of the doe-eyed looks Marvin called Charlie would get standing next to her in line, the perpetual knowing, the pitying.

This new Marjorie alters the scandal, giving some purpose, something filthy and sexy and titillating to pass the time, make conversation of, expand, fill in the details, something to reinforce that you're separate by your own good breeding from the likes of her, her moral deficiencies, her low family. Everything before is erased. The scandal defines and taints, moving forward, moving without her. She writhes against and clamps tightly to her defective chest this new fire within her that awakens more than her will to live. Without any weapons except resolve, she forcibly violates the bitter and stopped-beating heart with her own defiance. She will not die until she has filled her cup.

For those outside of the family circle, or too young, those making up the left out, the flotsam, the debris of all of this family scandal, this isn't something you learn about from polite conversation within the family unit. Etta and Jesse didn't speak of it. For them, it ceases existence, dies with their last remaining child.

"I hear she up and moved to Brookport!" someone whispers.

You learn about her from chatty distant relatives drinking too much, unsure of the extent the story has been related to parties present, so telling it anyway in a coarse whisper out of earshot from Etta and Jesse. They are the respectable intent on staying respectable, despite the scandal, the blemish, and the ever-evident tarnish sometimes found on the family silver that wouldn't go away because it was locked into the amalgam—a new part of the now dirty pieces of cutlery reserved for your particular table setting lest someone should see. You spare their feelings about their only daughter, who is diagnosed by the family as crazy, which is the only explanation for the new her, the new Marjorie, after her episode on the back porch: the scandalous Marjorie.

Conforming types become like them, elevating their own morally coded qualities by pointing out deficiencies in hers, so it makes the family feel superior somehow, even though it is on all their family name, this blight they keep alive with their ordinary speak. The blame for it lies sometimes on Jesse, sometimes on Marvin called Charlie, sometimes on her illness, or on all three simultaneously. The end result is the same. Rumors tell how she just up and leaves.

She doesn't give any warning and she doesn't write or call or leave any explanation. She walks out on Marvin called Charlie and the six kids, and she walks out on the respectability and the chores and the china and the neighbors who say hi in church and ask how you are. The biggest slap in the face is how she leaves Etta and Jesse in their weakening years and takes up with a man in another town, and the fallout is immediate and disastrous for those in her wake. On a quiet Saturday morning just after the chickens are fed, a deputy hand delivers that family's divorce papers with no words, a downcast gaze and a shaking head. It is at this time that Marvin called Charlie takes to the unusual habit of drinking coffee at the breakfast table, smoking one cigarette after the next, staring out of the window, as if waiting for something to make it right again. He would have forgiven her.

And it wasn't just any man, this one. Marjorie met him while she was looking for living with a capital L. She found him past the clothesline where the grasses became wilder, overtaking the pasture. It's easier to find when you're looking for it, you don't have any baggage, you don't have to worry about the consequences, and the caliber of the man isn't that important to help you accomplish what you are setting out to do, because time has already been wasted for way too long.

The new Marjorie finds one of those places with people searching for a freedom not allowed except to the truly free: the underbelly, the forgotten, the drunkards, the sluts, the sex workers, the lechers. She wades into that putrid end of the line for him. He drinks hard and he doesn't love so much as he gives meanness with a passion that confuses her, living in bars and dance halls where no married woman goes, except her new situation allows it, but he doesn't care about those kinds of things and he doesn't want a respectable woman. Marjorie makes herself over to the kind of woman he wants to hang onto. He takes, and that is the fun when it isn't necessarily given freely and he wants to possess. So she meets his lusty stare with white terror and defiance and want and more fear and cowardice and bravery all at the same time, and that starts a little spark of commonness between them, and he begins showing her a good time and she adjusts. She goes right in along with him.

And in short order, Marjorie learns to be hard too, because he brings her down that way, by force and hardness and persuasion, and by being louder and stronger than her. She learns all the tricks to be with a man like that, to be dominated by his force but to steal her independence by being there willingly. She is desperate to live with a capital L and she doesn't have much time to do it in, so she learns fast. She makes a lot of allowances. She gives away every shred of what she is to do it, to have it done to her.

They take up day drinking together, and then dancing until all hours of the morning, and go back to his motel and tear the roof down with fighting and lovemaking. Marjorie forgets her mortality, slights it. The drink ravages her and she forgets to care. The kids and parents and husband fade then, too. And she unhinges with all of this terrible newness that she doesn't necessarily like, but on a raw and primal plane doesn't dislike either. The motel is a reliquary for her few possessions and somebody cleans up after and she is liberated from responsibility. She discovers carnality. She finds that she can be base and wanton without an identity. In that mystery she is a phantom, lost, and in the loss she is free.

But some stories do not end well—hers doesn't. They have a moral codex and messages of redemption, of being redeemed and justified, of genuine retribution. Others must compare the sin and the sensibility.

Marjorie's catting yawns into the night with tiring sweet whiskeys and barbs and insults and insinuations and kisses and stolen thrusts and furtive hands. They are unashamed. Leading others on, lingering eye contact thrills, teases, and piques jealousies that boil the blood and get the claws out.

He likes it. She becomes accustomed to it. They rankle and escalate the stakes. The catalyst of her death is inevitable, given the path she lays while looking for living with a capital L.

The ending starts with the steel guitar spinning out the last refrain of Honkytonk Angels, trite even for those kinds of bars, when Marjorie and a stranger pass each other at the bar and she trails her thin white hand too closely to his sleeveless wrist exposed on the table. Eyes catch eyes and take it further. The ending is all but inevitable with the lead-up to that exchange: the flirting, the possibility of walking away, then catching again into each other's revolution, then pressing the envelope forward again so that others could eclipse that intimacy, so that it could be given with the slightest provocation, that each of them is capable of taking up with another, which sparks and then ignites the fury surfacing between them. Marjorie heads toward the chipped door under the white enamel Mademoiselle sign and the wrist follows. Before sealing the deal, before they can connect, her lover snatches Marjorie away from the stranger and away from the possibility of possession. Snatching her through the bar, he jostles and pushes her toward the exit and she laughs and cajoles him and curses. And nobody pays much mind because this foreplay is how it always happens between them and this night isn't any different than the many nights before that. Except it is. Or it would be.

He presses Marjorie into the car with the weight and strength of his body as she fights him off, but she gives in anyway, parrying with the game, and he whisks her away toward their motel room. This too is normal, him taking her from the clutches of another or others, potentials, reclaiming, owning. She is his until he determines otherwise, and that too is part of the game. Neither is sorry, yet both will be tremendously sorry in another way, in an unexpected way— in a way that makes the soul sad for the magnitude of choice, and the inability to control the outcomes of events. After fury settles and before the terrible consequence unfolds, the fighting escalates and he slaps her over and over again, but she hits right back and then they are exhausted and the game ebbs away to only the quiet of the room. She is suddenly tired of the play and drink fades him into the gentle comfort of bed linens, wasted by his excesses, and this is the moment she discovers she is waiting for. She does not know it but she has been waiting for this moment since meeting him.

With him in his stupor, with those slim, white, working hands of hers, it is easy for her. She effortlessly removes pantyhose from the slippery sink water and deftly loops and knots his half-naked body to that flaked and tarnished white enamel wrought iron bed, spread-eagle style, and taking one of his thick boot socks that doesn't have too much give, she puts a couple of bars of Ivory soap in that sock and begins her methodical castigation.

Like beating the wet out of a mop, she swings the makeshift weapon down on him.

There is no place sacred that she reserves from her calculated fury. With the *thud, thud, thud* of the carpet beater, she avenges herself with systematic annihilation of the pain and injustice she has suppressed; she pays him back for the beatings he gives her and for the shame she feels for having been beaten, for leaving all of her respectability behind, and because she is sorry for the long nights of drinking. But she isn't sorry about the living, even though this isn't what she really expected from the capital L. She beats him for the humiliation she caused Marvin called Charlie, for not being able to renegotiate the cost. She beats him for her children, who could not understand and whom she wouldn't see again. She beats him for Jesse and Etta, who must be heartbroken for losing her. She beats him for the defective heart that drove her to him. She ravages and breaks his body and spits out all of his injustices to her while she is doing it.

"You think you can do this, do this to a woman and not account for it? Think you can take from me and turn me into ... this! Break me?" The blows flail at him. Her deep-set eyes are wide and lolling as she half sees him through the rage and remnants of liquor. "This isn't what I wanted, not what I wanted, not what I was looking for ... not this, not you, NOTYOU, not what you DONE to me," she mutters between labored breaths. "You stole it from me! You stole it! All I had left, so much time ... lost ... used up. You used me up!" She wails it out of her like she is begging for it back.

And, with renewed vigor and clenched teeth, "I'll send you to Hell for it!"

But this last part, this liturgy, this beginning part of her final processional, comes out of her as an act of penitence and atonement, but invokes no mercy.

She redoubles her efforts. Under the first strikes, he shocks into awakening to what is inflicted on him. He is not accustomed to being on the receiving end of such anger and it momentarily silences him despite the blows. He sucks in air and spits slobber onto his undershirt as it registers. It does not click that a woman is capable of this. The bull is tied to the altar. Then he rages and meets her fury.

He begins screaming, "I'm going to kill you when I get loose!" He bellows profanities at her: "You good for nothing bitch of a dog, I swear I'm going to repay every fucking mark you give me ten over, I swear it! Let me loose, you fucking bitch! I'm gonna ...." And obscenities keep coming so the neighbors hear, but it isn't the kind of motel where people ask about your business, so nobody comes to help him.

The Ivory Snow keeps raining down on him and he fights against it futilely as he writhes and turns but cannot escape the blows of that justice served hot and white by a woman diminished. Finally, she does not hear him. The blood forces itself into her head and turns to a cool dial tone any noise other than what spews out of her own mouth. She watches his lips move and his spittle fly as his eyes bulge and redden with the flowing alcohol and the futile strain against the tether, but she hears nothing.

And when she is through, when she spends her anger and her hate and her self-serving sorrow, she sits and stares into the abyss of what is next, not at him but through him, through the dumpy motel, through the bars and the liquor. She stares into the void. She finds no answers there either, just a reverberating pulse of exhaustion and confusion and the flickering hot pink of the "y" of the vacancy sign visible through the window.

So instead, she pulls out that little white valise with the white Bakelite handle and puts what is left of her life into it. She does not know how long she sits there. Her breathing is normal again. She no longer looks at him, although she becomes somewhat aware of his twisting presence in the room by his still laboring breath. He is passive too and his breath is shallow. Marjorie mechanically walks through the room as if she is no longer associated with what transpired there, any of it, as if it never occurred. He begins again to heave his sweating and raw body against the tether but remains bound and bleeding as the hose cuts deep into his wrists and purpled fists and feet. She does not hear and she does not see any longer. The abyss has overtaken her and she does not resist. She rifles through his pockets and takes the $242 they have together and tucks it inside her patterned blouse, past the crisp white slip, and neatly into the thin bra cupping her perspiring skin. She takes the white Bakelite handle once again into her long, elegant, white hand and leaves him tied to the bed, bleeding and broken by her, to be found by others, found in his naked shame, emasculated by this woman. He would never see her again.

That isn't how her story ends. Ironically, he did kill her, but not in the way he swore at her that he would. Marjorie didn't die of that second aortic tear, which is a merciful thing, because this is what she wants least of all: the second shoe falling. The anticipation of that second sole slapping the earth cannot be drowned out with violence or lovemaking or liquor or nights without memory. It had been perpetually there since the delusion lifted, this continual dread. Yet Marjorie dies on her own terms, brought about by the complications of her actions. She summons one of those unexpected, randomly doled-out graces from God, the winning of some awful draw. The surgery had marked her with a pink and purple scar that takes a hard turn under her ribcage and left breast. Despite the blood thinners she must take, he has incidentally given her a minuscule clot of blood, a tangling of proteins that now travels to her brain and murders her, and she dies without visitation rights for her kids or saying sorry or reconciling with Etta and Jesse or Marvin. It is instantaneous and a small mercy. It is a thankful and clean end to a woman with no compass and no direction—her failed attempt at living.

There are effects for her left-behind children, now the half-orphans, and to one child in particular, now a granddaughter and no longer the daughter of Marjorie. Jeannie, on the cusp of becoming a woman at the age of twelve, teeters over the edge in direct and unknowing consequence of those stories she pieces together of the shocking end to her mother's life at the age of 42. It terrifies and perversely thrills the child that it occurs in some far away roadside motel, where nobody asks your business and nobody comes to help her mother either. Marjorie is found by the black cleaning lady, and when the police arrive she is laid out on the bed, still in her traveling clothes, the still-packed white valise sitting on the floor at the foot of the bed. The report makes note of the fact that she looked as if she was sleeping peacefully and had not resisted when death came.

Jeannie, Paducah, KY 1949

"That Cunningham boy" is what Etta calls him. It comes out of her mouth like an unpleasant surprise, like finding spinach from your supper caught between your gum and cheek in such a way that you can't discretely dispose of it or dislodge it in polite company, and so you fixate on it, wondering if you can do something about it when nobody is looking. They didn't find out about him right away. Jeannie Mae isn't suspect at thirteen, but she developed early. The Marfan Syndrome, a gift from her mother, Marjorie (they say Abe Lincoln had it), gives her unexpected height and a slim waist to go with her full hips and the small, culpable and buoyant breasts that sit high in her cotton homemade dress without undergarments, accenting her exotic, angular features in a field of moon pie-faced girls in Symsonia. She covers herself over to avoid the clumsy looks of older men who'd stopped having sex with their wives but remember those moments from bodies such as hers, with a sideways glance to her breasts and hips and buttocks on cool morning walks, when brisk air brings attention to such things. At school, she removes the button-up sweater Etta knitted from lightweight discount crimson wool the color of cardinals. Etta coincidentally makes it around the time Jeannie gets those breasts, insisting she wear it as resistance, as armor, to school, come summer or winter. Everybody notices, but nobody says anything to her about how she is a woman and how dangerous that is, or what the outcome could be for possessing a body like that at thirteen.

But that Cunningham boy notices. A big-boned youth displaying his sensuality in the way he wears his hair, with too much attention paid to it, too much attention drawn to it, is an advertisement. Jeannie notices. His pants are tight and low across his hips, so that his virility is visible to anyone who ventures their gaze below his Levi Strauss brass button fly, or when the light catches his khakis in a certain way where you can just tell he isn't wearing underclothes. And he stands against the wall in the hall of the school and juts that out, or crosses his ankles, leaning the small of his back into his car while talking with friends so that the light catches him the way he wants to be caught, full on with lots of crease and shadow where it counts, and he counts on catching somebody's attention. Jeannie notices that too but pretends she doesn't, as she casts her eyes down and rushes her scarlet cheeks to her next class.

She is a girl woman. Impossibly thick blonde hair brings her entire body into proportion and coils itself into thick ringlets without her trying to do it. White blue eyes remind one of morning light hitting chill creek water controlled by the thinnest crust of ice, just enclosing its swelling crest, yet somehow still rushing impossibly on just beneath, dangerous should you fall through. Transitioning, she demonstrates qualities of girl and woman, to the chagrin of those looking after her. She still has dolls and her grandfather's handmade three-story dollhouse in her room, and plays jump rope and hopscotch with other schoolgirls. She knows children's songs. But still, her thin freckled skin blushes across her gaunt cheeks when she glimpses that Cunningham boy's older frame, which has the leanness and slender but taut musculature of a teen growing, planting, suckering, shucking, and putting up too much tobacco at his age. The thickness of his hands belies his age. He has outgrown his own body, with slabs of muscle that make a young girl's mind wander.

His daddy owns a large swath of Cunningham County and he is expected to make it bear fruit, to drive it into flower and then to strip that wealth from it and wad it up in his dad's pocket. That is what boys like him do until he catches up; he overwhelms, takes over, and makes the next Cunningham generation, a son who will overshadow his daddy too, in the same way, in time. He drives his daddy's '34 Fleetwood-that-means-Business sedan, when few boys have access to a car of any kind, which means trouble and is a considerable advantage for that Cunningham boy, and he knows that too. Wide bench seats stretch from one side of the car to the other. He shuffles to school in that vehicle in such a way as Jeannie could tell he's done God knows what on that very seat, specifics she can't imagine but finds she wants to know about.

This scandal with her mother, Marjorie, that the whole town knows but pretends they don't in the presence of her family makes

Jeannie bold, to want, to seek out those kinds of lusty thoughts her momma must have had, but especially it makes the girl cautious and wise to the perception of those around her should she get caught being curious about this boy. It is dangerous for her. She doesn't care. She assumes she has the same hot blood within her that drove her mother to madness and she doesn't intend to go mad. Piety is a flavor she seasons well, and decency too, and what that looks like and how to give everybody that show. Etta has conditioned her to be an expert witness to lust that does not leave traces. So when that Cunningham boy pulls up his broad smile alongside her when nobody is looking, in that sedan-that-means-Business, and strikes up a conversation as so many times before, Jeannie is not caught off guard.

"Hey, Jeannie! It's way too hot for you to be walking and I can see you're sweatin' right through that pretty dress. Now say, I'm heading out by your house to pick up some rent, so why don't you let me give you a ride before you get all dusty from walkin'?"

He grins so pretty at her that she beams back before she means to. It starts as simply as that. She accepts a ride that is offered from that Cunningham boy at the precise moment when she knows she won't get caught, and then she talks herself into the belief that it is just a ride anyway, and Carter's General is close so she can ask to be let out there, and she isn't going to do anything with him, but thinking about the fact that he might like to kiss her overwhelms any thought of not accepting. And then she is on the far side of that bench seat, staring straight ahead with her knees locked together, and her books clutched to her chest and over her lap. She has left the cardinal-red sweater at school that day.

The Cunningham boy keeps talking to her, but Jeannie says nothing, which is even more exciting for him, understanding this instant power he holds over her. He has seen it before, in older girls, and he is able to overcome. He watches her vibrate like a pent-up cat. She decides that if he tries anything she'll skedaddle, even if she enjoys it. Jeannie accepts that ride, but in the back of her thoughts she knows she is accepting a lot more and that begins it all, begins the process of her giving up the thoughts of filling in for her momma, for assuming the yoke laid out by Etta and Jesse and Marvin that everybody calls Charlie, laid out for her by the 600 or so folks in Symsonia to do the right thing and to settle in and take care of, to replace, to do as she is told, like her momma (before she didn't). Jeannie anticipates that she is more like her mom in other ways, she probably can't help it, and it's in her blood. An excuse makes the transition easy, to do what the body calls for, easy. Marjorie's experience teaches her that when they whisper behind your back, it takes a while for you or those around you to get wind of it, sometimes a long while, and she decides to use that, should she need it, to get around and see that boy, with his virility and the knotting of back muscles under his shirt and filling out his pant legs, and that knowing look of his that makes her feel naked. Her thoughts take her eyes off their course just long enough to do a sweep over of that body close up. He observes that too.

Once it begins, Jeannie becomes an expert in slipping out, slipping away, of becoming a specter with illusory destinations, of late nights that don't show in her school or chores the next day. That Cunningham boy takes her, slowly building upon trespasses, to places she doesn't dream of going, takes her where Marjorie left off, drew a line against, and did not dare dream of transgressing, even in her own abandonment, of reserving the dignity of not even knowing that such places exist. Not right away, he didn't, but that slow intrusion builds up like dripping wax, so that it feels natural once you finally get there. Nobody talks to her about those specific, undetectable incursions that lead to the general wrong, so it becomes easy to convince herself that each little invasion is acceptable, each want is not an infringement but a stopping point that somehow becomes the new starting marker, goes a little further the next time, that she is capable of going only this far, until it is time to advance on the next little misstep.

That boy knows how to get past defenses. His body, his maleness, makes it easy with girls who want it, want him, to get through the murmurings of "no" and "please stop." The secret is to stop and let those girls discover how much their own words betray them, to discover that they are lies, to discover how much they want it, and let them pretend to be in control of the next "yes." That Cunningham boy has patience. This he knows all about too, but Jeannie doesn't. She has the unfortunate disposition that she is prone to what she is about to do next, that the next "yes" is predetermined, that in fact she has a predilection to "yeses."

And both master the secret. They drive that Fleetwood-that-means-Business sedan to Melber or Boaz, or to the Kentucky Dam, and park off the main road or down by Kentucky Lake and explore the curiosity each of them has for the other. It starts agonizingly enough with the accident of fingertips brushing the outskirts of a slim, unflinching hand, parked too close to each other on a blanket in the middle of the day, as the tow boats grind themselves against the steel of the barges loaded with coal and ore or more-precious cargo, slipping up and down the locks of the dam, and it is slow and lazy and kind of natural for their hands to touch like that, and to lie in the grass so that her shirt comes a little untucked and he points this out but accidentally grazes her stomach with those hard-worked hands. And the thought seizes her and lingers long after they leave each other, about what else they might be capable of, when Jeannie is alone in her room at the top of the stairs overlooking that backyard with that crucified clothesline that runs into a dead end at the close of the yard.

And those little movements become natural, the grazing and the touching and the hand-holding, so that the next slip is so much easier, almost ordinary, when he tries to kiss her like she thinks he will and like Jeannie secretly daydreams about while working, and she allows her fingertips to graze against her own hip or stomach or across the back of her neck, or to feel their way over the indentation of the elastic at the waistband of her panties through muslin, but it isn't even close to the same as when he does it. That shift, that movement from kiss to embrace, is logical in her mind because she pursues it, wants to be wanted, longs for it like a dime store novel or a movie with Elizabeth Taylor in it about a girl gone bad, and Jeannie sort of has eyes like hers so she emulates those kisses with the thin air. It isn't enough. She wants that kind of power over somebody else but doesn't really see it like that—more like having someone with the same kind of longing she furtively owns, but who knows how to quench it. These secrets fire off like the Fourth of July inside her, almost burst into her telling her sisters, but Jeannie knows better. Marjorie has made her wise enough to know that keeping a secret keeps it sacred, keeps it pure. It can't be tarnished with fact or with advice. That is what is mysterious in this boy, that Cunningham boy.

Jeannie also knows he somehow holds the spells to all that she wants to know, wants done to her, and to do to somebody else.

"David," she says to the fluttering clothes that whip in the March winds but remain strapped to the clothesline. It is like that for her.

So their embraces soon are prolonged and Jeannie is aware of his virility flatly between them and her own sex is meeting that same neglected, empty place that she never knew she had before this instant but now can't forget for even a minute. These moments intermingle with her daily life, as she loiters in adjusting the pliant zipper of her cotton skirt, while thinking about those coarse fingertips and how that would feel, or as she soaps her swollen breasts in the corrugated tin tub with the slippery scalding water, and her mind and her inner heat is on him. There is no amount of pleasure that guilt doesn't make more tender. And that is how it all begins between them.

Its secret lies primarily in its physical qualities, the banal physics of blood coursing to newfound areas, nerve endings finding new life, but for her, she doesn't know the difference. She has nothing to compare it to. The delineation between liking this boy and wanting this boy loses itself because, at her age, those things get mixed up and some people never sort them out. Jeannie does not know this; it isn't part of the parsimonious information about womanhood meted out by Etta, and it is special, momentous, all-consuming.

And what is true for her is especially so for him because he is ruled by the physical, which belies the emotional. A boy like him has never met a girl like that before in the history of boy meeting girl. That Cunningham boy rivets to the fact that Jeannie meets his want with such ferocity, with equal or more powerful need, without reservation. He has never been this far in the chase, not this far with a girl. He drives her the twelve miles to the back side of the flood wall outside of Paducah, and they spend hours petting and serenading each other's bodies on that big bench, and she quenches her curiosity about his sex and he finds ways to make her respond to him that satisfy his ego and his lust and leave her flushed and panting and sweat-drenched in such a way that Ivory Snow wouldn't be able to completely remove it, this change from a child to a woman. Such transformations reveal themselves and cannot be concealed. Her mystery becomes visible in her hips and how she knows her body and in her confidence in that newfound body, her body of sex: her body capable of sex.

Those around them notice the difference in her, but they can't sort out the potential from the act and they whisper, but it takes a long while for this gossip to get back to a family that has taken notice themselves. Her family waits and they watch for some sign that the potential has been breached, but not closely enough. Jeannie knows this, has counted on hesitation while she learns to live with a capital L. They are never seen together, dare not speak to each other outside of the confines of their discretion, but give themselves to each other with a passing glance or a brush of arm or fingertip if they can manage to obscure it. The two develop that secret language exchanged between surreptitious lovers, a familiarity and trust and bonding that only teens can have with each other after becoming sexual, that time when bodies harden to each other, adhere and draw toward each other without their owners being aware of the betrayal. Theirs is a relationship that grows inside of the secret, becomes ripe with it, splits itself open with its over-ripeness. The effort to subdue its ferocity cannot be contained and it presses its heat under the skin until its oppression consumes both of them.

Months into this pairing, the two break free of the barriers of the sedan, of hidden places, as is inevitable. That Cunningham boy overcomes resistance with the same patience that breaks down her defenses, and he seeks out other venues to celebrate and expand their proscribed isolation and talks of nothing else, and she is equally frustrated with the sequestration. He entertains thoughts of taking her to places he would only take a person with that kind of built-up trust. That Cunningham boy talks of places they could go where they would not be exiles, able to walk among people who understand the need to live with a capital L like those two do. It becomes an open discussion to reach an end neither of them could envision.

"David, you know we can't do that. I can never go back to that house and show my face again if we get caught! Why would you ask me to do something like that? Don't you know how my grandmaw is? What she'll do to me if she finds out? Daddy won't do nothing, but muhmaw will strip and horsewhip me!" Jeannie is too cautious, slow to come to the realization that want trumps caution.

That Cunningham boy takes her protests into consideration, decides it cannot be with the white trash that goes to the Clark's riverbank. Even those individuals have cause to speak of it. It can't be on the other side of the railroad tracks where half-breed Indians and whites live neither. Found there, you'll be spit on and labeled an Indian-lover, but the ramifications are a middling, a halfway. Even those lesser-than's are a step above what he is contemplating: people offering little or no risk to hiding in public. It is out of irresistible desperation, out of a preponderance of need. That Cunningham boy seeks out the outcast of civilized society, because they are not acceptable to a society that is civil, and he determines that the places they go will be socially outlawed pockets of furtive gatherings, makeshift centrifuges to separate the civil from the untouchable; places for those who side-skirt society like he and Jeannie are doing. He is up to no good. If discovered they will be killed and by people who know them and think it a death well deserved. The stakes have to be high to savor this kind of fruit.

In their current form, they are anathema and they both understand this. And it works. Because that Cunningham boy toils alongside his father's workers and knows them and is friendly to them like white people normally aren't, and because they are friendly back in a way that is a little more trusting than they give most white folks, because of all of this he finds in existence such hidden places where black people go to celebrate in the way that Cunningham boy wants to celebrate Jeannie and offer his revelation in her to the world, even if it has to be this one. That Cunningham boy goes there and he convinces Jeannie to go too.

"When we're together it's like we're dreaming it, and that's fact. It just ain't real. I gotta see people seeing me with you to believe it, Jeannie! You know I mean that honestly, that you gotta go with me. You just gotta go with me!"

"You think I don't know that, David? Every time we pass each other and you don't look at me, I wonder if all that we have together does really happen. I know it ain't enough. I get sucked up in emptiness when you pass me by without even lookin' at me. I die right there and wanna call out to you to look at me. To just look at me! But what am I supposed to do? You know if Muhmaw sees us she'd make a barrow out of you herself with a kitchen knife!" Jeannie doesn't laugh after the statement and her white blue eyes hold his gaze like an exclamation point.

It takes nights upon nights and building on facts that what they have is not enough. Convincing is made easier by the circumstance that they both are greedy for more of each other, to have each other in new ways; the luster is slipping from the pearl. Jeannie thinks about that Cunningham boy's frustration, his despair, about their misery, and finally doesn't want to miss out on life like her mother—whose quick death has somehow turned off in her that ability that most folks have to cast moral judgment. This is what convinces Jeannie to go with that Cunningham boy to this scandalous underbelly. And besides, that she is capable of doing such a thing is so outlandish that her family would never believe it, even if the rumor catches up to her. So Jeannie goes with him.

Desegregation isn't a legal action in Kentucky brought about by governments and officials, an abstract, but a terrifying set of events ripping away the sanctity of every community and shredding the fabric of society. Alabama and Mississippi are too far away. In this all are of one mind and of one thought. It is a preoccupation. All they know will be destroyed by mixing the races that God intends to keep separate, and nowhere is that as important as in this poor backwater of Kentucky. This is so, not because of racial purity, as the rest of the nation decrees, so much as because the only superiority a body has left in this small forgotten town is color. Everybody is secretly a mixture of Indian that nobody talks about, inbred with God-knew-what, dirt poor or working-middle-class poor except for a few ruthless families of worth. Those families are the ones that everybody wants to take a chip off of, because they live beyond the boundaries of possibility, snatching up all that is good and raking it in to themselves, and only sharing among the likes of them, as they all glut on greed and lies to keep what they have hacked off for themselves firmly amongst themselves.

Jeannie and that Cunningham boy live in a society of carefully kept have and have-not castes, in which farmers and sawmill workers subsist and do not intermix. So their meager town and its people keep each other in place by social stratifying, and simply ignore requests to take down the "Coloreds Only" signs over the two public water fountains, or to close off the side entrances to respectable businesses and public places. Colored folks just keep on using them like things haven't changed much, because really they haven't and this is what is expected in order to keep an orderly society. The two sides draw a cautious truce, and speaking—outside of a habit amongst workers—is unspoken and forbidden.

So Jeannie goes against God with him. She goes against all that Etta teaches her. She goes against all that Marjorie drilled into her about their kind. Full of trepidation and cold, balled-up fear at first, Jeannie discovers that going there becomes easier to do after that first trespass. The rewards are too great to resist. The fruit is honeyed there. That Cunningham boy uses the farm truck to drive her way out on Wildcat Road and then deep into the woods and then to tow paths that can only be accessed by foot. Winding tracks announce your arrival before you get there, in case any action need be taken were you not welcome. These are way-out-of-the-way, secret places where a certain caste of black people gyrate and grind and sweat all over each other like they are fucking in public and make a wanton display of that like Jeannie and that Cunningham boy do in the secrecy of the sedan-that-means-Business, and the people run hands underside heaving breasts and brush hiked skirts and naked thighs against rigid male flesh pressed wet and sweating into thin wool pants. And they dance, with the shadows hiding the deep valleys of sparsely lit bodies, so God only knows what touches in those areas as they drive each other with life and vigor and sex and sweat and need and hunger. And this is all that Jeannie knew of these people, and she assumes they are all secretly this way, so she watches with wide eyes and asserts that this is what living with a capital L is about, these kinds of places, this kind of freedom, so far beyond what her mother discovered in her longing.

They couldn't go often. It is too risky that someone talks, or sees the truck, even though they have driven miles out of the way to get there. When they are there, they drink and sponge up this spectacle for faltering, halting, long periods of time, working themselves into lust for each other with what they see. Jeannie and that Cunningham boy break away to the outside for fresh air and a hit of spirits he buys from the same Negro that sells to all of the folks in his juke joint, from the back of his rusted, pistachio green and white pick-up. They watch, and when the liquor and all of that elation hit them, they sometimes dance alongside.

This shocks even them as well as the black couples swaying around them, but nobody says much because they all know that that Cunningham boy from the tobacco fields and this white girl are going to be a lot of trouble anyhow, on account of her wild momma, and it was a kind of a payback to that bastard of a father he has. So the kind of people that go to the kind of place Jeannie and that Cunningham boy find themselves in let him do it to her, and in a way that Cunningham boy is doing it to all of the white folks of Symsonia and Alabama and Tennessee and Mississippi and Georgia that is in the news these days. And they keep it to themselves and allow these two white kids to go to town on each other and gyrate and grind and rub sweaty flesh onto sweating thighs and sometimes kiss and grunt with the passion and joy that well up inside them on those creaking floors of a hidden and no longer segregated dance shack lost in the backwoods of Kentucky. And this mainly works up to bigger explosions than Jeannie and that Cunningham boy are looking for by going to such places, and it happens in each other when they finally find themselves alone in that farm truck again. It becomes easy, natural, this behavior.

And when they are through and the chill of the early morning air slips into the cracked, sweat-streaked window, drying to faint salt stains on clothes clinging to their now chilled and satisfied flesh, he tells her stuff like how the colored folk could act that way in public because of the years that they were traded like cattle and weren't able to have families and emotional connections to each other, so that freed them because respectable white people treated and traded them like animals so they could writhe and grind and rut each other and be free about their sex and have an understanding about their bodies in a public way that society imposes and suppresses away in white people.

"You know, Jeannie, it's a damned shame that we got so many rules on us that you an' me can't be together like that. Hell, my daddy's already talking about who I should marry and when, when we've got all this. Why can't you just be together with me like that, without suffocating under that strangling noose of what everybody else wants?"

He tells her that white people make themselves respectable, but respectability also makes them like imprisoned cuckolds, lap dogs under the watchful gaze of everybody else so they don't get to let go like those Negroes.

Jeannie traces the genuine sadness in his face with her fingertips.

"You know it can't be like that for us, David. Nobody wants to step back, and us being together would be like steppin' back for your daddy and Muhmaw, but for different reasons. Your daddy's got his sights for ya and Muhmaw don't think it's a good match, plain and simple, because of my age an' that. They just can't see it and it'll never be let be."

And Jeannie thought he is smart to understand this, and she revels in this secret, worldly life she is living with a capital L, and she does it without anybody knowing anything about it, which also thrills her and lusters up the pearl again, and this is a secret he already knows about girls, how much they like it.

Jeannie begins doing it right after church, joining her girlfriends for a soda at Woolworth's and cutting their visit short to meet up with that Cunningham boy, or she sneaks out of the house by climbing through her window onto the back porch and shimmying down the Victorian latticework on the outside of the screen, and runs out past the clothesline to the road and hurries to where they already talked about meeting. He waits for her just out of sight, around the hard bend in Oaks Road, with the lights off, and has her back before four, when Jesse starts to rise. That's how Jeannie gets away with it for so long, how she does it right under their noses—with the help of that caliber of people nobody notices, in town or outside of it either: the day laborers, the chattel.

But that kind of passion in a teen boy can't be contained to only slaking his lust. It can't be contained by increasing the stakes. It spills out in other ways too, into everyday life, and that kind of thing can't be held in to just one part of life, once it's unleashed in a boy like that Cunningham boy, and that's what did it in for them. He is the kind of boy who knows better. They are at odds, him and adults. So he stops asking and he starts doing. That is how the beginning of the end comes about with their affair.

Protocols do not mean much to a kid like that Cunningham boy. He doesn't understand how his opposition can't see how right everything is for Jeannie and him, how important all of this ecstasy is. Without introductions by his family, without following the proper channels or presenting himself as a proper suitor (which would be rejected by Jesse and Etta and his parents too as preposterous anyway because Jeannie is only into her thirteenth year by this time), without understanding the consequences of his reception, he drives that Fleetwood-that-means-Business sedan up past that hard turn in Oaks Road, right to that Gothic white farmhouse in the middle of the day on that Saturday afternoon that changes everything for Jeannie and for him too, for everyone really.

Jeannie is on the back porch with the Kenmore and the *ugg, ugg, ugg* of the gyrator covering the sound of the engine as he pulls up to have a talk with Etta and Jesse and Marvin. Jeannie is thankfully deaf to the plea he is making to Etta about how he is going to take her away and marry her and that's what he set his mind to, even though, admittedly, Jeannie has expressed reservations about the whole thing. Jeannie is pleasantly ignorant to the fact that that Cunningham boy has it all worked out as to how they will live and what he'd do for a living to support them and how it wouldn't disrupt any of their lives too much, as she'd just be down the road and, for the great finale, that Cunningham boy finishes with the happily-ever-after of great-grandchildren for Etta and Jesse and for Marvin too, and all thanks to the magnitude of his and her happiness. The urgency and the pleading in his voice reveal much about the depth in which Jeannie has already indulged, and Etta silently comes to know this. Jeannie, however, remains, for the moment, blind to the fact that he has exposed everything.

It is one of the rare occasions that Jesse is out in his workshop, which isn't so much to continue making furniture as it is to escape the house full of women, and Marvin called Charlie is still working at the sawmill. Etta is the one who comes to the door when he calls to her from the bottom of the wooden stairs with the gray paint rubbed thin from wear, although it still remains ingrained in the wood, leaving traces of what once was on those aging boards. The sound of the engine alerts her to company, but she calls for someone to go to the door as she is peeling apples in the kitchen. Nobody responds. So she carries that pleasant smile that all folks have in Symsonia, that is half expecting pleasant company, or terrifying news, but mainly covers the turning wheels and questions a grandmother has who's raising her dead daughter's children, and who lives out the shame of what went on before in good grace, even though she knows people talk about it still: what happened when her only daughter was driven to madness with her broken heart, as everybody collectively decides to label it. Etta peers down the long fresh hallway from the back of the house with arrested surprise and dull wonder.

Etta is wearing house slippers and her simple cotton Simplicity pattern shift crossing over her heavy chest, with ties on either side, the shift that was once a radiant pink with a pattern of floating, individual-cut fence roses on it but that has been bleached white from hard wear so that you look hard to see that it had color at all once, or notice that the sweetness of those fence roses had faded off some time ago. Not expecting visitors, she dresses it up with a gay apron she made from a McCall's pattern that she pulls over her housedress as she shuffles her way to the door. None of that is on her mind just yet as she steps out from behind that wavering Victorian screen door into the dancing heat of the day.

This is Etta's feminine armor, which she uses to keep her large house and family running past the time she expects to. It is what she wears day in and day out while cleaning and cooking and tending the little kitchen garden, and tending to her husband and grandchildren and her daughter's widower, Marvin called Charlie, and it is these things that have stripped that house dress of all of its color and vigor and sweetness. It is comfortable in its age, this old thing; it is easy to keep sparkling clean and it suffices. This unknown boy in this unknown car is altogether a surprise, and Etta doesn't know why, but she has four girls in her ward and is instantly suspicious.

So it occurs to her that it is even more surprising that he drives that Fleetwood-that means-Business sedan up to the front of the house and announces that he'd like to see her granddaughter, and not even the oldest, now fourteen, but the second one.

"Is Jeannie in? JEANNIE! JEA-NNIE!" He calls her name out as if garnering support for his deed, an accomplice of sorts.

This does not go unnoticed. Although there is no visible change in expression on Etta's face, she has recognized this kind of urgency before. She asks why he inquires about her granddaughter and does he know that she is only thirteen and keeps no company of any kind at her age?

"Mrs. Jones, you gotta see here, your granddaughter and me, we've got something special here…." He shifts, he fidgets, looking up at her from his place the yard. "I know what you're thinkin'…." The words keep coming and he keeps going and leaves no auditory space for rebuttal, accepts no argument, and does not reason. Overtaken by silence, Etta notices the emptiness in the boy's words.

The strength and force and nervous constraint with which that Cunningham boy speaks reveal all kinds of things to that old woman on the front porch as she listens to what he has to say, and to all that he isn't saying. Etta notices how his body moves in his tight khakis and tee shirt, how his hips jut out slightly as he speaks, how he rocks himself into the rapidity of conversation with his sex, and she takes all of this in as the boy proclaims his love for this grandchild of hers and speaks of taking Jeannie away because they are in love. Shaking her head, Etta acquiesces to his demand to see Jeannie and calls into the house for her granddaughter, through the long hall cooled by the afternoon air moving from the front of the house to the back without interruption, all the way to the back-porch pantry where that Kenmore is churning. Jeannie hears the call in a voice she doesn't recognize, the pitch of a familiar voice changed, made odd. Jeannie freezes as she kills the engine switch and peers into the dark corridor leading to her future. The eternity as she pads along those long wooden planks, from the exodus of the house to the entrance, weighs on them both, Etta and that Cunningham boy, knowingly, cautiously watching Jeannie make her way to the door.

Etta also watches, hawk-like, the two together for a bit, noting how Jeannie nervously puts her hands clasped self-consciously over her feminine parts. Then Etta fades back into the comfortable shadows of the house, leaving the two of them on the lawn, standing by the Fleetwood with its bench seats where so much has transpired. The girl takes it all in, everything now coated in blanched terror—his urging and his words, the Fleetwood, which was so delicious and private in the furtive dark but now catcalls at her so that her shock and shame are revealed for all to see in the light of day, in her own front yard, in front of her grandmother—and the horror of what is happening by his being here strips away all of the carefully laid secrecy that drives color to her lean cheeks and flees it simultaneously.

Etta's disappearance gives Jeannie a few distorted moments to collect herself. But Etta witnesses that registration from behind the screen, in that cool hallway that her husband laid, that is where she realizes the transgression that Cunningham boy has laid on her grandchild. His hands have been on her. To what extent, Etta wonders. How far has this gone? Is the child in her ward still intact and can she be saved? Etta ruminates and turns these thoughts over in her head before her next move, which comes in short order. Protecting a girl's sex and morality is paramount for the structure in which they live. Fallen girls don't go off and get married and they don't increase familial stature in society, and they don't make good wives to good men. They become social pariahs. They become her daughter Marjorie. The child's mother was debauched by such a man as this and Jeannie should know that it rubs off on good people. They are good people.

That is what Etta is protecting when she lithely slips out past the screen, and it is with fortitude that Etta raises the double-barrel shotgun and levels it at him.

"This won't be goin' any further than the end of this here shotgun, boy."

He turns as the gravity of the situation registers with full force, and it is with that same force that the first shotgun blast peppers him across his back and thighs and dapples the paint of that Fleetwood-that-means-Business sedan as he dives for the sanctuary of the driver's seat. Jeannie floats above them, above herself, as she watches the second blast take out the back windshield and stipple the trunk and the back of his head as it speeds away from that old white farmhouse at the hard bend in Oaks Road. Etta doesn't say anything more. She turns and gives that look to Jeannie that tells her everything that is wrong with what just happened. It tells her about the filth of a girl her age having interest in anything but her studies and hard work and innocence until told to do otherwise. It tells Jeannie that she is just like her mother, cut from the same cloth with the same pair of scissors. It alludes to the fact that this old woman knows the sordid things she has done, has allowed to have done to her, and it rankles Jeannie's entire body as if it were a physical blow. And it sinks into her with suppressed defiance. She gets it, all right. She takes that message to heart as she falls to her knees watching that Cunningham boy go.

But it isn't the same message that Etta is sending out with that cold-dead look reserved for whores. It gets twisted in the switchboard somehow, gets rearranged. It makes concrete what Jeannie has suspected in herself all along, and speaks to her that she must be more vigilant, learn how to further hide in plain sight to get good at it—and haven't they been good at it? This is a game to be carefully played if she is to win it. And that is her intention; Jeannie needs to win. She knows that she needs to be more heedful and prudent and restrained to get it by them again, that she needs to get it right the next time or there will not be a next time and then she'll never get away, get out from under. Never once does Jeannie think about ending this living with a capital L.

They take up where they left off, but it takes him many months to heal. Etta had removed the buckshot from the shotgun, thankfully, but loaded it with rock salt instead. The salt burns through the meaty flesh and cures it, so healing takes longer, sealing up is more painful, and the wound is a reminder of the offense that Etta took great pains to punish. And that Cunningham boy learns too. What can't be overcome by willpower needs a different direction. So he set out to find it and to transgress by those other means, not upright, not proper ways, but ways that get him and Jeannie what they want, which is each other, to have unfettered access to each other's bodies. Sensibility frequently gets mixed up with youth and needs time to recalibrate, like a choked-out tractor engine. It gives Jeannie time to recollect, to deny, to build the false fortifications she needs to pass the test.

And so it goes in those healing and calculating months and beyond that Jeannie spends double time convincing her brother and sisters, Etta and Jesse, and Marvin called Charlie that she has reformed, that it was an innocent crush, that they all overreacted to a mere triviality, and that nothing like that is going to happen again.

"It's such a long walk from school and I don't get new shoes very often, so I was really thinkin' about saving on that. And I'm always soaking wet by the time I get here. So what if he gave me a ride? What's wrong with that except what's in y'all's dirty minds? It's downright unsanitary what y'all're thinkin'! I don't wanna bring it up, but this is all because of our momma, so why don't y'all just say so!" And then she'd turn doe eyed and soft: "I'm sorry about causing such a fuss over a ride, Muhmaw. I just didn't know y'all'd react like that. I mean look at me. I'm just a girl who had a crush on a boy an' he took it way too far and out of the actual situation, really. Stuff like what y'all dreamed up, well, that never entered my mind what y'all're thinkin'! I don't like boys. No, not like that, not at all like that."

She uses her guile and her deceit like a weapon against their morality and suppression. She vilifies their vileness and she acts out a childhood for them, spending more time with her dolls and with children's games while under their gaze. It is what they need to believe and it slowly dissolves their mistrust.

Jeannie spends double time making sure that her double life is not discovered. She and that Cunningham boy snatch smaller, hungrier moments in plain sight of her family, perpetrating the ruse now where she is visible, exposed, and blatant, cutting the minutes to a desperate amount but doing so in the light of scrutiny—the public library, sometimes minutes behind an unguarded bookshelf, sometimes hours at a time locked together in the broad daylight smashed into the unseen parts of the stifling cabin of a hay bailer—whatever she can get away with. The result of such actions makes the moments intoxicating, but the interlude between meetings compounds frustration.

Want doesn't slake itself in denial. Unslaked lust twists the bedsheets and culls sleep. It takes a toll on the body and on the mind. Finally, there is one particularly cool evening that follows the dry dead-heat days that drain you of energy so you're too tired or too hot to sweat properly. That exhilarating cool breeze takes you up and out of yourself, revives you, releases you, and that is the evening they decide to do it.

"David, how long are you gonna pretend before we get caught again, before the odds turn on us? They watch me, sometimes two at a time, to make sure we ain't together. How long do you think that's gonna last before they catch us? Sometimes I don't think I can breathe with them lookin' at me! Listen, something's gotta change and it's gotta be us or them, and I don't see them changing."

"I've been thinkin' about that too, Jeannie. God Jesus knows I love you. They just gotta understand this. They will too, by God. But it's our job to show them we really mean it, that we gotta teach 'em, Jeannie. You an' me just gotta stand up and show 'em how I love you—that we ain't kids just messing around or somethin'."

Jeannie owns few clothes and even fewer personal belongings, which she places in her white vinyl valise with the white Bakelite handle and brass snaps that she has never used, she climbs onto the black tarpaper roof over the back porch pantry, and with some effort climbs down the gingerbread lattice work over the screened-in porch to the dew-sopped grass below.

"Okay, Momma. This is real now and I'm scared. But I swear to God it's really gonna happen. Me and David's gonna stand up together and we're gonna finally be living just like you did, Momma!" She smiles his name into the night wind as she alights and pauses to take one last look at the old porch and the clothesline, the constraint and hampered ambitions, and all that her Muhmaw's house represents.

Jeannie makes no noise as she slips from behind the house and around the gazebo that is really a carport, careful not to crunch gravel until she is well away. She makes her way to the hard bend in Oaks Road as you head into Symsonia. That Cunningham boy meets her there in the Fleetwood-that-means-Business with the lights off and pushes her head down and into him and they head out to Missouri. He has already scouted it out. In Kentucky, sixteen is the legal age to get married without your parents' consent, but not in Missouri. So they open the road with a one-track mind. At the courthouse, Jeannie presents her mother's death and divorce certificates and tells the Justice that she doesn't know where her father is. They marry, ready to begin again with a little of his daddy's money stashed away, and God damn the rest. Their illusion and their passionate living with a capital L last a total of five days.

As determined as the couple is, Etta is just as determined to set things right with her family and to varnish over, tar over if necessary, the kind of scandal the family is headed for, but Etta is a respectable woman and uses respectable means to do it. And so they are found out, holed up in a motel there in Missouri when the police discover their whereabouts. The Fleetwood is one of those cars that are unmistakable and easy to find, especially when it is on the backside of a sleazy roadside motel close to where the cops are looking.

Even though that Cunningham boy has a marriage license in hand, the cops arrest him, on the word of the old woman, for kidnapping Jeannie and transporting her across state lines, and they call his father to come pick up the car. They take the girl back immediately to her waiting grandmother, who is the very epitome of frailty—hysterical, all hand-wringing and tears, standing on the front porch of that respectable old white farmhouse at the hard bend in Oaks Road. The policeman lectures Jeannie on the ride to Kentucky and is sorry for the family having to go through this again. He explains to Etta the story Jeannie gave of a mother's death, and how the courts were deceived into believing that she didn't need consent and so married her to that Cunningham boy, and that by talking to the judge that married them, it would be just as easy for Etta to file for the marriage annulment. The policeman gives Etta his number and he helps the old woman get it taken care of without anybody knowing except the two of them. And with the Cunningham boy corralled for a bit, the marriage is dissolved discretely, felicitously, without his consent. The courts do not ask the opinion or preference of the lawless. But it cannot be done quietly in a town like that, no matter what the police officer promises.

Months later, after the tobacco is cut, stripped, and railed to dry, Etta's family realizes that five days is more than enough time to get a girl knocked-up in some sleazy roadside motel with all the comfort of a bed and the convenience of nothing but time on their hands to celebrate their not-yet-annulled marriage. It is too late for Etta to save the family by having something done about it. Not that Etta would anyway, so she pens a letter in her too-thin cursive to family services, who comes with neatly typed forms on onionskin paper stapled up in robin's egg blue official covers, that transfer over the custody of this bastard child born to an unwed minor. Etta demands that Jeannie sign it, and the infant is taken away to Iowa. Jeannie would keep those onionskin papers that typed up her future and the future of her little baby girl as filmy and brittle memories of what had transpired, and of what Etta was capable.

And the neatly wrapped bundle of a baby girl, first named Marjorie but, like fate, quickly changed, never knows that she is adopted or about Marfan Syndrome, why she loves horses, or why she dies at 29. Instead, in that lovely white, comfortably familiar turn-of-the-century farmhouse there in Iowa, a family cares for her as their own and teaches her to be a good, upstanding member of society and attend church on Wednesday night and have Sunday dinner with family, until—just before she spreads her wings—a sudden heart event stretches the miles back to Kentucky and her lost family, just as suddenly as she came to them there in Iowa.

Authorities release that Cunningham boy almost immediately, with a lot of help from his father's connections and a little warning about statutory rape and a chuckle from the officers about keeping it in his pants. That boy and that girl see each other now and again, but it isn't the same, no matter how much Jeannie tries to make it out to be for them. The baby is gone and the spark is gone and the reality of a world set against them sets in and makes it no longer natural, simple. Their binding, minus the clarity love has in the young, stains bitter. It isn't directed at each other but somehow intermingles with what they once felt for each other, and it is no longer savory. The luster diminishes to hardly noticing. That Cunningham boy and Jeannie turn on one another with the longing of the space between parents and absent children but aren't sure why or when it happens. Still, the complication of melded feelings about the turn of events does not keep them from the want, and so they both continue battering their feelings and excess constraint against each other's bodies, in search of strength again.

By January, Jeannie has stopped caring whether a muddier affection does or doesn't diminish, and it no longer matters anyway. She and that Cunningham boy arouse such passion, yet watch helplessly as the other part, the finer part, withers away. It is then, in the suspension between hope and resignation, when tobacco shoots are inching up in the greenhouse, when Jeannie, trying to prove to them both that everything is the same, finds she is again with child. As in all of the stories that don't quite make it, right after that Cunningham boy learns about the second baby coming, he drifts away, leaving her to the responsibility and obligations of a woman in that kind of trouble, because he can no longer recover the intensity, because he knows it is never going to be the same way again, and he should really listen to his father after all. The mind clears after the lust slakes and the sweat dries. Neither of them quite recovers from the losses imposed by those around them, imposed on each other, and on themselves. It is in such unions that one is reminded that Romeo and Juliet once served as a warning.

Jeannie is fifteen when her clothes betray her and the pregnancy reveals itself in her body. It is too late for hand-wringing because Jeannie has lived with a capital L, and she realizes her lapse of second guesses, trusting that Cunningham boy, giving like she had given to no one else, and bearing witness to its abrupt and fruitless end with the worst possible consequence for a family already slandered by the actions of a mother. She has executed her destiny too soon; the flame of youth burns up inside her, and the baby is now extracting whatever is left. And Jeannie decides then that she is no longer determined to get out of that house, and that freedom concludes at the end of that clothesline before the open fields that lay after it. Living with a capital L tarnishes and loses its luster.

It is summer and Jeannie's a burden now. She finds that it is not possible to shake the yoke of her mother Marjorie as it descends onto her young square shoulders. She wrings the life out of those clothes and resuscitates them again in the wind and the sun. She no longer leaves the farmhouse. The weight of the yoke also carries the shame of looks and stares when she isn't supposed to notice. Her family knows that she notices and that's why they do it to her. Dismay bends her under its weight and the weight of the child in her. She wavers. She stumbles under the enormity of its banal ramifications. She is not welcome. She adds to their burden the betrayal and the furious indifference made obvious in every waking moment of her day, just what her carelessness and her incomprehensible need to live with a capital L have cost the family.

Although not quite silver, a lining of sorts for those clouds over her bastard Cunningham child appears unexpectedly in late August. Marvin finds him for her. The Riverboat Man sweeps aside her baggage, Jesus to the Magdalene. Broken himself, Edward Earl is only fourteen, but he has already been his own man for two years now. He is seeking out a wife, but for different purposes.

Etta cancels her call to social services and releases the child and two generations of scandal. This is the first stride to the salvaged family grace that Etta so completely needs, and her tears are selfishly for herself. This would do. It scours away reminders of the kind of child Marjorie and then Etta raised, the failure, the humiliation of faithless lust that slopes into her granddaughter's belly so publicly it could not be eradicated. But Jeannie refuses the old woman her salvation. At childbirth, she refuses to give her new husband's name to her child, branding the child a bastard to spite Etta and adding to the brutal consequences. But for the moment, the sun is on Etta's face, on both their faces. They turn to the light.

A Woman's Winter, 1964

It lasts five years. Witness collapsing destruction and it gouges its path of assault just under the skin. Jeannie's family has track marks vividly mapping the end of this coupling, the viciousness of two people in the throes of divorce, after Jesse Earl and Jennie Kaye are born and add to the mix all the trouble of his wife's flagrant first bastard, Lisa Jo. They remember better the bitter ending than the hopeful beginning, her false start. The ensuing days and months and years are banal before obliteration strikes collectively. Jeannie (or Jeannie Mae, as she comes to be known in the family after Jennie Kaye arrives) spells it out for her children as love festers, ruptures, and is abruptly over. It is in this way that children take upon their thin backs the lashes that break apart the pieces. The torrent of wrath crashes upon some shore. The smashing mass of failure that comes from a fourteen-year-old boy and a fifteen-year-old girl's marriage collides in all directions the instant Jeannie stops trying.

It isn't just the one thing: that instance when Edward Earl, the Riverboat Man, impugns upon the neighbor, when he takes the girl home and lingers. Jeannie and Edward Earl are buying the little Brown Street house their new family lives in. Once neighbor, now conspirator against his family, against Jeannie, she drives the wedge between them. Edward's indiscretion isn't the destroyer. Not *only* it, that is; it is a part but not all. The bringer of annihilation enters this household by taking Edward's final son, that last baby. That is a part of it, too, toward the end of Jeannie Mae's second marriage.

In their first year together, Edward Earl and Jeannie head out to Fresno in '64, just him and her and the bastard girl of that Cunningham boy, leaning a little bit on Edward Earl's mother and picking oranges for a living. Jesse, his first boy, comes, then the last girl, Jennie Kaye, as the couple makes babies but no progress, no traction. Jeannie wavers, pulled by the ostensible tethers to her family on that hard bend in Oaks Road and her Riverboat town. They drive back to Kentucky but return to Fresno once Edward Earl is doing better and making some financial traction. It is going to be better, but then it starts to slip again. The last child comes, that last baby boy, but dies out there in California, and so do all of Edward Earl's hopes.

You can't have kids with sometimes work and no money. Edward Earl and Jeannie return again to their Kentucky town, from all of that happiness they thought stretched before them like orange groves, with Jeannie's bastard girl and his firstborn boy and then Jennie Kaye, and then, finally, that last dead hope that was the youngest boy. Through the ceaseless setbacks, the last false start the Riverboat Man places his hope for a new beginning on is that boy, and suddenly the long shot seems too long, so he returns with her and they give up on Fresno. Edward Earl goes back to working on that towboat called the *Trey*, because the dream of making a living in California doesn't pan out. But Jeannie Mae and that Riverboat Man are too restless for their own good.

His second boy had lived a few sweet weeks, born into all of that concluding possibility, but he was tethered too tightly to his mother. The umbilical cord strangles off his oxygen, cutting off his existence, and the tiniest little infant, imbued with hope, struggles against these odds for a little while, strains to latch on to life but finds that there isn't enough out there to hang on to, and finally can't do it on his own. Fighting for an existence that isn't coming, he can't compete hard enough to make up for it all, for all of that defeat and that struggle to make it among the hard living that is still to come. So the baby boy dies and Jeannie and the Riverboat Man put that tiny body in a baby-blue coffin the color of the mother's sorrowful eyes and trimmed extravagantly with white lace, and they name him and seal up all of that opportunity in that box with the child, and put it in the black Fresno ground. The Riverboat Man doesn't show any emotion about it, but it gut-punches him losing that boy, that new hope among these two girls (one his natural child and one not) and Jesse Earl, the firstborn boy he has somehow already lost over to Jeannie, before this final boy of chance is lost to perhaps his own dissonance.

It doesn't start off like that, putting so many hopes in that bundle, in this new son, his boy. For the Riverboat Man, his firstborn, Jesse Earl, is lost to him in the summer of 1970, really after Christmas 1969, when, along with a pair of Buster Brown shoes and a blue-and-white double-breasted blazer and white pants, the boy receives the hard plastic, taupe-colored Geronimo action figure (because he is a sidekick and therefore cheaper) with the red face and hands; black hair and eyes; and a buffalo cap with horns, a bow and arrow, a peace pipe, a shield, and a tomahawk. The catalyst starts because that firstborn leaves Geronimo in the front yard one evening in the beginning of spring, leaves it with the distractions of children, forgetting the doll and going to bed. The Riverboat Man tosses the toy in the trash barrel. Toys cross the line and encourage peculiarities in his boy that can't be tolerated, so he disposes of it. It is the beginning of a father's suspicions. A second incident forces the lesson and makes it stick. That is the man's undoing.

The episode begins on one of those days when the Riverboat Man works but does not come home at night and then suddenly appears midday, out of the blue but without explanation, because he doesn't need one, this king of his castle, and that is when he uncovers evidence of his suspicions about his firstborn boy, discovers his own mistake, his folly. Carrying with him his scent of sweated-out coffee and a pack-and-a-half habit, the Riverboat Man is aggrieved by his own hand in raising this child, leaving his firstborn son too long with a house full of women. The Cunningham girl has spread across the braided rug her array of Barbie's, including the darker, particularly offensive Francie Fairchild, and there is his son, holding that red-faced Geronimo (taken from the trash where it belonged, goddamnit) that should have been made for girls. Suddenly, everything was wrong.

The Riverboat Man knows then, too late, too late discovers his grave error, when the predilection is already in full nurture behind his back. The discovery makes Edward Earl mad, makes him look for excuses as to why it isn't his fault, why it isn't him that needs punishing like this, having this doll-playing boy, but somebody else, by God. It isn't going to be him this time. But it is his job to correct it, and I mean right now, teaching this boy the right way, the way to be a man, that no ifs, ands, or, buts about it he is going to learn his lesson. It is his God-given right and responsibility to do it. The Riverboat Man flies into one of those rages that makes him a man and calls on him to show 'em all who's boss and makes him put his damned foot down. It is about time to cut those apron strings, but the line blurs between his wife and his own mother. Too much time with all of those women does it to his first boy, and he works his ass off and can't do everything himself—and what the hell has Jeannie done to his son? He'll stop it, and he means right now.

Without hesitation, the Riverboat Man drags Jesse Earl out of the back bedroom of girls. He forces his firstborn son into a white-and-yellow Easter dress with a quilted pink elephant embroidered on the chest and white scalloped trim, pulled from the closet nearest to where he finds his son, sitting there quietly with those two girls, playing with that red-faced Geronimo and the plastic, mixed-race Barbie from the white vinyl case with the brass hinge and the white Bakelite carrying handle, the one Jeannie got from her mother Marjorie after she died.

The dress fabric is an impasto-thick yellow the color of buttercups, trimmed in white. The cheery elephant stares up at the incongruous little boy sticking out of the trim collar. The boy feels stitched into it immediately. It traps his panic and rising body heat inside its unnaturalness. It is repellant to the touch, and the boy struggles against his father's quick hands to get free from it, from him, to get away, to hide from the shame of his skinny and welted and beaten five-year-old body, at first clad in nothing but his blue-and-red Spiderman Underoos, but then in this foreign and wrong object that strangles the child and cuts off his breathing and paralyzes him with fear of what is going to happen to him next.

The child has a lesson to learn, so this madman shoves Jesse Earl's little-boy feet into his sister's red patent leather Buster Browns that do not fit him but are strapped, skewed, lopsided around the part of the boy's foot that can be forced, and the man drags by the shoulder and tiny wrist this androgyny of his once son, now entering the parents' bedroom, mashing his wife's lipstick into the firstborn boy's face, already red with heat and humiliation and sick and exertion, mashing the oily paste deeply, in gashes, across and into the child's mouth and across his teeth so that it looks like matted blood and mixes with it so that the firstborn can't really tell if he is bleeding or if it is clumped lipstick or both, but the taste of it chokes him all the same. While Jesse Earl mouths out the screams that no longer come, or perhaps that he can no longer hear from the ringing in his battered head, and kicks and fights for breath and for a way away, for that escape, for that death that will not come, the child is dragged on limp legs outside and into the withering white daylight.

The Riverboat Man hauls this five-year-old body from neighbor's house to neighbor's house, pounding on the door until they come, frantic and bewildered, in the middle of the well-ordered noonday sun, so that all is illuminated and no detail is left un-scrutinized and hurls the words:

"Congratulate me! Jeannie and me, we've got ourselves another goddamn girl!" and "Isn't he much prettier, a fucking girl?" while the little boy mimes out the screams, contorts in the face screams make, tortured muscle and skin pulled rigid, though the noise no longer comes. He no longer kicks and struggles against the man, but allows himself to be dragged in his sister's dress and shoes and his mother's lipstick gashed across his face and across his teeth and mouth, down the block to the friends that played with him in that big corner lot just this morning, shirtless and sweating, with lithe boy muscles and smiles, and now this. Incongruously, the free hand of that Riverboat deckhand still clutches the Francie Fairchild Barbie between white fingers and knuckles, knocking the back or side of the boy's head with the doll when he remembers to do it, etching little welting lines from the hard plastic hands into the boy's face and head.

The unnerved neighbors close doors but also peek through the windows or scuttle to the curb after, observing this curiosity from over at the next house. The firstborn boy, who stops struggling and instead allows himself to be dragged by this strange man as if he is a towboat tie line, this strangling man who can never be his father again; the unfortunate boy instead simply floats away from it all, watches this odd commotion from above that is now happening, as the mad man brutalizes and shatters him. Sweating profusely, panting out the unfiltered Camels, the Riverboat Man, still grasping the child, finally ends their loop on Brown Street, circuiting from their house, northwest, up the street to the electric tower, turns, drags the child southeast down the other side, across the street to the house with the old Mimosa tree in the front yard that the boy climbs to watch bees and hummingbirds in the morning. The boy wouldn't recover his innocence.

Afterward, after this incident, the Riverboat Man really needs his last little boy, the new one, the one who'll finally be the one he wants. That would-be child, the one that the Riverboat Man will not make the mistake of leaving alone too long with a houseful of damned women to be defiled and corrupted like his first born, this mistake. In this way of thinking, the Riverboat Man starts over, starts over again to finally get it right, with kids, with wives, with places. The Riverboat Man musters his hope that the new one is normal and will hunt and shoot like his dad, will take pride in the bruises the butt of that 12-gauge leaves. That Riverboat Man will be proud passing down to this son his own daddy's shotgun and explaining to that hopeful boy how bows and arrows take down something really big, once the child gets good at it. With this next child, the Riverboat Man will gift these things to him instead. With this next one, maybe one day Edward Earl will give him the keys to his '54 Chevy truck with the V6 110hp manual and custom sideboards, and he will appreciate what that means, the old man giving over the keys like that, knowing how much his daddy loves that truck and swearing to drive it to his grave. And that Riverboat Man will have a boy who jerks that motor and rebuilds its V6 from the ground up, and who talks about how the seals are blown or the pistons bent when it threw that rod, but together they will fix it right up, with that secret language of working on engines passed down to his little man. He forgets about Jesse Earl, the firstborn, who one time left his limburger cheese sandwich on his daddy's motor and ran off disinterested-like to play, leaving that awful, scalded dairy smell that lasted a month and reminded that Riverboat Man of a firstborn who does not like to rebuild motors or learn that secret language or talk about the big tits and ass on that one or hunt or inherit shotguns or Chevys. The Riverboat Man hates dairy, and he's reminded of it every time he turns on his engine. It sickens him, like his firstborn sickens him. And as he places that newborn in the cerulean box in Fresno, he no longer has shit to show for his hard work; his last real hope is gone and all his anticipation of starting over goes into that box with his lifeless boy.

Catching Herself, 1970

His children don't know him, a vacancy who spends his time
on the Ohio River pushing down his disappointment about
the girls, the remainder of a son he now has, and his failed
life picking oranges in Fresno that brings him back to the only
work suited to him. Edward Earl knows those rivers and what
makes a towboat churn the muddy waters of the Ohio and the
Clarks and the Tennessee and the Mississippi, he knows how
to tie off barges and how to back that engine up and shove it
through a lock on the first try. He knows that his coffee is going
to perk all day on the stove and be bitter and black, which is
good for choking down regret, and that his meal is going to be
greasy and hardly fit to eat and is probably going to kill him
one day, but he pushes forward into those locks and past those
dams and up and down rivers like the hardworking man he is
supposed to be, with hardening arteries and a beer belly and

a pack of Camels in the rolled-up sleeve of his white Hanes t-shirt or in that impossibly small pocket over the left pectoral, and he is satisfied going like that and forgetting the rest.

It is progressively easy, the hard labor that keeps hands too busy for fighting, which is something else he knows about. Edward Earl is missing for weeks or a month at a time, and returns home or not. If Jeannie asks, he was hunting but he didn't bag anything. Sometimes, fifteen days are missing and not in his paycheck, and sometimes not. Jeannie and her kids are stumped by this stranger, who is sometimes in the house but more often than not absent.

It isn't the words but the easiness they have with each other when Edward Earl is gone. Jesse Earl is meeker now, seeking escape, is able to sit quietly, to be no trouble, to read. He reads all of the Laura Ingalls Wilder books, descriptions of the town the Ingalls family lived in, like the way his papaw and mamaw still live in their house with the tin roof and no insulation out on Starr Hill Road.

Jesse Earl now draws because his mother Jeannie sometimes draws.

"You get that from me," she says over his shoulder, but he is better at it than her.

Years later, long after the Riverboat Man remarries, Jesse Earl demonstrates some skill and eventually wins competitions that encourage the kind of behaviors his father worked so viciously to thwart. He develops English proficiency when nobody watches, and a love of history. At home, nobody likes a braggart. The boy unwittingly ends up outside his counselor's office waiting out the clock, long into his 20-minute turn at guidance from a counselor, as she chats up the student from a better family in her office. When Jesse Earl enters, he doesn't have much time left.

"Boys like you, in your socioeconomic straits, your upbringing, well, they usually go to trade school, not college, Hun. You ever give thought to working on cars? We got a real good program for that." The counselor pulls at her dyed perm as she looks at the clock for her next session. He should like cars, at least.

This Riverboat Man doesn't trust the educated because they use that education to take from him. Those first five years, his boy hides his interests, because all that the Riverboat Man thinks might be true about his half-of-a-son is, that he is in love with words. Jeannie knows the boy is different, so she helps keep secrets, but Edward Earl knows without knowing. Fathers who hunt and have extramarital pastimes and work on cars notice when their son does not have interest in such things, even at so young an age as five. So it does not congeal for that Paducah family right away, the ramifications of a night when the Riverboat Man takes up with the neighbor after dragging his son through the neighborhood, after breaking his marriage vows and breaking his family. It does not congeal about what it all means for Jesse Earl, a five-year-old boy, or for his four-year-old girl, Jennie Kaye, because they can't know what such things cost. But the six-year-old Cunningham girl, who isn't really his, she knows. There's something in the blood of a bastard that makes them wiser, makes them wise up fast. Lisa Jo has that at six.

Lisa also takes onto herself the assumption that she has a predilection for a bastardized life, only capable of achieving a status of less-than. Her siblings perpetuate that myth. Jesse

Earl and Jennie Kaye witness Lisa's proficiency on that night that ends their family, in Lisa's sixth year, in that last year of an unraveling marriage, stretching consequence through three generations.

The day after his adultery, Edward Earl leaves his house as if nothing had transpired the night before, as if infidelity coming home to roost is a natural succession of events. Edward Earl then returns home to Jeannie as most nights, without any margin of error, complicit and demanding complicity to his exploit: emotionless, without request, and without asking forgiveness for that which is not forgivable. But home changes in the interlude between act and denial. Jeannie turns the latch, barring entry to the Riverboat Man, locking him into the intermission with his misdeed, his belongings boxed up in Kroger produce boxes and placed on the porch. He does not notice, bypassing this anomaly of his possessions, refugees from the little house on Brown Street, and misunderstanding that they are now exiles. The produce advertisements gaily hawk the freshest lettuce and the juiciest tomatoes, stamped with colorful pictures of goods larger-than-life. But what a surprise when you peer in to find sweaty socks and Levi jeans and stacks of white V-necks and colored tee shirts with the sleeves cut out and that teeny little pocket that stretches just enough to hold a soft pack of Camels. There are no photos, no letters or personal effects—now burned—mingling with the green can of Barbisol shave cream, the cinnabar-colored Naugahyde hygiene kit with the shiny brass zipper, the bottle of Faberge Brut (unused and still in its scraped-up, forest green box), and two pair of cowboy boots, one black, one brown, that he purchased in Mexico.

All of that regret of hers is in there, too, but you have to look harder for that. The Riverboat Man does not see it because he is not the kind of man who takes notice of such things in women. Jeannie's children do not know how she accomplished it, have no idea she's done it, weren't clued in on the evening's performance. Jeannie is everyday calm and simply packs up that chapter of their lives without consulting with anybody, separating out all of the Riverboat Man memories and his clothes and his shortcomings and his distance from those things that belong to her, which is mostly her dignity. Jeannie arranges them in neat, orderly piles in two cardboard boxes, along with his betrayal and his coarseness and his anger, and just like that she places them on the porch and leaves him.

The children wake to hear Edward Earl crashing down with all of his might on the front door. The pounding and the yelling seem to penetrate every fiber and cause panic in the body. Jeannie sits purse-lipped on the sofa in the living room, motionless. Houses must be made of stronger stuff on Brown Street, because the door and its casing steel their resolve to bar him. The layers of paint over the thick metal hinges with the heavy pin keep them right there, keep them rigid, and keep him on the other side of that white ingress. Edward Earl stalks around to the back of the house, growling what he will do to any of them if they do not unbar the door. He pounds on all the windows as he circles the house. All three children scramble out of bed and scurry under the hand-me-down, 1950s-era Formica table with the yellow-and-white top and double chrome legs with white rubber tips, and they pull up the matching chairs like a fortress around them. The kitchen, being the most exposed room in the house, has the brightest light for clarity of the situation, feels safest and farthest from the darkness of bedrooms, as the Riverboat Man connects with the back door.

He arrives at the door before the mother can hang up the telephone that tethers her to the bedroom. Edward Earl appears oversized and illuminated, stark and flat white like the belly of a trout, with eyes to match. He is infuriated and daunting in the kitchen lights, through the small glass panes of the kitchen door, and his children cower closer to each other in panic at his obscenities and gestures, and the panes sprinkle their caulk in a tiny white cascade onto the linoleum and dance in their loosening casings as the rampant man pounds wrathfully against them. The years of sudden night beltings have demonized Edward Earl, and this abruptly proves what he really is. Trepidation riddles their white faces as the children squeeze bulging eyes tight to avoid looking at him, working desperately to shut out both him and the surrounding alarm.

And then it is decided. The Trojan in the horse is the firstborn boy. It is such an easy thing to do. Jesse Earl does it with hardly any effort at all—a scamper of knees and palms, a little flick. That slight clack of the latch on the big brass box lock that is screwed into the fascia of that white-coated door, and the Riverboat Man is inside.

Punishment, beltings mostly, befall fatherly duties at whatever time the Riverboat Man arrives home, no matter when the crimes occurred. Now the children are dazed and terrified, as if a closet demon has descended, and all the terrors they have of the dark ring true when the Riverboat Man arrives. Jeannie keeps a list on the refrigerator for him:

neat, handwritten notes in three columns underneath each child's name. Women do not raise their hands or voices. These are not contracts children are privy to.

Castigation requires no reason. Edward Earl's two natural children instinctively run to him and hug his legs out of fear and confusion and as a pleading, so that whatever this misunderstanding is can be cleared up, but also so they all won't get belted for whatever it is that they did, although none of them could imagine being so bad as to cause all of this misperception. Jesse Earl and Jennie Kaye hardly have time to notice that they stand alone, suddenly separated from the herd, because the oldest one does not run, does not clutch, and does not beg. It is, in that instant, a family cleaved in two.

This is how the firstborn boy betrays them all. As the windowpanes dance and the Riverboat Man crashes against the door, the children know that they'll get it if they don't comply and convince him that all this is some kind of mistake. It happens too quickly to register when that Cunningham girl falls back, watching from under the yellow-and-white Formica table, because somehow, in the difference of a single year that is between their ages, Lisa has learned more about the influence that comes with allegiance, and about treachery, and knows how this surge already turns. She lines up her ducks.

Lisa moves behind Jeannie, who enters the room in silence as Edward Earl crashes around: she is unmoved, never utters a word, never grimaces. Edward Earl does not strike her. He knows his sin. Lisa's face, the bastard child's face, is taking in what all this means and there is no going back for her. There is no mistake about which side of the coin will drop and hers is facing up.

But it is in Jeannie's face that Jesse Earl and Jennie Kaye find the message. It conveys understanding to them without words, just a glance, a hardening of the jaw, a pursing as blood flows out of primrose pink lips now running white, now the color of blood just under the surface of an avalanche. Those lips are now drawn into a line over the slight under bite she has, and that's how the firstborn boy gets it, that's how he too late picks up the shift, that knowledge that five-year-old boys don't have but six-year-old girls do. The betrayal testifies against Edward Earl's natural children, and it crystalizes into a hardness held just around the mother's eyes that hadn't been there before, as she watches two of her children cling to him. Betrayal is an ugly fact lingering in this room, where each claims his or her ground. It is fatally apparent for Jeannie Mae and the bastard.

The firstborn son and the natural daughter are instantaneously associated with the enemy, are conjoined to his failures, the disappointment, the regret, the infidelity. They are tarred with it. After his slow discovery, Jesse Earl wants to protest that the mother did not explain why the Riverboat Man's life was separated into produce boxes and his children left behind, that they have no knowledge of how unfaithfulness can end everything so abruptly, that children do not know these rules and are too young to maneuver the secret and unspoken language of women and feelings and retaliation, when it comes to lovers breaking apart and destroying each other with knuckle and confrontation and actions and silence and spit and sweat and empty nights and the chasm of sorrow it all causes. These are not conversations adults have with children. It is not a language children would understand, should it be told to them. In this way muteness extinguishes the flame of love, extinguishes devotion, and extinguishes the temperaments of children.

The firstborn and the youngest receive no trial in which to exhort all of this, even if they could articulate it for themselves, because Jeannie Mae never speaks about it. The bastard does not dare give away the secret. His children are unlabeled as *they*, without the mother or the sister, and now without the Riverboat Man, too. They are silent and grieve ignorance in the inability to speak. Jesse Earl and Jennie Kaye, exclusively the Riverboat Man's children now, suffer their confusion and pain and fret in silence. His children don the mantle of traitor, ripped so recently from that little start, that little beginning of a family, that beginning of a life that they all created on Brown Street but that ends that night with so few coherent words. In the fatal moment of turning a latch, the coming of winter enters that room where those natural children stand their ground, and it lasts until the time when two entities branch apart, and distance ebbs and flows and overtakes and laps silently at the back of each of their minds, raging again in the mother or the father with no explaining, without justification. It overtakes each of them in its own way. It envelops, and it does so in the stillness of a little family extinguished.

The latch turn begins the unraveling, that separation of the "us" and the "them" that is inevitable. It comes that night, but without recourse because they all can't really understand that they do it to each other—that the cleft entities all play their parts, that they subsidize the colliding into one another and the cessation, not of themselves but of their own collective.

It is easy enough for the Riverboat Man, walking away, and that is what he does: disowns, disavows, and ceases his part. Being alone condones forgetting. There is nobody there to be ashamed of you when you walk away, when you forget, when you move on. He has that. His children do not. They are abandoned to each other, to remember, to feel shame, to give and to take blame. His children harbor it. They swallow it. They eat it when the Riverboat Man leaves nothing else for them to eat. They consume the vacancy and it consumes them in return. It fills them and leaves them empty, except for the parts stuffed to overflowing with resentment and venom and desire for vengeance. But mostly what is left behind is barrenness. And mostly his children keep vigil over all of this within themselves. It wells up in other ways, some petty ways, and then subsides by never directly seeking out the cause, by covering up so that the main does not heal. Abandonment scabs. It festers. It subsides and it flares. That is the game, really, being tougher than the next engulfing, despairing wave and not caring that there is only one side to take, to be part of. His natural children do not believe the front, not really. They secretly harbor some love still for the man who walks away. It cannot show, not to Jeannie, not to them.

This union tears itself apart and, in the tearing, they pull away pieces of each other, leaving the fragments exposed.

The cardboard boxes disappear from the front porch, leaving behind in their place only those effects hard to see, and these are soundlessly fastened onto his natural children's little bodies. Jeannie parades the captive children, spoils of a terrible war for the neighbors and for the family that are left from her side, the family that continues, her family—their family, but more mainly hers. They all take sides, too, like the children do. Those who stay revile him and all of his faults and lies and cheats and drinking and womanizing, hissed through teeth at low whispers, and the trough fills itself with these things through Sunday dinners and kids' outings and birthday parties and summer cookouts in the park and at Etta's, and his natural children pretend it doesn't matter that they now exist without him. The remnants of that little family now demonize the Riverboat Man. His children haplessly churn in his wake, and those left-behind children are somehow responsible for all of his shortcomings, of which they had once been unaware, but now all fingers point in their direction, but not really, not overtly—not on purpose. His children cannot defend his absence as they cannot defend themselves, or their association with him. So they learn how to hate him like the rest.

The popular house fell. The fresh, handsome couple had been popular, too. That once-together family knows all of the neighbor kids because of the big, empty end lot next to their house on Brown Street, where children draw together after school to play children's games, while the neighbors stand on porches or are absentee, knowing where the kids collect, taking the time-out adults need too, sometimes. The kids play kickball and tag and outdoor games that kids play in those seemingly endless five summers, and they play them at that once-fine couple's house in cutoffs and no shirt or shoes, and they all beg to please stay longer or to maybe stay for supper if there's enough, and the mother acquiesces and allows the pandemonium to disrupt her house in a good-natured way, but she finally shoos them all home when it gets close to bedtime. Jeannie makes Kool-Aid and the parents gush agreeable, because their kids exhaust themselves elsewhere, out of their hair for a little while. And besides, the nice, fresh, and handsome couple is a beacon and sentinel for their perfectly ordered neighborhood. Theirs is a popular family, but mostly for superficial reasons.

After the divorce, attitudes seize up, ground still. Neighbors do not know them as well as they had supposed, and certainly not as individuals at the conclusion of a marriage. No longer the nice couple, Jeannie is a Divorcee now and therefore suspect, and all the conjecture about what really collapsed their paper-thin veneer of happiness everyone else secretes away in their own lives. Ruin happens to her, not to them.

These badges of miscarriage, these unwanted trophies of an unending war: His kids. Those kids. The pitying looks that sometimes come are harder still because his natural children do not want to be pitied, seen in different light, as separate. They secretly harbor hope that this is still a misconstruction and the cleft will somehow heal. But Edward Earl leaves and nothing follows. No acknowledgement comes that his natural children are left behind, that the Riverboat Man remembers, that his family had occurred.

Jeannie Mae and Lisa Jo are a subdivision of two; they bond that night and forge a new family without meaning to, weighing more than the two natural children now only half belonging to Jeannie, but with looser bonds now. It occurs not by resolve but by a fissured family distilling from the rawness and the hate that is produced when the stuff that brings two young bodies together violently repels one from the other, after the burn of lust dies down and the problems mount up. That's the stuff kids don't know about, the mysterious stuff that kids can't understand, those rules that govern those things. In hindsight of that moment, it sprang up in the seconds of that undefended door, that Trojan horse spilling out its chill night air, letting discord slip in between the two newly formed ranks of foes that once so easily had been one, to pool around the feet of the mother and her child, where his children stand, and whisper vicissitudes of division.

The chasm, the divide; they are separated. They are isolated and they know but do not want to know, because it is a quiet shift for Jeannie and it isn't always, it isn't every time, and the good-together times mask a lot of it. So Jesse Earl and Jennie Kaye have to pay attention, and maybe even Jeannie Mae does not know that she does it: actively seeks out, presses into their flesh, and pulls the two apart.

It isn't his fault really, how Edward Earl treats her. How he treats his children. It starts for him before he is a Riverboat Man. He tells you his momma is three-fourths Cherokee, which her genealogical line denies, but it's what all Kentuckians say about vicious women, as if having savage blood can be the only explanation for how cruel she is to him and his siblings.

At the age of fourteen, Edward Earl is for two years already impassive to his parents' ramshackle and homemade house of five kids and is searching out his new life. He builds a family of his own that isn't forged from the clay of his cast-off parents and siblings. Edward Earl is hard because of them, and his own profligate refusal to return. The Riverboat Man is hard because of his hard mother, Jessie, whose licks he says, after he belt whips his own children, are nothing like what he'd got when she hit him with cord wood for good reasons, or sometimes because she didn't know which brother was the culprit and so beat them all.

Papaw Ed and Mamaw Jessie: their house of want leaves Edward Earl with a fifth-grade education and a childhood apprentice's knowledge of shoeing horses and mules and then riverboats and then getting away. When the Riverboat Man loses his round of the perpetual battle that rages between him and Jeannie over the next few years, it is here that he exiles his two natural born kids, on Starr Hill Road, where Ed and Jessie Stark are already raising two grandchildren, Billy Joe and Starr Renee. Instead of taking his children inside, the Riverboat Man drops them off, and his refuse adds to a parental house of cast-offs. His losing the battle but not the war is only temporary, and it is his parents who get the lousy prize.

To this couple, to his parents, the Riverboat Man's unwanted children are awarded, no longer part of Edward Earl's life as he defines it, no longer fitting the definition of what he is searching for. His methods are routine: the same quiet drive, the quiet talk as his two children stand wide-eyed and pensive on the porch, then him driving away with a head pat or a pinched shoulder. Words are not something Edward Earl commands.

Mamaw Jessie: her white, heavyset, grandmotherly roundness is a fluke, a lie. Hardness, and a rawness that sometimes finds itself in bonier women, is masked in her by obesity, adorned in gay, homemade shifts of plain-pattern cotton with simple white trim hand-stitched around the sleeves to make it prettier.

But it does not hide her edge. It is in everything she does. Winter or summer, Jessie wears no shoes and she is uneducated. Chickens sometimes wander into her house and she feeds them there instead of shooing them outside. The woman takes the leftover chicken feed and left-behind shit and crushes them between the cracks in the boards of the floor with her bare feet. She eats with scooped fingers raw hamburger from the brown paper package from her husband's slaughterhouse.

This grandmother tells you that being educated leads to sinful thoughts and prideful ways. She leans into you as she tells you this, stoops down so you can more clearly hear her, and her tone and her direct way of looking at you while she fervently nods her head underscore her certainty. Jessie's pride stems from humble thought and deed. She drives by the dictates of the good Old Testament rather than the New Covenant of a more lenient god; a good wife and a good mother needs that hardness, driven by hard ultimatums. You do not spare the rod. These are the chores assigned by her God to her, and she bears that weight unquestioningly, unerringly, even when she doesn't like what it directs her to do, and she tells you that—love sparingly and discipline severely because praise only leads to pride, which leads to the fall. She has none of it in her house. This is women's work. Her roundness fools people. It does not fool the Riverboat Man, and his children learn his same lessons.

Jessie believes in miracles, like the one that saved her life by the astonishing hand of Jesus alone. Lying in bed with pneumonia and Papaw Ed ardently praying over her for hours, as she dances on the doorstep of death, Jessie is wracked with coughing and sputtering. Ed increases the volume of prayer, is shouting to his God, when he suddenly reaches down into that old woman's throat and pulls out a softball-sized globule of phlegm, and with it the evil that is in her that is now expelled by prayer and the endorsement of an Old Testament God. She also tells the story of her favorite uncle when she was a little girl, who dies while delivering produce in California while, simultaneously, her family's house catches fire in Arkansas, and she wakes to find her uncle wrapping her up in a blanket and delivering her from the flames out of the back of the house, leaving Jessie alight in the fresh night grass with the blanket and his fire-damaged watch, which she clutches from his wrist in her delivery. She shows the watch several times as a relic of the most holy kind, as this is surely an angel set to deliver her from the fires of Hell. These are the acts of a God that she does not question.

From these loins and these thoughts Edward Earl is made, birthed in the same home where they live, but he does not say much else about the white-hot hell he and his brothers have little hope of escaping. He does not speak of the apparitions he sees there, of the vapors, of being cast down. Edward Earl does not speak of the tasks this God commands his mother to demonstrate on her children to show Holy submission and obedience.

The Riverboat Man speaks only of the fact that he is proud of leaving that house when he is twelve and of becoming his own man. All else is pieced together from hearsay. Wives of men borne from that breed, who live through it, tell few tales about it. He does not speak of hard labor, long into the 1950s, in his father's blacksmith shop, which had been his grandfather's before him. He does not know that his line originates in Scotland and Ireland and in steerage compartments of big boats as blacksmiths and maids. Edward Earl does not care to know his past or his predecessors. He does not speak of severing from all that is associated with Mamaw Jessie or Papaw Ed and this house, but quickly leaves without glancing back except in times of dire need, like when he has the inconvenience of needy children. His mother, Jessie, figured out that at the age of fourteen he needed a wife to join him in his escape. It is her edict that seals the arrangement between Jessie and Marvin who everybody calls Charlie.

They are farm folks, they tell you. Until the slack and draw that came with a proliferation of vehicles in the 1950s, his smithy shoes horses. All of the boys learned the trade of his shop, back when people still used mules and horses in that part of Kentucky. And Papaw Ed refuses modern conveniences. He is not cheap, but he loves God and living off the land and having no debtors or creditors, which brings him closer to Him by living close to the ways of the Savior. After the smithy fails him, he loves farm work and taking wood from the forests and bartering his work for necessities, and he loves toiling until he is exhausted. Papaw Ed does not question being the man of the house, the breadwinner, the provider, the human drudgery that keeps a man's mind clean and his hands busy. The fact that time and technology outpace him does not trouble him. Instead, he holds tighter to his ways, holding himself in higher regard for living low and avoiding the lure of conveniences.

He keeps a kitchen garden out back like generations before him, where he grows most of the potatoes and onions and beans and whatnot for the house, but also stuff to keep in the dugout space under the house for the winter. After there is no need for a smithy, Papaw Ed builds a slaughtering house from cinderblocks painted with white barge paint, because it lasts longer and doesn't chip. He slaughters for the neighbors too, out there on Starr Hill Road, and trades services for meat for his own table, and some he sells for necessities when he thinks to, or when his wife asks for it. He uses money for essentials like flour and coal oil for the lamps, gas for the car, and used parts he isn't able to barter for. He sometimes surprises Mamaw Jessie with new cotton material for a dress, after the other wears through.

His is one of those old-fashioned enamel white-like-the-hospital slaughtering houses where you drive a piston into the skull of the sacrifice and hoist it up on winches with thick chains wrapped and locked around the animals' feet, weighing the animal down so it can't get up and can't get away, and you cut its throat with the last gasps of breath still in the animal and let the blood sluice out to a collection pond around back, and it is still hot and steaming from the struggle, still twitching and kicking, when you start cutting off the parts to put in the butchery.

Jesse Earl, the firstborn, is ten when Papaw Ed decides that he is man enough to see where his food comes from, so they haul him in to help shut the gates where the cattle are herded, and they pick off the one they all agree on and then open the smaller gate at the other end, and Jesse Earl chases the cow into the narrow gauntlet. There is no going back then, only forward. The animal is run through to the final gate that shuts her up in the front and shuts her up in the back, and she is trapped and a man with a captive bolt gun holds the rope steady and pulls the trigger and the iron rod penetrates her skull and her brain and she falls to the ground, chained and dragged to the middle of the bloodstained cement floor for the ritual. It finally takes five men to do the deed of doing her in.

The boy watches on as the men hoist the cow upside down, and the machete long knife fresh from the whetstone slices through her white throat so that the forty-eight quarts of blood she holds quickly cover the entire cement floor. And the boy hoses it away, all that life, all that waste, rinses her life into a neat trough, draining away into that collecting pond around back of the slaughterhouse where lesser animals feed, where crows drink. Jesse Earl wants to not know this thing, wants to find a way out of there, but to be a ten-year-old man he must linger there, must witness; he is required to know how those five men rip her apart and tear away her skin to get to the meat and the organs, and pull away at her until she is in manageable pieces. He must eat up death so that he will not forget what gives men sustenance. Like all demises, he forgets the sounds of spilling organs and the sounds of cutting away the hide and slopping blood still found in vessels and muscles, her body's voices. What he cannot forget is how she is undone by those men, and his doctrine of participation. That snuffing out a light stays with a man.

Papaw Ed chops fallen wood from the hills and trees that surround the house to feed that black and round potbelly stove in the house, and to cook those pieces of meat he has cut out of cows and sows all year round, and also as a pitiable attempt to heat the homemade house with the corrugated tin roof and no insulation, and with the floorboards where you see through to the dirt below, the color of meat-packing paper. Mamaw Jessie keeps a cast iron casserole pot with water on the top of it, helping to heat the house and for household uses like heating bathwater, but also worse purposes.

The house covers a well room off the back porch that is falling in from bad corrugated tin and rotting timber. A red hand pump in the kitchen pulls well water into a sort of tin sluice gate to wash up in, if you properly prime it. The roof is bad only over the pantry part of the back porch, so that falls into disuse and then holds cast-off stuff like black trash bags and broken furniture and old lumber. Out from the dry timber porch, beaten into the red clay, is the path to the slick cement well, greened up the sides from moss and lichens feeding on the sloshed-out water from the corrugated bucket on a length of chain tethered to a round cut of wood, with a hand crank for drawing up and letting down the bucket into the cold black hole below. The well water is ice cold and sweet from the bucket, and that's how you drink it. The tethered ladle dips out drinking water any time of day and, hauling it up, you hear that tin bucket *ponk* and *ponk* off the side of the cool, slick cement of the well walls. Frogs perpetually cycle themselves somehow down there out of sight, singing their night song, and a boy can barely make out the shapes of the tip of their nose and eyes in the reflection of the dusk sky when that underground stream swells high enough in the spring and you wait for the moon to cast itself down that dark hole. The boy does not know where those frogs come from or how they get in there, trapped down that deep cell their whole lives. He lowers the bucket, moving the chain to drag the bucket toward those noses, those eyes. In their fear, the frogs dive deep into the blackness of the water, eluding their salvation, misunderstanding the offering.

"They must be pretty stupid to get themselves into a mess they can't get out of like that," he thinks as he walks away from trying.

Each year, they are still here, calling up to the left-behind children to help them up from those slick, wet walls, or send them a companion, but they remain perpetually, generation after generation, trapped down that nowhere place at the bottom of that dark wet hole.

Papaw Ed's shanty holds three big rooms and a kitchen of sorts that he adds to the back, which holds a number of appliances no longer in use, or, more likely, purchased with the intent of updating the house, which never ensues. The gritty porch glass separating the house from the new kitchen entombs a shiny aluminum and white enamel Hoosier pantry, with the unused flour sifter now rusting; a bright green enamel gas stove (with no gas lines on Starr Hill Road); and a white and chrome Monitor Top Frigidaire, all standing like sentinels, patiently awaiting a second chance. There are two bathrooms in the house. One is in the second large room where the kids sleep, behind a curtain on zinc wire in the corner of the room, mostly for night use, or inclement weather. It is a dark-stained wooden Victorian chair, but the chamber pot has long since disappeared, so Mamaw Jessie adds a ten-gallon white plastic lard bucket with a galvanized steel handle and the spinning white plastic grasp at the top. She flatly carries out that bucket to the second bathroom, the outhouse in the back. She does it barefoot and pours that shit and piss into the dark stinking hole and pays no mind to the flies and the maggots and the stench and the spiders, because this is God's work for a woman. She does not complain. She does not wish for running water or a real bathroom, or better insulation, or the new kitchen that never comes, not for a television or even a mirror for the house. Jessie does not ask for more than she has. The house is not electrified. The sometime-occupant children stay out till dark, in the rain, in the snow. It is preferable to getting under foot. They return to a bath in a galvanized tin tub on the front porch in the summer and in the kitchen in the winter, although it may as well be on the porch all the same.

Jesse Earl, Jennie Kaye, Billy Joe, and Starr Renee: They invent games with anything they find in the abandoned gravel pit adjacent to this house. Once, the children discover a box of unused Pampers on the side of the road, fill them with gravel and red dirt and sand from the gravel pit, and spend the day pitching them to the sky to see who is the first to run as they comes crashing down on their heads. Those diaper bombs pummel rocks and dirt and sand down on or around them, but either way, the four of them are covered with red dirt, and the clay and sweat-caked, filthy mud wedges in the cracks of their skin and mats their hair. They return after dark, covered in sand and grit and red clay with dirt-ringed necks. Seeing the children, Jessie pours water fresh from the underground but refuses to add any scalding water to warm it since they are filthy on purpose and need a lesson.

The four children climb one by one into the limb-numbing cold of the corrugated wash basin on the front porch and are scrubbed as near as you can get to clean in a tin-tub full of spring chill on a front porch. The trick is to not be washed last in that filthy reddened water, but also to not make a fuss about it because then you get it, wet and naked. Jessie's less brutal castigations rarely deter the children. Sometimes they slip off to the stream before home and strip down and swim for a while to be cleaner before they return, beating their clothes out on tree trunks.

"Starr Renee, careful to hit that wide-open spot there just before the big flat rock! Moccasins don't like to hang out in the open. You won't see a one in that open water. And you can see 'em comin' if they do." Billy Joe calls it out to his sister as she hugs her shoulders, afraid of jumping in.

The four children spend nomadic hours in the woods, careful around the beds of pine needles and dry underbrush, fearing timber rattlers. They avoid low ground and overhead ledges where wildcats hunt you if it is after dusk. One early spring, while coming back from a little privacy in the privy out back, the firstborn boy rounds the corner to the front porch, face to face with a black bear sorting through the assorted furniture for a better vantage point. The boy waits him out in the driver's seat of the broken-down Buick Skylark around back.

Papaw Ed isn't like Mamaw Jessie. Opposites attract, and he is quick to hugs and corny clean jokes and toothless grins over fine weather or fat chickens or the bewildering number of green beans he is getting this summer. The frail, thin man talks for hours about when the right time is to pick squash and cucumbers and 'maters, and the first one every year goes into a Wonder bread sandwich with mayonnaise. He nicknames the first boy Junior and June bug. Papaw Ed has pretty names and sweet ones for Starr Renee and Jennie Kaye, like Buttercup and Sugar or Sweet Pea. Mamaw Jessie is quiet and talks when she has something to say, and she calls them "kids" collectively and never by their names, like it doesn't matter anyway. There is no purpose in addressing a child individually.

Jessie is mostly hard and mean and lets you know that this house is her house and her rules and not to cross her. Offering an opportunity for a "Bible-teaching moment," not that she really thinks of it like that, is a mistake you do not make more than once, and the resulting punishment is hers to decide and it rarely fits the deed.

Raising obedient children means they take orders, do chores, don't fidget, don't talk back, and get homework done without her having to ask about it. Kids stay out of your sight, are seen and not heard, and cause no trouble for you. Raising kids is woman's work, she reminds you. She quotes you the passage that gives her rights to the job and to your body. She hits with her words and the word of God, and with her hands. The thick leather belt is for not sparing the rod, and she does not go easy because you are a kid or a girl, because she taught you better. Mamaw Jessie takes exacting interest in teaching through the use of the rod.

Shortly after the abandonment of Jesse Earl and Jennie Kaye, the previously abandoned Billy Joe and Starr Renee are fighting over the old Ford tire that is tied to the oak in the dirt-packed yard the color of meat-packing paper. Jessie does not speak to the arguing children but walks her broad bare feet out to the swing in an almost careless gait and catches each of them by the arm. Jesse Earl and Jennie Kaye look on and observe the almost uncomprehending look on the two victims' faces as the old woman leads them to the altar.

Mamaw Jesse brings the two children to the front porch, where an assorted number of cast-off chairs end up for finishing off the day with cold water, and the old woman pulls down their shorts like she mashes that chicken feed and chicken shit between the floorboards with her bare feet—with that same nonchalance. She takes the thick leather belt off the nail by the door. She places the whole belt into the scalding water on low heat on the black, cast-iron potbelly stove for household purposes. She does not scold them; instead, the old woman forces two of the chair legs between their legs and over their downed shorts so the children cannot get away, and she twists their protesting and naked bodies over the seat and lays their flesh open with that belt with all of her considerable might until they stop crying, as if having gone into shock.

That old woman does this without anger, but she does it with determination.

Thwack! The wet leather connects with pale skin. *Thwack*! Skin wells crimson and lines with blood. *Thwack*! Blood smears across pale skin and wells again. She quotes Bible passages through the whipping and she beats them simultaneously, straddling their writhing bodies with her tremendous girth, keeping them from moving away from the blows. It is a lesson they must learn, and the time for lessons is now.

The firstborn boy sees and knows it is not the first time these lessons have been taught to them. He suddenly is aware of the scars that crisscross their legs and backs and buttocks. He understands now. She does it like she takes out the shit and the piss in that white lard bucket. And the youngest girl sees too and it hurts her more than it hurts the eldest boy, because she knows it will happen to her.

Jennie Kaye is crying again in the way she mastered in the kitchen on Brown Street, without any visible reference on her face. The tears keep welling up and running down the freckles on her perfectly round cheeks, and her too-small of a chin hardens into that little ball. You have to pay attention to see it. You have to look at her. Nobody really does that except Jesse Earl: he notices. The Riverboat Man's natural children do not speak. Not to each other, not to Billy Joe and Starr Renee, and not to Jessie and Papaw Ed. The children think it isn't polite to mention it, after it is over.

Months later, the Riverboat Man had seemingly forgotten them, but he hadn't. When he returns, the instant he drives up is when Jesse Earl decides to speak his mind. He does it for the youngest. Jennie Kaye is too small to take on such an obscenity as that old woman gives.

The Riverboat Man doesn't really speak to his natural children after he spends some time on the porch, whispering to that old woman and Papaw Ed. When he enters, that's when the boy tells him that he isn't going to stay in the house with that bitch, putting extra emphasis on the word *bitch*, and it comes out in a little thrill at being so grown as to say something so shocking as that, but before the boy can get it all out, before he tells the Riverboat Man about the lashing and that he has no intention of allowing that woman to do what she does to his sister, the Riverboat Man strikes the boy full force in the face with his fist.

The Riverboat Man's face did not change, so the firstborn boy could not see it, did not see it coming, and doesn't even feel the blow, instead wondering how odd it is that he is suddenly on the floor with his head ringing. It is a moment incongruous to the logical argument the boy presents to the Riverboat Man. She is, in fact, a bitch, and the boy, in fact, does not intend to stay in this house. The firstborn boy cannot reconcile those simple facts with the fact that he is now on the floor. Jesse Earl lies there looking through the floorboards to that packed dirt, swallows his blood and watches it trickle out of his mouth into the unvarnished floorboards, and thinks about those frogs trapped in that well. He figures that this is pretty much how the life of the Riverboat Man was all the time, living with that woman, and that's why he had to get out of this house at twelve years old.

The firstborn boy isn't twelve yet, it occurs to him. So the child also wonders how he is going to do it, how to get away, much like those frogs, when the concrete sides are slick and dark and as wet as his own blood.

The Riverboat Man says, "Now get up and sit your ass down over there and don't you say another fuckin' word, boy."

Jesse Earl does not know how to shoe a horse and he does not want to work on a boat, does not want to be anything like this man, but he would do it. And he wouldn't tell this man about it, because he does not deserve it. And the boy learns his lesson about talking about those kinds of things that happen to kids. He learns how you just let it happen and hope everybody else doesn't see or guess or talk about it, and if folks do they don't talk about it either or do anything about it anyway, and Jesse Earl imagines that is how the Riverboat Man did it too. Nobody throws anybody a bucket.

Edward Earl leaves them there again when night comes. His natural children are particularly quiet after so many incidents in a row, and in the silence of the left behind it is hard to say exactly when it happens. You don't notice it at first, and when you do notice, it seems like it has been there a long time already and you can only be aware of it because the house is so quiet. It emanates from the early part of the night, as the crickets sing and the night air comes together and stealthily slips into the house. It comes in through the grimy, gaping screen door with all of the white paint worn off around the handle, and through the bottom corner where you catch your foot to hold it open, the door that doesn't exactly equal its opening. His natural children are in bed listening to the hush, drowning in their thoughts, and gawking slackly toward the darkness that is the ceiling. It happens when the coolness slips up through the gaps in the floorboards, and past the rusty screen windows. There, that moment, is the instant Papaw Ed and Mamaw Jessie leave the children.

It is at that juncture that the old couple slips away to their bedroom to read to each other from the Bible by the light of the coal lamp, kneeling on the rough, unpainted floorboards, and then the two of them quietly pray, eyes closed, foreheads pressed together, hands entwined. And the prayer continues and rises in tempo, in unison. And then the prayers turn mournful and then wail out loud and ferociously, the two kneeling and facing each other, with locked arms gripping, grasping, clawing each other as they tremble, swaying, stillness turning to rocking and now hips churning back and forth, grinding their knees into that hard wood floor until they are both wet and exhausted with exertion and tears and exaltations.

Only after achieving their Glory, their ecstasy, after completing their ritual, do the flush-faces cease their tremors and jerking, and when the murmurs cease to come any longer and the quiet once again creeps back into them, the old man releases that old woman. And she in turn releases him. Only then does he turn down and then put out the coal oil lamp, and the old couple both crawl into bed, heaving and pushing away the last vestiges of sobs and sighs, leaving wild-eyed children in the next room bewildered and unable to sleep, wondering what it is that the four of them do, or who it is they know, to warrant that kind of absolution, or what happens so terrible inside this homemade house on Starr Hill Road in the middle of the country that nobody pays attention to, that needs somebody to pray like that over it or them, or to remove such a stain of sin.

Slowly, in dread, each one nods and drops off, leaving three, then two, then the last of the children standing sentinel over the others, locked together in that big bed, in that big black room, in these strangers' house, in the middle of this vast country so peculiar as their little strip of Starr Hill Road. The darkness stretches further down from the ceiling and engulfs them all, and sleep finally slides in between those thoughts and songs of crickets, and the final futile cries of frogs from creek water flowing up into that cement hole around back of that ramshackle house, and the firstborn fades finally into rest.

Perfecting the art of not listening, Jesse Earl comes to know about the existence of a mystery woman, the one who no longer exists, the one un-talked about. She has black hair combed away from her face like Jackie Kennedy and water-colored skin. She first appears in a black-and-white photograph, holding two squirming children close to her breasts, one in each arm, all three looking mournfully at the photographer, as if they hear the prayers emanating from that house. Their faces are unusual because they do not smile, not in the mouth or eyes. The woman assumes a brief half-smile, a non-smile that is more sadness than smiling. The photo's corner is torn, a little Polaroid holding some of its scalloped edge that isn't cut away, cut down to fit inside a little plastic sheath inside a dusty box of keepsakes.

Jesse Earl discovers the association between this woman and the time Billy Joe and Starr Renee are forsaken, left to reside with grandparents by accident, by being in the wrong place at the right time. Hers is a story the family hush-talks, cautiously evoking the spirits of the dead in repeating it, and people fidget when a scallop-edged Polaroid incongruously appears, or inquiry is made, or when a child heavy-handedly figures it out. The conversation just goes cold and faces change. This is a hidden story of when that woman's daughter, Joyce, marries a man who isn't in his right mind, is suspicious and jealous and mean: a keg of dynamite. It is straight from the Testament of Jessie, what happens to Joyce.

"He is the kind of man who should have been locked up away from people," Aunt Ruth mutters before she checks herself.

Ruth is Joyce's sister, sister to Edward Earl too. Joyce, in contrast, is a quiet person, simple and pretty, with a smile that somehow reminds you of rain, or that mist of rain that rises up off of hot concrete after a summer storm, indulgent and tempering those hard lines around her. She is the kind of woman with eyes that are servile and eternally downcast, a soul that cloaks itself around a family.

Joyce's demise comes on the day her husband returns from work and lays into her with his anger and his threats and accusations of her fucking everybody while he is working and making a joke of him, and he and everybody else knows it, and demanding to know who all in the hell has she been with. And he does what he hasn't done before except yell. He strikes Joyce full in the face. And, once released, he keeps on hitting her and she doesn't defend herself, is incapable of it, and hasn't been taught that she can, or that a woman is allowed to do it. Joyce is powerless to comprehend that her husband is this man, in this moment. Her lack of resistance thrills him and he feels more virile, so he ratchets up his blows. His wife shoulders the assault, covering her children's bodies with her own, and then flees this house and this man she suddenly doesn't know, stumbling her way by foot over the miles to her parents' homemade house with her two small children, one under each arm, and begs for clemency from her mother and for guidance, for a mother's love to take all of that unkindness away, to give her shelter, to once more take her in and accommodate her children.

When Joyce winds out her story, wiping away her own blood and terror and hysterics, her old mother refuses her at the door and does not open the faded white screen standing between them to welcome her or her children. Joyce does not know a mother's kindness or protection in her last moments. Jessie speaks over her daughter's cries, ignoring Joyce's lament for her children, instead quoting Bible passages, and commands her to leave her parents' house and to cleave to her husband. She has no place there. Not with them. And Jessie closes the door and turns her back on her child, her grandchildren.

Spellbound by the conviction of what she assumes is her mother's love, taken in by the falsehood, Joyce returns to her husband as supplicant, as commanded. He shoots her in the head and her body traps her two children, Billy Joe and Starr Renee. He then shoots himself in that same bed, and the two lie there, Joyce on top of those two babies imprisoned beneath her dead body, touching her, beholding them, absorbing the demise, captivated by the end, covered in their mire. Billy Joe and Starr Renee's minds are now a fixed disfigurement that takes years to become evident.

Although it is not officially documented by professionals, not signed into the record by the four rooms of teachers at their elementary school, they all know. They are aware but say nothing. Papaw Ed and Mamaw Jessie know also. The family eats up the secret and keeps it as a non-subject, a branding their family must endure, as so many other travesties are endured. The two babies are unable to age much past eight or nine in mind, even as their bodies develop. Starr Renee marries a man three times her age who controls every aspect of her life for her, and she remains a child for him and dies young from her ovaries destroying her body, mistrusting science and the refusing medical care that might have remedied her ailment. Starr Renee is happy with him, knowing no better happiness to be possible. The man-child, Billy Joe, is a burden to that old man Papaw Ed for the rest of the old man's life. Unable to fend for himself after the death of the old man, Billy Joe slips away into oblivion and dies a recluse in a government-subsidized apartment, unwashed, untended, corpulent, and obscured in his own waste. Jesse Earl suspects that such savagery visiting on their house, such ferocity resulting from those events, must be one of those things the two old people pray about so hard each night: how to live with the results of these actions, since it is God's doing and His will, but execution is by their hand.

After Papaw Ed and Mamaw Jessie are gone, the boy would remember the undeniable love of these two people, who were certain that the hard simple life they led, and the rigid life they administered onto those around them, were done in the conviction that it was right, and the way life should be led, and that realization becomes easier and more understandable too, but only from the distance of years and states away does it register. Only after both of them die and the emotions dull and fade and are almost forgotten does Jesse Earl understand how this world worked for them, and how so many generations before have been handled in the same manner; that what is right for the previous generation is accepted but resented by the following generation. Those same roles have been rejected and resented but have instilled themselves in the next generation from time immemorial. In that distance, from three generations, from these two people, it becomes, if not adequate, at least putative.

Before the demise of Papaw Ed and Mamaw Jessie, that Riverboat Man administers rules for controlling the lives of Jesse Earl and Jennie Kay in his absence. Like Martin Luther, he posts the edict for his parents. He could not know the enormous consequences it would carry, even if it seemed inconsequential to him at the time. This one little oddity in him shifts the young girl's perception, and it resists shifting back, unable to regain the trust that breaks apart in her that small but eventful evening. Edward Earl's statute when he was married had been overruled with disastrous consequences, in his mind, when he lost his firstborn, Jesse Earl, to those women. The Riverboat Man enforces this decree doubly now that he is untethered. He does it with conviction. His natural children could own no toys. That Riverboat Man lived with none. They would have none. It is such an incongruous thing.

He despises their dependence on crutches, hobbling through a childhood he never had. The room his children occupy is vacuous, because there is nothing to pick up. The large bed and its coverings, one dresser for all four children's clothing, sawmill-board floors, slat walls, one window, and a white sheet on a clothesline partitioning off the makeshift bathroom make up their living quarters. Books, dolls, toy cars, plastic horses do not exist there. But, in his absence, the rule becomes a suggestion and then the suggestion is forgotten.

On his return to that shanty of his parents, he finds that his children have accumulated a few odds and ends, pieced together from cast-offs alongside Starr Hill Road, or handed down with an insouciant wink to children with nothing. Particularly, the firstborn boy discovers an oversized Tonka truck with a hard plastic T-top in a box of trash left at the gravel pit site adjacent to the house. Jesse Earl finds and covets it away, bringing it out when the adults are otherwise occupied. The boy sits on the T-top, the color of a robin's egg, and drives down the steep hill that runs parallel to the house but doesn't lead anywhere. It is a dead end. No one objects. The jeep is almost as good as a bike. Without steering, the truck only goes in one direction and makes no forty-five-degree right turn at the bottom of the hill, which sends the child crashing through the underbrush of thorns and blackberries and into the ditch alongside Starr Hill Road, for which Starr Renee was named.

Jennie Kaye is particularly shy and unsure, still bewildered about the turn in life she never makes. Her voice mumbles and whispers if she asks for anything at all. She is a year younger and doesn't take the partitioning of their family well. A girl needs a mom, but Jeannie Mae grows tired and is sometimes weary of them, and of all the insurmountable obligation. Three are too much. One is just right. There are no crumbs of bread, so here the remainders are, and the young daughter, the one who got picked over, mourns that loss as an abandoned six-year-old will.

It is early evening when Edward Earl enters like old times. Edward Earl slaps open the screen door that snaps back into its facing by the long spring nailed to it, just after the evening damp had slid in. In an instant his face transitions from unreadable to rage.

"What the Hell is all of this shit in here? Who bought this shit for you kids?"

Edward Earl yells it into the voiceless, motionless people standing around him, as he snatches at the magazine pages Scotch-taped to the wallpaper remnants that still cling to the darkness of those peeling slat boards. The Riverboat Man gathers anything in sight—tiny, puffy animals you get for a quarter at the county fair or from a vending machine. He claws at the dresser top for the firstborn's collection of exactly four toy Matchbox cars—a green two-door Mercury Cougar, an enamel-white ambulance with a red siren and a red cross, a white Camaro with a black stripe and chrome rims, and a blue Studebaker Wagonaire with Bakelite trim paneling. Edward Earl snatches up the books hidden away in the top dresser drawer, which the four children took from the box of trash to play School and Teacher.

"You all know better than this." He stabs the words into Jesse Earl's and Jennie Kaye's faces as he drags them by their shirt collars, along with the piled-up children's trinkets, to the front yard.

With a little kindling wood in the dirt-packed front yard, under the big oak with the Ford tire swing, the Riverboat Man pulls out the red steel gas can that Papaw Ed uses for the block engines of the defunct vehicles he tinkers with, collectively rusting up and down in a stalled parade alongside the left of the house. The fire is in his eyes and in his hands as Edward Earl sends them all to Hell.

"I don't care," the first boy mumbles over and over again, to himself.

He has taught himself how not to care about a lot of things in his seven years. But for Jennie Kaye, this is different. She stoically watches, without flinching, as another incomprehensible act is committed upon her, toying with her life, as playthings and books and diversions and bits of paper that give a little dignity to her cast-off life are consumed, purged in that little Starr Hill Road bonfire.

The first boy watches too. Thrilled at the inferno that ignites the imagination of a seven-year-old, but also hypnotized by the fact that these little things are so easily snatched away, the tiny pylons of a restart, the little foundations those natural children are able to muster. These little gatherings that they so foolishly commit an emotional value to, this substance of little matter that does not mean much to anybody but them, disintegrates in moments, purged like the lives of Joyce and her husband. Jesse Earl says nothing. The children constrict in those squirming flames and the contraction purges the Riverboat Man and his bonfire, and then there are only two. The cleft is complete.

As Jesse Earl and Jennie Kaye watch, they see the others watching too. Billy Joe and Starr Renee and Mamaw Jessie and

Papaw Ed, they watch from the front porch as Edward Earl shows his natural children who is boss, who is the man; shows them that he owns them, and there isn't anything anybody is going to do about it. The Riverboat Man demonstrates his parents' teachings in front of them, taunts them with his deed, and cannot remember if he is mocking those lessons or reenacting them, or showing them how well he has learned.

Jennie Kaye had been in bed when the Riverboat Man came, and absentmindedly brought it with her: her greatest treasure, miraculously cast off or lost by the side of the road. That is her mistake, but it is the slip-up made by a six-year-old and should be forgiven. The Riverboat Man does not forgive.

"Give me that filthy fucking thing!" And he pulls the pillow with the face of a bear on it from his little girl and slings it into the crackling inferno.

As the flattened blue tufts burn brown and then black and then split open, feeding the whiteness inside to the licking flames, his little girl's understanding whittles down in front of him, transfers to the round and ratty hand-me-down pillow. On ordinary nights, Jennie Kaye secrets away her icon like a talisman, warding off such disasters, the little contrivances she manages to bide out her childhood. She needs it. The bear comforts in the last ruins of blurring evening lines as they elongate into shades: a shield against the shadows. It permits unnoticed, charmed specters in among the children. When nobody is looking, she pulls in close the lifeless object, a form of love that is solid, real. She exists once again and is not transient.

The four children know. They sleep in one big bed. They pretend not to know that she hides it, that it is the size for embracing, for murmuring her deficiencies to. That Riverboat Man should know it. But he is not there to know, so he does not. Edward Earl, instead, burns up all of that meaning.

"What I say goes. Y'all are gonna learn!" He spews spittle into his mustache in his efforts, and the orange firelight highlights the spray of his spit as he barks. He turns and full-hand slaps each of them across the mouth, knocking his natural children down into the red dirt of his father's house.

Jennie Kaye stares up and her eyes swear to him that she will never absolve. Those incongruously hard little tears are back in her mother's blazing white-blue ice eyes, not attaching to anything, not attached to sound or expression. She hangs there, emaciated arms and legs unanimated, fingertips slightly drawing up toward the fire, only the little tightening of that knot in the bottom of her too-small chin, that motion of despair that comes upon her, remains with Jennie Kaye for the rest of her life, that balling up of the knot in the bottom of her chin, that furrowing.

But you have to know to look for it. That isn't something the Riverboat Man is going to do, as he shows them all that he means business.

It is a moment in which something delicate fortifies in her, something like the firstborn boy saw before with those Kroger boxes. All that is left when that Riverboat Man leaves and does not look back for her, all the substance drifting out of those boxes, somehow clings to his sister. It spills out again in that moment and her eyes change. The lesson is passed down in a girl so young as that. Hardness. Jennie Kaye saves it up for her own kids: a lesson of how to be hard, of desensitization, passing it down as a gift to her children, and to the men who try to love her. That grain of hatred instilled in a six-year-old grows fertile, builds up the living layers, and this is what festers inside at that moment. Edward Earl's natural daughter calluses over to every facet of this Riverboat father/man, and she takes that hatred to the grave with her. She never, ever absolves. The father, in turn, knows that he remains unforgiven, but he does not know the moment it happens. All of the rest of them standing around that fire in the night, they know. Some things cannot be forgiven.

Edward Earl does not mention the incident again—no explanation, no apologies—and proceeds as if it had not occurred, like infidelities and walking away. After the show of who's the boss, he doesn't stay.

Hard Winter, Paducah, Kentucky, 1972

Divorce is quick for two people who have nothing to fight over except feelings. The way the court system works is that the woman gets the kids, every time. The courts also suggest that he pay for his children; which he ignores. The "sometimes all of us" and the "sometimes only them" is not articulated between mother and children but it foments in the sometimes neglect, in the sometimes care that hadn't been there before. It comes when hard times sneak up, when there is an assault, when she has a run in with the Riverboat Man. His natural children labor to understand the dynamic. The mother picks up part-time work and then full-time jobs, and then adds a part-time job to that, but the ends never meet. There are few options for a Divorcee with a tenth-grade education. This new dynamic keeps Jeannie Mae out of the house most of the time now. Her children bend to the tasks necessary to feed and clean to her standards, which means baseboards to cupboards, and to get all of the laundry done, but now at the very public Coin-All, with once-friends driving by and gazing through room-sized plate glass windows onto the pool of unfortunates there. Who is going to fold and put away and bathe and dress for school and make sure everyone is up and at the bus stop before the children miss it? Somebody has to be responsible for all of that, so her children struggle on as she struggles.

"I became a momma too early. I thought I lived until the kids came," she tells you, and nothing more.

The abstract fantasy is a hard-edged reality by the time she discovers the lie. Her story begins as circumstances mutate into this lesser life, when her life and the world around her no longer coincide because of the lie that overtakes her. She arrives at this place where she can't sync events, the daily occurrences, the details. She finds that the days and the weeks and the months and the years, the minutes, move forward at a pace that overtakes her own movements, that overtakes the actions they now collectively execute or do not execute. She is unable, and does not have the resources, to react. She is unaware that she is flotsam adrift on that large and deep junction between the Tennessee River and the Ohio, the current so close, so compelling, that she is unable to break free from it, to move away from its muddy hold, to span its treacherous, fickle depths as do the remarkable iron-bridged structures that carry the trains and the cars away, to Illinois and to Tennessee, but not her. This family is mired in the marshes of the game reserve she loves so much and cannot leave.

"To where?" she asks.

Her children are spun to the banks, as if in the wake of the towboats that traverse those rivers with their bounty of coal and timber and cars, heading to Michigan and to Louisiana. These are craft far better than she at manipulating the environment for which they are suited. They have direction, purpose. She is mercurial but chained to her compromises.

Mired through the fallacy of the mother, her children are people-propelled by the enforceable actions of others at first, and then by each other, by resentments, by feuds and bitterness and newfound hardness brought about by hardship. Jeannie Mae is no longer in control. Her core, her contempt for how others plot her downfall, her excuses, are therefore not by her own volition but the direct result of the will of others. She, this family, is now the result *of*, the end result. They are unprepared. She finds too late that it has not been explained to her that she is without a plan, ignorant of the need for planning. It happens to her now and, by proxy, to her children. They accept but simultaneously rage against, cry foul, do not understand, but they themselves must pay because no one else is listening. Action and consequence have no connection because they refuse to see; she cannot find the link between their misfortune and why or how it befalls them. Life moves forward for others, but for this family it is the water gone stagnant, yet still trapped in a whirlpool. They are sidelined by the rapidity of action put into place by others, to castigate, to mar, to vilify them in their downtrodden state.

Collectively, they futilely wish their lives could be altered in a lovely sense—a loving sense—but are unable to build such structures. Beguiled by inaction, Jeannie Mae perceives that life is more sublime through the stories of others. She reads, cover to cover, anything to escape.

They are locked together, reduced together, in misshapen apartments culled from the more regal life of past inhabitants—those once great houses that are now on the skids, on their last legs, with shoddy plumbing and holes in the walls from loutish tenants, and rattletrap windows taped into their casings, floorboards letting the draft in, with working heat sometimes and sometimes not, that forces dressing with the covers still wrapped around bony shoulders and protruding ribcages, hovering over the coal oil floor furnace that blows weakly into the thin blanket like a teepee. Jeannie Mae delves into literature of any caliber to not see.

Bellies swollen from want, a month passes with only rice to eat, so her family ingests it three times a day, with heaping tablespoons full of Domino sugar in the morning, then seasoning packets at night, and anticipating the rich spread of school lunches during the weekdays, graspingly forgetting that mother does not get a share.

"If you don't cry, nobody gives you milk," Jeannie Mae's grandmother told her long ago.

Defiant, this mother does not cry and nobody sees her want.

Her house is made up of discarded objects fitted to their new station, what they have become. She improvises with whatever utensils of everyday life are shed by others as no longer good enough, but which then must be good enough for them. This entails endless searches through yard sales and thrift stores and curbsides for what a few extra dollars can buy in some semblance of a chair, a stained pot, a few pieces of silverware pieced together into a habitat naturalized by poverty. This puzzle pieces together her home each day: building upon, then losing, then rebuilding; casting off and then acquiring these items of marginal value fills an intrinsic need in her, an endless cycle of change—at first an attempt to swap up, and then just swapping for swapping's sake.

"If y'all wanna stay home today, y'all can, but we all have to clean the house," she says.

The ritual scrubbing clean of these objects only highlights their shabbiness, but they do it all the same. Her children miss a day of school, scrub-brushing baseboards and degreasing cabinets with straight Pine Sol, and burnishing thin and scuffed linoleum floors and windows. It takes longer than a school day to do it right. Mix-and-match furniture masquerades under easier-to-obtain pieces of cloth, covering over the chagrin of stains and fabric tears, filling in the sunken, the broken, the shored up for a few more years of use. Flannels and shawls, quilts, and colored tape to hide splits in forest green Naugahyde and shiny white vinyl laced with silver flecks, the pristine white cotton filler erupting, then fading to a kind of gray with grime, or shabby brown couch plaids and chairs thirty years out of date, where book stacks or cans of soup stand in for missing or defunct legs—until she needs the soup.

This family eventually trains the eye not to notice and no longer invites in those who do. Culling from their lives those who cast judgment, limiting social strata to the local and transient hustlers and whores, to the criminals, to misfits, runaways, forgotten people who, like them, are minutes from exile, from utter poverty, from homelessness, and sometimes even to the homeless. Jeannie Mae shares this succession of little disowned spaces, divided and now divided again, chopped up into lesser parts, obscured from the majestic home it had once been, reduced by neglect, and then passed off from successions of consecutively less-important owners from a time when it was just a bit better, a descent to the less-than that the space has now become. It is here this family takes up temporary residence. These shelters are all that she can afford in her new circumstance, and most times she cannot keep up the rent, sneaking off before the final cut-off notice arrives. She comes from something, and that is a hateful thing that she is unable to forget. Forgetting would be a mercy.

Still, she takes pride in having enough to share. They are welcome. Unmet cousins arrive from Arkansas and, when they leave, take with them her only can opener and a new bottle of hot sauce. She swears. She calls them thieves and gypsies, vows they will never set foot in this house again. She invites more anyway, and the door rarely closes. There is always space on the couch, an extra blanket for the floor, her animal pound of human refuse. Jeannie Mae takes her time to learn that living like this does not happen all at once. It is not a free-fall for her. These eventualities, this descent, like the decline of the once elegant and now cramped apartment quarters they briefly inhabit, take years of use, of abuse and neglect, to fall from grace. It is another one of those twelve-step processes.

She copes with her new surroundings by affording herself a few creature comforts. She is avaricious for something not shared, something just for herself that is off limits to those who come in and out of her temporary shelter. These are not great things: a scented bar of Dove moisturizer soap, a special Clairol Herbal Essence shampoo, a second-hand paperback or *True Confessions* magazine, and occasionally a prize more rare: the glossy-covered adult comic of strong, barbarian women and men in tantalizing and revealing outfits, protruding manhood and breasts and pubic mounds scarcely covered (although these are the most expensive of her vices and seldom appear). These items all have one common denominator—escape. The covers, when present, depict the fantasy of sex, with titillating headlines that advertise illicit sex and discovered liaisons. It is an odd juxtaposition that she does not speak directly of the act of copulation, or even once appear in front of her children in so much as her undergarments.

She satisfies herself with these petulant luxuries, just as more elegant women vacation, or lie in the torpor of Dead Sea salt baths or mud wraps, or pedicures, or schedule salon hair and face appointments. These extravagances make do in the stead of those things that are unobtainable. Although most times she hovers over her children like a sparrow hawk suspended over the body of Osiris, attempting to fan life back into them after this family descends, there are other times, too, when she gluts on the stolen moments of solitude as if she is starved for them, gloating over those moments of forgetting all that is around her, forgetting this senseless maze she is endlessly repeating, and forgetting them.

The coveted distance from reality is never so great as when she vacates for her real vices: reading and coffee, both of which she is seldom without. The narrative does not matter so much to her. She savors, yields to this other string of eventualities without resistance, and it is better than this, her own life, and momentarily she forgets and lives within that instant of forgetting, free within the immediacy of somebody else, someone better than her, living days that are better than hers, made from better choices and better luck, but she does not comprehend why she escapes in such a way. A radiance overtakes the hard lines she masks behind; her mouth, although not a smile, develops a vulnerability, a ceding of responsibilities that are too heavy a burden for her, a decidedly feminine quality she perhaps once wore easily. Racy words ravish her in the carnal sense, and she lingers in them as if she has just been ravished; she lingers in those stolen moments of complete solitude, locked tightly away from her life, constricting herself within the vastness of possibility contained in those words that mean everything that is not her reality. She needn't voice that her story is not on these pages. She isn't required to read about her kinds of people. She lives it. Her story does not waver in fortune as these do, but remains the same, a constant. Words are not written about her.

She performs her Houdini tricks in the ritualistic and systematic way that is required with all magic tricks. Her children read the signals like braille, hard to pick up at first but, once learned, coming lightly as fingertips. She first drapes herself with one of the cloths shrouding the furniture, so that she seemingly becomes one with the line of the couch, unbroken. The cup of coffee would have gone cold beside her, but is still absentmindedly sipped, ringing the table with its condensation and ignored, as she apprises herself of page after page, until it fills her, saturates, gives her means to continue with the banality that follows after the book closes. Extricated, she does not hear, or if she hears, ignores those events that occur in the lesser reality that has continued around her, without her. This deceit takes her out of herself, out of her life, out of this small prison of poor decisions, and out of her uninformed and misshapen sometimes rage against/

sometimes love and care toward she knows not what. It is a beautiful thing, this moment of desertion: thoughts of what she should have done better or how things could have turned out if only, neglecting to summon all who have abandoned her to this place, to this now faded place.

She has no choice but to do it. The escape is infectious. Instinctively, those pushed out, removed, know to make themselves smaller than her pages, to disappear, physically and figuratively, to go away and blend with the mismatched furniture, to occupy quietly, to excise to the outside or to the back bedroom or to a neighbor's house when she escapes from this pantomime of reality and into the world of who she really could be, only without trying, without engaging. It is also in these moments that her children become the little savages they are skilled at becoming, each bullying or being bullied; going to the Kroger so the eldest could pretend to shop while the others steal bags of candy bars to devour, hidden away behind the bushes that line the sidewalks on the way home; or hurling themselves with abandon into the bunk beds with wrought iron railings, until a misjudgment splits the boy's skull, spewing blood down his face and torso until he becomes the creature from a horror film and forces the youngest girl to run screaming into Jeannie's fortress, thus shattering her carefully constructed illusion; or playing with the wild-haired mulatto twins down the dead end street, until they shockingly demonstrate in the back of an abandoned car what their father liked for them to do for him, and ask the boy to join in the fun.

Jeannie Mae gifts it to the boy and to the younger girl too, this desire for escape, this gift of deceit. The elder is immune, too pretty to need it, relying on that crutch alone to help with her own kind of escape, the illusion of escape. The boy begins stealing stories as young as six, in the bathroom, locked away from the rest of them. He furtively stalks around Jeannie Mae, observing but pretending not to observe, searching, inquisitive. While the rest of their now-reduced number gluts itself on television after losing the father, Jesse Earl scours words like his mother, trying to make out meaning, to find understanding in these little vignettes of other people's lives just after Jeannie does it, looking for the secret, looking to get away too, or looking for a way to get in.

Certain of his stealth, he thieves them away just after the *True Confessions* with the curled edges and coffee cup circlets makes it to the tattered magazine stack, left on the rusty shelf that holds toiletries, along with toilet paper lifted from the library on a short month. He also pilfers the paperbacks with covers ripped off, which she gets for a quarter at the dreary concrete-colored discount mall with its endless halls and stalls, used up, cast off, damaged, but with the words still intact. Only when it is buried inside the hard, brown, plastic swinging doors of the coffee table, cast in the vestige of a genuine country antique, but fooling no one, or pressed, immovable, on a multicolored shag rug of golds and greens and browns, years out of date, does he steals it away. She pretends not to notice his interest, or perhaps has other urgencies: hers is an expert observation, but as with most topics of discussion concerning the welfare of and care for each other, they avoid the subject. Perhaps she imagines that repeating her is an emulation of flattery.

The reading material sates an inquisitiveness in the boy, and this slaking of an unknown and curious thirst becomes as habitual for him as it is for her, and it again repeats in the youngest, one year the boy's junior. It contributes to his salvation. He scrutinizes and studies how Jeannie Mae does it, this better-than-lifestyle stunt of disappearing, of letting go, of becoming subordinate to the page. And it is better. For her, it is easy to forget the start (or the miss) she once had in the beginning of her life, which began her descent, and then once again when she believed that she was ready. It isn't just this small-but-important matter of learning to emulate the forgetting. It serves as an easier example from all the rest of the handed-down lessons. She makes the boy thirsty for this secret knowledge she hoards unto herself. It is those pages that define his understanding of sex and affairs, of how men handle women, how women want to be handled, but most important, how families outside of their hovel conduct themselves: faster, more elegantly, and more regally. It isn't reality, but little is. Her habits, and this absorption, unknowingly create a persistent feminine perspective to the boy's overview of human interaction that does not leave him. He is unable to eradicate the nuisance.

The Cunningham girl finds loopholes, and tricks Edward Earl's natural children into doing her share, freeing herself for a good time. She studies her guile early.

But there was also "them," excluding the natural born ones. The secret trips told the story of the fact that the Cunningham girl weighed more now, maybe always did. It is because she is left over from times that were not hard, from a true love as opposed to a necessary one, even if memory serves to impair, or maybe it's that the Cunningham girl simply is not one of his natural children and therefore not part of the equation, the end result of all this grief and hardship. The natural children punctuate despair, are reminders of it.

It begins with little intimacies Jeannie Mae affords the Cunningham girl and intuitively reminds the child not to tell: trips to the grocery or Dollar Store for cleaning supplies and a reason to slip in to Munal's Donut Shop for just the two of them, for something with sprinkles and a chocolate milk that Lisa later gloats about anyway, victoriously rubs his natural children's faces in while they eat boxed mashed potatoes again with Kraft Italian style spaghetti, or with macaroni and cheese and canned corn, because they cost a quarter. The Cunningham girl recounts the time she gets a soda on the Two-of-Them trip to the very public Coin-All Laundromat and didn't have to stay with Bumpaw Marvin, who had moved in but every single day sits at the kitchen table and stares at his never-ending coffee cup refills, or out the window like he is looking at something in it, or like he is waiting for somebody to come back, as he wastes away in his blue-and-white pillow-ticking coveralls and slippers and chain smokes. Jeannie starts calling him Bumpaw shortly after he loses his sawmill job and moves in, another burden on a strained budget. He is a party of one.

After the Cunningham girl exults, taunting his natural children, Jesse Earl and Jennie Kaye fire back, "That's all right because you're a bastard and we've got a daddy" or "Where's your daddy because you don't know."

They all know his natural children really don't have one either. In the end, the taunting inflicts wounds on both sides, which, although not mortal, scar deep into the tissue like rock salt curing the flesh, which heals, but leaving the texture changed, thicker, tenderer, for all three of those leftover children.

Cruelty also has another purpose, more ready, more beneficial. It comforts his natural children by pretending in the moment that they aren't the baggage, the leftovers of some unimportant calamity of a kind best forgotten. But how can you forget with two kids latching on to you always to prove it all happened? The Riverboat Man also does not save them. And when his children ask the mother, Jeannie Mae promptly is annoyed because of course she loves equally, but they all know better. It isn't really a lie, because nobody believes it.

The mother with a tenth-grade education and three kids and no husband can be forgiven by an ever-watchful town, even on that side of the tracks, except for the last part. Working class becomes white trash pretty quickly when the paycheck dries up, requiring them to evacuate the little house on Brown Street with the great Mimosa tree out front where the hummingbirds and butterflies and bees visit in the summer. The sheriff evicts them for not paying the rent.

There, the crucible splits, spilling its contents into their faces. His natural children remind Jeannie Mae of that time, too, reminders of failure. The terrible thing, the laughable thing, is his children remember, too.

Men whore. It helps relieve pressure between young couples. It is unwritten, presumed. Whoring's parameters keep it clean, discrete: don't get anyone pregnant. The interloper is always guilty, for a multitude of reasons: unwanted strings, expectations or hopes for the leaving of wives and kids, or she might get pregnant. If that happens, the agreement is disagreeable and the union dissolves and the bastard dealt with. Scorn lies with the man, but blame is shouldered by the woman. She is ostracized.

Men are weak and seducible. Women are suspect, and there are a myriad of labels for single women who work around men. Career women are a novelty for Kentucky, for the country, dangerous to the status quo and to men's egos. Divorced women are a different breed because they have been had. They are more desperate or lonely or sexualized and, therefore, more untrustworthy, pariahs loose among the patchwork marriages tenuously bound by the slimmest margin of tolerance for each other.

Jeannie Mae could not know that Edward Earl got to be single and she got loaded with the baggage train. He sends no money. And the rent is ignored, the groceries are not purchased, and the light and gas bills go unpaid. She expects the Riverboat Man to honor his obligations to his children, to honor the court edicts that define the obligations of fatherhood, but he walks away from it all instead. He, like all men, has options like that.

So they move to a place that is "affordable" for a woman changing sheets and washing bed linens on a gargantuan scale, cleaning shitty bathrooms in the morning and scrubbing restaurant floors at night. She steals in well after her children are in bed and has just enough time to look them over before they leave for school and she leaves for her morning hotel job, but she can barely pay the rent, so they move once more to a used-up one-bedroom walkup, where she sleeps on the couch. The place is on the south side of town, where mostly black people live, and they look at her with distrust, this white woman who moves in with too many single men sniffing around. Her family is in rapid succession run through the lower regions of Nowheresville, landing smack in the middle of poor white trash.

Their place is a rattletrap shotgun house just past its usefulness that nobody has torn down yet. The living room leads to a bedroom that leads to the kitchen, with the bathroom backing up to the kitchen. You get to it from the bedroom. The floors are cold, and the pipes freeze up in winter. And sometimes she can't pay all the bills, so the electric company shuts off the lights and they retreat even further into that tiny house to hole themselves up in the kitchen with extra felt blankets nailed up on the open doorways, and they heat the single room with the oven door open and sleep on pallets, or the occasional mattress dragged out onto the floor if winter outlasts spring. When the electricity is on, space heaters near bathroom pipes keep the water thawed.

Jeannie Mae does not speak about paying, so living without one utility or the other becomes something that begins. Her decline is gradual but urgent. Clawing out a new desperate existence, her descent from lower-middle-but-respectable class to utter poverty does not go unnoticed. Friendships are the first casualty. Teachers treat her children differently: suspiciously and piteously. Students call names, tell them they smell like blacks do, and tell them they are trash. The firstborn, mystified at the new hierarchy, manically screams at the teacher to stop the taunts and laughter of his classmates, but Mrs. Bowles instead snickers herself, and her jowls waddle with mirth. She instructs the boy to return to his seat because he is disrupting the classroom, encouraging the peals of children's laughter. After several variations on this theme, the boiler comes to a head and bursts. The boy goes mute, marches out, and heads to the adult education center next door, where his mother takes part-time business classes, and he recounts his little horror and how nothing is done about it. The end of the story gets lost in his wracking sobs.

The classroom is electric as Jeannie Mae forces her way in, holding the child's hand, and bellows at them all: "If so much as a word is said, if this shit happens again, so help me God I will personally stomp a hole in your ass and your parents' asses alike, even if it means going to jail for it! Do I make myself perfectly clear?"

She moves within inches of the protesting teacher's face, and the rotund Mrs. Bowles leans back heavily onto her creaking desk to stop the trembling. The principal hastily enters, telling everyone to calm down, and the kids gape wide-mouthed at a mother talking in profanities.

Strangers then come from the government to probe the mystery of whether a single mother is capable, observing whether her children are raised properly and asking secretive questions in private rooms about the cleanliness of the house and the quantity of underwear the children possess, about the kind of food consumed at home and whether the mother is a fit parent in their estimation—as if such a thing as an acceptable single parent exists. They speak furtively among themselves in the presence of the three children about how skinny the three are and how poorly their clothes fit, about how their shoes are not appropriate for the weather or a coat is too short, about why the children don't have hats or gloves, and these interrogations end with more microphone announcement calls to the principal's office and more questions about the Divorcee. The huntsman sounds the bugle, but the children are astute at covering the scent. They steel themselves in solidarity against this supposedly sincere and off-the-record inquest.

The reduced family ceases to talk to outsiders about their home life, about the oddity of sleeping together huddled up in the dark on the kitchen floor, waiting for the lights to come back on and hoping the pipes don't freeze or the water get cut off for nonpayment, because that means you can't bathe and the toilet doesn't flush unless you fill it with plastic gallon milk jugs full of water you get from the gas station spigot when most people are off the streets. And sometimes well-meaning teachers take one of the children down to the Dollar General store to buy a new pair of pants or a shirt or a pair of shoes, and the mother rages and calls up the school and screams bloody murder at whoever answers the phone. That is what happens to the poor. Others take over one's life. No amount of frugality keeps them from sliding backward into white trash, no matter how the children assist and no matter how much the mother works. It is inevitable.

The courts order the Riverboat Man to pay Jeannie Mae child support, rule in her favor to facilitate the care of his two natural children. He doesn't. Edward Earl doesn't pay until the cops come and make him pay. The mother files grueling, endless documents with the courts and with his employer and with the government to garnish his wages, and the Riverboat Man quits in retaliation and takes another job, prompting her to sleuth out his new employer and begin the tiresome process again. It is time-consuming and it costs money she doesn't have. When Jeannie Mae corners him in the street, making a spectacle of herself with her kids in tow, Edward Earl simply moves to another state, making any attempts to collect now futile. States have no interstate agreements about such trivial matters.

"I can't make that bastard daddy of yours pay for you all. Does he think food and rent's free, that sonnovabitch?" She seethes at his natural children.

It isn't her fault, really, that she doesn't have food for the table, and the Riverboat Man leaves for Florida or Louisiana and works down there and gets away with it, gloating about how he got her, his natural children not a part of the equation, just a byproduct of the getting. He knows the system, too. But he misses that riverboat town because, after a few months, he sneaks back and Jeannie Mae finds him, and she packs her kids up into that black Comet and drives wildly around town looking for his car. When she finds it, she puts a brick through the windshield and says, "Let's see if you have money to pay for THAT, you sonnovabitch." Or she waits until late in the night and pours soap or sugar into his gas tank ("That will remind him not to fuck with me, that motherfucker"), and her children are quiet and pretend that they are all on the same side. Afterward, she stops the car whenever she is overwhelmed by it all and puts her head on the wheel and shakes all over, but she does not say anything and she does not cry. Not that her children see, anyway.

The meanness amplifies and sometimes consumes Jeannie Mae but does not break her. It drives her. She is single-minded in her fury and indignation over her failure and her shitty jobs and never seeing her kids, and over doing it all by her moral code of what is the right thing to do by leaving that cheating bastard, and this is the payout she gets. Jeannie thunders and he isn't there, but his natural children are, so it comes out in little restrained and vicious ways, from a woman who is both a woman spurned and the conflicted mother of the children she must keep for the man who works so diligently to destroy her. It rubs off on his children a little bit, the blame.

One of those ways is when she moves into a cheap and small house quickly vacated by the previous filthy tenants, who leave broken furniture and carpet stains and dog shit all over the house, and nailed over a particularly large hole in the hallway wall, an inspirational cardboard "Footsteps" poster, unframed and still in its plastic cover, with faded images of a sandy beach. A large pile of abandoned metal oil cans, partly obscured by tall weeds, lies in the abandoned lot adjacent to the back of the house. As the Riverboat Man's natural children play together in the way they are used to, with nothing at all, the Cunningham girl asks to join in, which she is not prone to do, so it seems to them like a pretense or a ruse of some kind, one of her ways to get them to do something for her without a price. His natural children ignore that Cunningham Girl. Lisa throws the oil cans from the debris pile by the house, one after the other, at his natural children, who would not let her join their game, making her assault a game of her own in which they are both target and participant. That's when it wells up in their mother, and his natural children find that they are part of a mother's anger.

Jeannie Mae watches from the back porch for a bit but doesn't intervene or say anything, refusing to rule for or against. After the wails and protestations erupt from his natural children, Jeannie joins in the game.

"Don't throw them low, Lisa, you keep missing! Arch the can, throw it over your head at 'em! That's the way!" Jeannie gleefully laughs at the connecting cans and at his natural children running from the assault.

This continues on for some time, a contralto of squeal and wail, and the older girl takes better aim and hits another one in the head or the face, and his natural children yell for their mother and their half-sister to quit it, and the mother laughs again.

"Defend yourselves! You mean you don't like this game? You don't wanna be excluded either?"

But you can tell the bitterness behind it, the surprise of anger, and the baggage of a woman trapped, with nowhere to go and three kids and a second-hand set of jobs and a house full of hand-me-downs. Those cast offs. And the Cunningham girl gloats in her victory and how well she learns her lesson.

The times when it is acute like that, with sub-camps and diminishing units, are glossed over by the all-together family time too, by the sacrifices she still makes for all three of her children: the sandwiches eaten together, made from white bread and luncheon meat, with their own soda, and Little Debbie Oatmeal Cookies with cream filling or frozen Hostess Ding Dongs, while they indulge in a TV she isn't able to afford. Sometimes Jeannie Mae borrows a station wagon from the neighbor, who lets her if she puts some gas in it, and by emptying out the spare wheel-well and stuffing two of the skinniest kids in there she sneaks them all into the Drive-In Theater. Those times take sacrifice.

Jeannie Mae takes only one thing of value from the divorce. It is her ticket to freedom. She makes her getaway from Brown Street in a black 1964 Mercury Comet, and that is her only real prize. From the south side, she drives decidedly north in that Comet that she takes away from her rotten past and rides her children into their collective future in that battered automobile, a way to get to the grocery and to her jobs and to doctors' visits. The tires are bald, with no traction and no money to replace them. It is deep into that first long winter after the divorce that stretches into and overpowers spring, when ice covers rows of quick-assemble house eaves in long bars stretching down to their cement steps and covers the sidewalks too, and the intersection laid in that riverboat town long before the Civil War, and that is when it happens to her, that first blow, and the reality that Jeannie Mae is unmoored.

Jeannie's black Comet eases into the intersection and she is unprepared. Preoccupied, she doesn't notice the spectacles around her - that brittle ice has overtaken the ancient grove of oaks along Charity Avenue, which heads out toward the Confederate monument, or that the weight of winter has already snapped off generations of heavy limbs secretly rotted from the inside, crashing them to the ground with an ebullient *Snap! Snap! Creak* and *Snap!* The old guard of sycamores, the chestnut and hickory, straining under the burden, piles the dead and the unhealthy at their roots – winter's sacrifice.

Winter distracts her. The flashes and arcs of prismed light present an expanse of glitter and glassy tree debris just now apparent to her, and Jeannie Mae takes it all in as she edges into fluid drive on those unsure tires, that Comet spinning its black start on the clear ice. She is unaware of another vehicle, also spinning out of control, of its imminence as it slams sidelong into her Comet, that long low howl of metal grinding through paint seeking metal, opposing forces disfiguring, crushing, setting her into a tailspin, and pitching her out of control and into a freefall. The firstborn son has already grounded himself, nestling down into the floorboard to the rear of the driver's seat, just behind her, and clasping the spot in the vehicle where pools of warmth collect from the humming transmission to heat the floorboard hump that runs between the two floorboard wells.

The girls, eager to emulate, are scampering to and fro— the youngest on the back-bench seat but hanging over the front, and the Cunningham girl riding shotgun, closest to the mother, in the passenger side. Like the mother, the impact pitches the two girls into the tumulus as the vehicle leaves its course, simultaneously spinning out of control, unrestrained, and woman and girls are repeatedly battered by the centrifuge that is now the black Comet. The boy alone inadvertently secures himself, constricting into the small space that spans just beyond his fetal position, preventing flailing limbs, which are jarred but not broken, aching but not bleeding. The women are unprepared. The trajectory of the black Comet on slick ice catches the stationary utility pole on the other side of the journey's ill-fated and unexpected turn of events. And then they are rocking.

And then it is over.

Impact and damage and without insurance, the black Comet now publicly exhibits the scars of that incident, just like the scars of their poverty, just like the three women are marked by the impact of unmooring in the most unexpected way, finding too late that their ticket to freedom isn't so free as that.

And the hard winter yawns further into March. The last of the month calls to them and still the thick layers of snow and ice keep coming, plowing into ever higher, blackening mounds, now stretching into April, and the heating bills are mounting up, pushing them a little more behind. It is the first time that the lights are cut off, and the first time Jeannie

Mae makes the concession of reconnecting the utility in her children's names instead, to get a fresh start on getting ahead, to last just a little bit longer, but now the gas bill grows too great and it happens again and then the water bill overcomes her and she makes mental notes, tallying bills associated with her and her children that need to be paid before they are switched over again. The Salvation Army and church services no longer assist her failing enterprise. The Divorcee has no credit, and cash goes only so far. The landlord extends no passes on the rent, and this is the first time that Jeannie Mae leaves like they learn to leave myriad place after disremembered place, negotiating a new apartment or house or renegotiating a slum tenancy they already left for a new try at making it, of showing them, and grasping at some small break to begin normal again.

Their focus on the ever-looming present occludes their rapid slide to the back of the bus. This next start will not be that break, that little success. Jeannie Mae finds herself without a receptacle to lodge the worldly loose ends of their last new beginning. It is a paltry assemblage she has managed to scrape together from yard sales and hand-me-downs and bargains from the Salvation Army, and it is the first time she leaves everything behind but clothes and those memories more precious to her than all of those other, finer pieces of a life: photographs documenting the past events, locked tightly in vinyl photograph albums in greens and yellows, with adhesive on the side so none of the memories will get lost. The mother boxes them up and puts them in her battered black Comet with anything else that will fit in somewhere, including her children, and she asks her sister to take in her and the

Cunningham girl, and it will be the first time that she drops his natural children off at the house of cast-offs—because she doesn't have a choice this time around, she said.

Jeannie Mae has to start all over again, really start over this time around. She's lost everything and she can't make it on her own and she can't show him, she can't show anyone, and her children can all tell that it breaks her down just a little bit to live through those next couple of months on the back of somebody else. After all of those first times, it gets a little easier to do it after that, after losing everything, after taking that first defeat. It never gets easy to have no expectations.

Jeannie Mae's abhorrence for the Riverboat Man does not subside. It remains relentless, becomes pure, unpolluted in its limpidness. When she finds him, her temper rises up to meet his ambivalence and the clash is breathtaking, and the odium and rancorous words and deeds consume both of them. She leaves in a fire of ferocity and invectives and scratch marks, if she manages to get that close. And sometimes Jeannie Mae will abandon his natural children to him, the two that still have tethers to him. She leaves the "them" portion standing there with Edward Earl on the side of the road as the "us" portion peels out in a rain of curses and screams, because this is a way to get back at him, these two human volleys. He has to take his children to give her a break, and if he isn't paying for them then he can damned well take them for a little while, and she tells him and anybody else who is watching or listening, and his children stand there, stricken, wide-eyed, wondering if they will eventually be abandoned by both.

Since the Riverboat Man left, since the divorce and the subsequent battles for lack of responsibility, the game becomes routine. Jesse Earl and Jennie Kaye learn to expect the next inevitable step, as do Edward Earl's parents. In silence, he collects the two children from that spot where the mother has abandoned them, and he transports them to the cast-off house without a word: that old falling down house. That house he'd grown up in and couldn't wait to get out of, that house full of his disposals. That's the house he take his natural children to, and he makes a deposit. It is banal in its regularity. The children mostly think Edward Earl will never come back, but in his action of leaving behind, of disposing of the dilemma they have become, the abandonment is complete; his relinquishing of any responsibility for his past is complete.

Edward Earl's sneaking away and running off gives Jeannie Mae some power over him, and there is enough distance in the hate because of the miles that separate them. They get their roles down, and the leftover family settles into a little better apartment, or at least one they get used to, settle comfortably down into all of that poverty. It is with resignation that they learn how to move, and they are always moving. There is never enough money to keep up the rent, and in six months' or a year's time the rent will be two or even three months late, and the landlord will throw that reduced family out, or the family will pack up what little they have and move, sometimes taking the furniture or the better pieces of it if they have a way, or just the essentials like beds. Sometimes, they will take nothing at all and start over, buying a little here from a yard sale or the Salvation Army, and getting donated furniture to begin that next new start.

The lights or the gas or the water will be on a few months, but always in danger of being turned off, and her kids know enough to be worried too, even though they don't really know why, but it would set into Jeannie's mood and that would just carry over to everything the children did or said, and they'd try to be extra good during those hard times, or stay out of her way at least.

Cherokee and We, 1972

That light. It's that light that streams through the window and becomes a curtain of radiance. It illuminates the swath of room it touches but is so blinding in the gloom that it transcends, veils. And it's difficult to see through, that light. The dust and grime and particles of so many years being moved around, the refuse of so many who had come before, colliding, flooding through that light and pauses and then moves again, alighting but does not clear away. It does not completely leave them, does not leave her. That brilliance makes all visible, even when you try so hard to collect it up, to rub it out. Being clean is important to Jeannie Mae. She takes great pains to keep everything scrubbed up and tidy, exactly in its place. Presentable. She wants to leave this past place clean, scrubbed through. Sterile. The outside world both makes her defiant and intimidates her. Being judged is intimidating. Friendly neighbors peeking out the window or standing on the curb to see what's going on in your life intimidates Jeannie and simultaneously makes her defiant, bristle.

Only one man overcomes her, forges a bridge. They are moving in together and it is marvelous to see.

Perhaps he is a redeemer. Cherokee brings out all that is good in them, makes them want to be good, to work to be a family. He teaches her son what being honorable is, and that his actions and not words speak for him, and that a body can be motivated by good and by actions done to help and not to hurt. He gives Jesse Earl that. Jeannie Mae has five years with him, as a collective, as a true north *us*, and those years promise to wipe away that other winter of a life they'd all gotten through individually and as best they could somehow, when that Riverboat Man walks out, walks away. Edward Earl had not returned after passing off children; he has become blurred at the edges, a memory.

Their poverty solidifies as a lifestyle, a routine, a scarlet badge each had adjusted to seeing upon himself or herself or affixed to each other. Her children wear it with nonchalance in these later years. They have also collectively become adept at raising themselves. The Cunningham girl is de facto the new boss-of-them while the mother works and goes to night school, occupied against the odds in business school. On some days, Bumpaw Marvin watches over, but, really, he is a presence, like the floating dust, a non-entity standing vigilant over the void he stares into after the sun had left. The old man uselessly idles away the day in the kitchen, waiting. They collectively do not bother to ask why he gawks into the street, inspecting the lives of passersby, or for whom he perpetually grieves. The children do not ask why he is relentlessly wretched.

Years later, the college boy came to realize that it must have been the enormous weight of losing love, and the burden of its consequence, that riveted Bumpaw Marvin to the thin twin bed in the back room, the traced steps to the kitchen table and back again. The old man had consumed himself for Marjorie all of his days and thought of no other woman, did not pine for, did not resume life without, did not pursue. He remained infatuated with his silent abandonment, his unquenched waiting. Watching over his daughter's children was an afterthought, as was everything after his loss.

Lacking parental guidance, the children were placated by the television. It became custodian; it stood in for. This a mother knows. When it finally met its demise and she couldn't afford a new one, she and Cherokee packed up and took the Riverboat Man's natural children to the cast-off house of Edward Earl's parents, and they took Bumpaw and the Cunningham girl to a sister's house, and Jeannie and Cherokee lived alone in a big silver Buick by the lake for a while, all by themselves, utterly free, camping out under the Egyptian Goddess Nut's bloated belly bursting with stars, acting as shroud and mantle, protecting a sacred thing between them, with nothing but a few covers, a Coleman butane stove, clothes, and a cooler for comfort. This continued until the two had saved enough money to buy another TV, and then they regrouped, collected her children once more, and together they moved on to another rental in another neighborhood. Cherokee and the mother had done that for her children, for them, for their family, for this newly defined *we*. In those early days, when there was enough love to go around, Jeannie Mae looked out for her children like that, but it took her three children a while to understand what sacrifice meant, what these things cost.

But for now, the empty room was warm and dusty and comfortable as *we* moved the big cardboard canisters with the tin metal tops into that dusty, happy room. Her joy was radiant and palpable in the way Jeannie Mae moved without that heaviness she had been carrying these last years, nimbler now that she wasn't doing it alone anymore—that litheness of a woman who can rest, let down defenses.

"Hon, I forgot the lunchmeat and the Cokes in the front seat. Could you grab them for me before they get hot?" She called out to him as he stood shirtless and sun-sleek and beautiful in the yard.

He caught her face in his gaze and they both stood there for a millisecond, basking in their connection, everything else fading for an instant, and it was just the two of them, and then he flashed a brilliant smile, pulled out of his eyes a long dense length of undulating black hair glinting shiny onyx in the sun, put down the boxes and sprang attentive to her request before carrying in more boxes. For her children watching them, their new story was a movie with colors clearer, more brilliant, more vibrant. Cherokee was moving in, a thaw had commenced, and a new summer was beginning. Maybe not one of those endless summers of myth, but one that was measured instead by the numbers of days when a family could be happy and together, not fractured, not separate, not stingy, but something fine and something lasting: a union.

This sensation had to last for all of them. For the firstborn boy begins a summer whose days he could all remember. Days that stood in contrast to a murky past, which still occasionally lashed out with malice from the shadows, abstract scenes witnessed through the thinnest sliver of alabaster, then fading, of things best forgotten. The former days began to seem inconsequential with this new beginning, and the faded father all but memory. It was a summer when darkness didn't shroud the truth and the light wasn't the artificial kind that circles and isolates us and them. That light and that room and those few canisters of that new family's belongings were a new prospect for a collective *we*.

Her children begged to hear the story again as they ate their sandwiches on the cream-colored carpet of this new beginning. They'd met as they both were hitchhiking, she to Louisville and alone, when they paired up for the company. Jeannie Mae was at the Greyhound bus station and had neatly folded two 20s and a five-dollar bill into quadrants and stuck them into the left back pocket of her bell-bottom jeans before pulling her powder blue Aerosmith t-shirt over the low waist of her hip-huggers. Those 45 dollars were for the trip, to eat on, and came from her second job, scrubbing floors at the Denny's attached to the new Drury Inn hotel, where she also worked cleaning rooms. It took a while to make that kind of bread, so she was adamant when telling her father, Marvin (who nobody called Charlie anymore, or even Marvin—he was just Bumpaw), to watch the kids while she escaped in some tiny way, to get out from under the pressure, to be a girl again, even momentarily, under the guise of seeing the city of Louisville, where she'd never been.

Marvin knew that look and he had agreed without comment. He was a man who rarely spoke unless spoken to, and his responses were short, to the point. They were the answers of a man who could not be made whole. He'd given it all away in the quiet look that wasn't exactly a stare at his daughter, and it showed in his resignation to let her do what he had not had the grace to give his late wife. For her, it was as if some of that desperation to live and cram it all in had resurfaced in a gentler, less urgent way. Marvin recalled when Marjorie had had the same urgency that last year, even though they did not speak of it before she left, and he knew about the consequences of actions—and inactions, too—but he didn't say anything because it was not what fathers talked about with daughters, and these were not topics to be discussed at any rate. The dead should be canonized whenever possible.

It wasn't the sort of thing that just goes away, this need that he saw in Jeannie Mae, which had once been in Marjorie. That was a lesson you don't forget, though you sometimes must wait a while to do better. Jeannie was now at the same brink, that moment he had entered before without speaking, without action. His wayward daughter would get away, change, and live (but maybe not with a capital L, he hoped) either with or without his consent. So he let her go.

In the terminal, Jeannie Mae and this happy stranger, both of whom had perfected that affected hippie vibe that attracted one to the other, immediately understood the cues each began to display for the other, and it warmed them to understand the context of the conversation even before it had begun.

"I know you, Miss. I've got you all figured out, you know," he said to her from across the polished concrete, with a genuine smile Jeannie hadn't seen in a while. "You're that new actress Jane Birkin and it's pretty clear that you're here incognito, don't want nobody to know it's you. Am I right?

See? I can tell in your eyes. You have movie star eyes, so that for one gave you away right there."

She animated her movements and fluttered her lashes at him.

"Let me guess: You're studying lost boys like me for some big movie part about a too beautiful soul, abandoned right here in Paducah, some good-lookin' stranger on the go? That's right, I caught you lookin' at me," he said as he moved closer to her on the floor, kick scooting his pack as he spoke, never averting his gaze. She smiled back before she meant to.

Shoulder-length black hair that was full of loose waves and a thick black mustache that welled up and into his dark skin made him look like an exotic Bain du Soleil suntan advertisement. He had black eyes that were kind and impish and sexy and held your attention when he pulled you into his easy and straightforward glance. His smile emanated from those eyes like a sun disk. There was no malice, no hiding. There was no end to the pupil and no beginning to the iris in all of that forthright darkness. His were the thick, long lashes girls labored to have, that curtained those black eyes and seductively fluttered over them in a sort of Josephine Baker fan, but without the intent to seduce. It gave him the far-off look of a man who had seen a great deal in his 28 years, which excited her right away like Jeannie hadn't been in a while, and those eyes seemed to understand about a woman who married too young and was tied to three kids and an old father who didn't work but helped with the bills from his social security check sometimes when times were hard, but only after he bought his carton of Marlboros and his Cheese Nips and his sardines and limburger cheese and maybe a new pair of overalls.

This happy stranger seemed to take it all in and was willing to completely accept it all in one glance without reservation or hesitation, if you equaled his acceptance, and it began with asking the right question. He had a way that made her want to talk to him about all of the injustices of her life, and to do so without making it sound like complaining, to give him the chance to get inside this woman who was already shutting down to chances like him, to be with him a hundred percent, to trust in his eyes that those secrets wouldn't get away from him or be used against her. He wouldn't judge. He would accept. It was all this woman had wanted from the other two before him. It seemed to her that he knew all of this already and all she had to do was say it. Jeannie Mae got all of that from those eyes and their easy conversation, as they sat together intimately on the vast plane of hard-polished concrete floor, with the random gray specks made up of shattered bits of lesser stone ground into it, and found something more valuable on the floor of that Greyhound bus station.

"Where is this movie role taking you, Jane?"

"It's Jeannie. You can call me Jeannie." She pulled a bit of her impossibly thick, strawberry blond hair out of her eyes and put it behind her ear absentmindedly as she cast her gaze down toward the floor.

"Wow. That is a perfect incognito name for you, Jane, er, I mean, Jeannie."

Her smile opened up to him just a little without the immediacy of defenses and turned her face into a girl's again as she leaned into him, cautiously, just brushing his thinly muscled shoulder.

"You wait right here, Jean. Don't go away. You hear me?" His eyes danced mischievously as he back shuffled away from her, but never not looking at her.

When he found that she was waiting for the first leg of her ride to Louisville, he decided to go along with her and made his way to the counter to change his ticket, to alter his course, leaving her to watch after him in amazement at what had just happened between them. Just like that he decided to be with her.

And he had one of those bodies that good genes and being 28 gives you, lithe and hard but not forceful; full of vitality and sex, but not obscene. It flowed from his confidence, from his having enough in not having anything, in making decisions that alter lives with a moment's notice, of being his own person. His name was a mystery and she liked that too. She supposed he got the name Cherokee maybe because of his looks, or maybe because of that affected hippie vibe, or maybe because he really did understand it all by not having anything, which gave him everything, and she wanted to find out. This felt easy. At last, Jeannie could breathe. Any reservations left her as she pivoted without a central mass to hold her in place. She chose to live. This was one more chance to make it right in this world that had beat her ass.

She liked that he called her Jean. It wasn't what the other two had called her, what had made up her identity to this point. It transformed her. She was able to forget Jeannie Mae and be Jean with him. It was what she needed without knowing it. When they came back from that trip of the mysteries, away from her children and family, away from the all, he spent a lot of time with her. With *us*. Her children were included. It wasn't that conversation she'd had with the Riverboat Man, that strange kind of talking about children as if they didn't exist, about how it was time to get shots or that they were going to the dentist tomorrow, or that this kid or the other had gotten a bad grade or a good grade, or the myriad of conversations adults had about little people as if they were possessions.

The firstborn boy did his best to be noticed, to stand out. To matter. To him. It was a novel feeling to have a man notice, to take a part in his life, to concern himself with the boy. Jesse Earl was mesmerized with the happy stranger, with the figure he stood for, stood in for. The three children had been sidelined by those conversations, made into a non-entity, a second citizen in that house and in those aberrant exchanges. With the Riverboat Man, it could have been the car oil he was discussing with her when he discussed his natural children, or how one of the towboats got sunk because of some stupid-assed green captain who didn't know what the hell he was doing and how he would have handled it better. Those were the conversations they'd have, but it wasn't with children. It was about them. They didn't get a vote, didn't count. It was almost always bad news too. And they'd be scared of what would come next. Always. There was little affection, only force, only smashing and putting you in your place and ass whipping and slaps in the mouth and solitude and silence or yelling and then silence.

This. This was different. It wasn't like that with him. They'd be in the middle of a conversation, Jean and Cherokee and her sisters and their husbands, collectively the grownups, and he'd see them standing there on the periphery, or watching TV while the grownups were piled around the kitchen table playing cards or shooting the shit and he'd call out: "Jesse! Come over here and tell me how you got that scab on your elbow!"

The boy would grin and importantly tell him all about it as Cherokee grabbed him up and pitched him onto the table and into the middle of the cards, like they weren't anywhere nearly as important as this story and to take a better look, or he'd tickle one of her children or spin one of them around until they squealed, and he'd go right back to his conversation while he pulled another onto his lap and hug real tight until they could almost not breathe but didn't dare complain in case Cherokee thought to let go.

Her children didn't want it to end, that embrace. The affection and warmth had been parceled out like a modicum of food to the starving. It wasn't customary, wasn't how adults treated kids. Spare the rod was the motto in families like Jeannie's and Edward Earl's. Work and effort were good enough, but never great. Praise begat pride, so praise was withheld. The boy had been able to count the "I love you's" before this happy stranger. You demonstrated love by busting your ass and providing for, and clothing, and breaking the will.

But not with Cherokee. It happened to all of her children as a collective: the newly formed islands just as mysteriously recoupled and merged into one of their own accord, without the Riverboat Man and his natural children and the other bastard Cunningham girl. They were equally his. There wasn't a favorite. None fought for his favor because he gave it freely and there was an abundance of it. Finally, there was enough. He lavished each of the three children with it, coated them in it like an armor.

And her children were electrified to be part of the grown-up conversation and sitting at the grown-up table listening to grown-up things, so they wouldn't respire too loudly or talk, but just feed themselves on the instant and the warmth and the attention and the togetherness they realized they had never experienced before him. And it would end as it usually did by Jean telling her children to go play or go outside or go watch TV, but it wasn't out of fear of consequence or jealousy or worry.

Still, Jeannie Mae coveted her time with Cherokee, was greedy for it also, and hungered for it, all of it at times, because there had been so little of it in her lifetime, too. It wasn't something she had been able to slake and she was starving like her children. The other side of damage, the result of it, Jeannie Mae couldn't discharge her own upbringing. She couldn't meet the expense of affection and so she maintained a distance at times, panicked at the thought of its demise, maintained a nervous disdain for his abundance of it, and sometimes, not always but sometimes, remained wary. Jeannie kept quiet for fear of losing this unfamiliar euphoria herself, tipsy on its heady exhilaration already. In her silence, she reviled it and simultaneously craved it, because it was from some other place with which she was unfamiliar and couldn't quite determine if it was too great a risk to accept. She had become out of control of herself.

In those untroubled five years, in all of that plenty and elation, this sometimes silence of hers, this reticence, would wear away at the base, disassemble what Jeannie and Cherokee had built as if it were a neglect, what expressing love from only one perspective can do. But those five years were glorious. This family had seen the other times and understood those times of need in her too; even the viewpoint of children exposed it. Her children got it. This new family was in love with him.

He was better than them in every way. He came from an upstanding family but didn't care how far hers had fallen because he joined her there. He understood the power of his affection but didn't wield it as a weapon against her or her children; he didn't abuse his power by parceling it out or withholding it. He saw each one in that collective as an individual with merit and strength and with the capacity to love fully. He didn't tell her children to get the hell out of the room or to go out and play. He was not selfish. Thankfully, thankfully, he taught Jesse Earl this lesson before he went away.

Cherokee expressed his interest in her children by hearing their voices, by giving them a voice. He saw past the insecurities and the shyness of her brood, a confused and sometimes mute boy with little confidence and a desperately shy and small gangly girl who sometimes wet her bed in terror of the world she had been left to. Lisa flirted outrageously with him and he took it in and flirted back in a mocking way, but he wasn't mean about it. He saw each of them and instantly they were his own. Cherokee spoke to each child as if he or she were important. When that firstborn boy thinks on this history, it is the only interval that remains perpetually present, as if the boy still lives those moments. The clarity of the face and the affection are illuminated, lustrous and not a recollection, not a memory. With him, every detail is fresh and the boy is in love with the incandescence, the purity of the channeling, the sweetness of the detail; he is complete. The other times, the times outside of Cherokee, are the detached ones, untethered, disassociated events in the life of someone else, moments made for somebody else. But these, these commemorations, are not faded. They are rubric. They are significant.

That new summer that recreated the unit into a singular element again, the summer that began the process of stitching the bone, this interlude of sealing fractures, this remaking of we or to whom we could aspire, that summer began with breath, with the ease in which one breathed. And it was going to last because they were all going to be good and not fuck it up, like mom would tell her kids not to do when they began to stray from their common purpose of being a cohesive unit. And this period of exhilaration and of simultaneously being scared of fucking it up went on for months in the rental that was attached to the back of that brick dive on South Sixth Street, with the row of kitchen windows that looked out onto Kentucky Avenue, where Bumpaw who nobody called Charlie any more would sit and watch the spectacle of the outside drive itself by. It took on and still holds a shamanic quality cloaked in his immense temperament that was able to accomplish what Jeannie and her children alone had been unable to do for themselves. They healed. Her family became people of optimism.

Her mood of a divorced woman in the company of those who did not divorce, of being perpetually without, cut off, alone, her family of deficit, and the depressed years on the chart that would be outlined in the red that previously dominated her family, dissipated into a happiness that was not characteristic of her or of them. They were without scarcity, and that raised the plane from which they viewed each other. Her children were no longer competitors encouraged to outmaneuver each other. Blame dissipated, too; so did regret. Her children seized upon the small kernel of receiving and it blossomed of its own accord.

The beginning months gave them time to extricate themselves from the delicate ice on which they had ventured, which had begun to thaw with this new spring. This metamorphosis, this transformation, this alteration to their reality, was not completed in one hawk swoop. The pieces of the broken vessel must be gathered before it can be made whole. Their shards had been swept from stagnant waters, out of the rushes, and whisked along into the clear current of this new personage that developed within each of her children, infecting the mother with optimism. Jeannie could not believe her good fortune in having been found, reassembled. In those moments in which that family was changing into what *we* could become, as the muslin began to heal the broken and raw skin that had been pulled tender from those previous times, she overcame her most egregious setbacks.

The event that helped along or maybe hindered healing happened one day in the yard of their South Sixth Street back apartment with the wire clothesline. It was here where Jeannie and Cherokee's children played a sort of makeshift softball/baseball/whiffle ball, because she owned none of the effective pieces to play one coherent game. The equipment included an aluminum bat and a mismatched ball that wasn't quite whiffle ball and wasn't exactly a baseball, but the family was together as Cherokee pitched for the oldest sister. Lisa drew back to really knock it out of the yard but instead connected unexpectedly with the zinc clothesline, and the bat ricocheted off of that taut wire and came hurling right back to her, catching her along the side of her head and blackening her eye, as Jesse Earl and Jennie Kaye watched the slow motion of that bat giving her a beating like the two secretly had wanted to give her at some point for her bossiness and her conniving and her pressing them with the work she should have done, and the homework she wouldn't do, for her laziness and her cunning but instead, on impulse, they ran with a genuine concern for their sister, lifting her arms and head into their lap as if all had been forgiven somehow.

That was also the house with the rat that snaked itself up through the drain of the toilet as Lisa sat peeing. Seeing it, she ran screaming and naked into the yard, shorts and panties still around her feet, tangling her in her escape. The neighbor wounded it with a gun in the kitchen but it still got away anyway and now that old house, so rotten then, has been gentrified and turned into an Historic house with a capitol H, but it still holds the DNA of Jeannie and Cherokee, Lisa Jo, Jesse Earl, and Jennie Kaye (and the cigarette smoke of Marvin), and that bullet hole is probably still there with all of that abundance and wholeness and good fortune. Now forgotten, the incident closed one more remnant fissure left between them.

Jeannie's was a family of demonstration. Ingrained, it was like that already when the family found that Cherokee too was a man of demonstration. It happened on one of those evenings when friends were over, their group was together, and Cherokee was strumming out lyrics while never taking those eyes with the heavy-lidded lashes off of Jeannie, except to glance down at his moving hands, only to glance up again, fixing her with the gaze of desire where he had left off with her. More friends gathered and the apartment, two stories, became full of the young and beautiful types these young and beautiful people attracted. Mostly 20-somethings, girls in halter tops and cut-off shorts and boys with jeans and no shirts, talking together, listening to music, some bringing alcohol, some bringing weed.

And the mother would make certain that if these kinds of times stretched into bedtime rituals for her children, that she would not neglect them, but excuse herself and take up her mantle of domestic duty, shooing her children into their beds, tucking them away from the night. Her children revered her for it. Jeannie hovered over her children, sparrow-like, as the last few rays of sun filtered through the window, with the tranquility and patience reserved for Egyptian goddesses carved on stone temple walls: stoic, immovable, eternal. In those days, Jeannie did not shirk her duties, was dutiful to her children above all other duties; she was dedicated to them.

As this particular night wore on and the party became livelier, she drank. It wasn't her custom, but she had been enraptured by this man, her life, the night. She found herself deliriously drunk. Her children had taken advantage of her slip and crept out to witness the spectacle of so many beautiful people enjoying their two beautiful parents, watched everyone having a good time, slipped themselves into the midst of a full-on party, and then watched the mood suddenly shift and come to a standstill. The mother's bedroom door was locked and those present, standing around, murmured to themselves and to each other.

"She's falling out that window!" Cherokee's drunken sister shrieked, caterwauling.

"Quick! Everybody, come outside! She's up there!"

Heavy and awkward, squealing for attention, yelping this time from the front porch stoop, the heavy, lonely girl stood pointing to the second story window. Everyone rushed outside to see that indeed, Jeannie had her head and arms languishing outside of the upstairs window, limp, temporarily overcome by the potency of the alcohol. Through the drunken gasps and remarks from the spectators gathered outside, the firstborn boy saw that she was not alone. He was there, enshrouded in darkness, patiently standing just behind her, a protector, his arms spread out to engulf her, over her, watching, holding, protecting. He was the watchman keeping the night at bay as she rested in this in-between state.

"I ain't worried. He won't allow her to fall. She won't never fall again with him around," the first boy thought.

Satisfied that with Cherokee she was finally, thankfully, safely locked in his protective arms, ever vigilant, the boy returned to his room and slept soundly, knowing there was nothing any longer to fear.

On one of those long afternoons of endless summer days, the boy walked to Kroger's for Bumpaw to get his Cheez-its, or his carton of Marlboros, or sometimes just a Sprite, and bring it back for him. It was on the return trip that he'd drink just a little of it and fill back up with spit so the old man wouldn't notice the difference. It was on one of these summer trips that he found the Evil Knievel stunt cycle with the Evil Knievel doll and the accompanying wind-up zip line lying on the curb. Accustomed to salvaging anything of value from the curb on trash day, of yard sale finds and Goodwill choices, of scraping together any semblance of a Christmas tree from Etta's farm and a lifetime of Dollar Store presents under the tree and some new clothes that were really for the coming school year, the young boy hadn't really ever had a toy. Destitution didn't support having them on her two-day labor jobs. The boy took it home under his shirt and, fearing discovery, left it in the yard where he would discover it later when there were witnesses to the deed. When Cherokee noticed the new toy, he knew before asking, yet asked anyway.

"I found it on my way home from Kroger. It was just lying in the street…. I looked around but nobody was there so I brought it home."

The crime was heavy on the boy's head and Cherokee knew it. The boy saw that it pained him, that which they were both aware of. The first boy fell apart and immediately told him everything.

"You know this isn't yours and that you can't keep it, Jess."

"But it didn't belong to anybody or else it wouldn't have been in the street in the first place," the boy protested.

"You have to return it to its owners," Cherokee stated, more firmly than the boy had ever heard him speak. He held the gaze of the boy and the child put up no more resistance. "Look. To make it easier, I'll go with you, but you have to know that this is the right thing to do. I can't always be with you to make the right decisions, so you have to learn to do the right thing for yourself and only for you, OK? Do you understand that? Do you understand why you have to do this? Not because I make you, but because you should know to do it, Jess, that only a pure heart matters. Nothing else, Son."

The boy's lip quivered but he understood completely. They both walked, toy in hand, to the place in front of a large and elegant house where the boy had found it. Jesse knew this house and it filled him with dread and terror of the talk in school that he would endure when it was discovered what he had done. The world seemed to collapse.

Cherokee stood alone on the pavement. "You fucked up, Jess. You've got to be a man and make this right. It's best not to think about anything except what's right and just walk it right up to the door. When somebody answers, tell the person answering the door that you took it, that you knew it wasn't yours to take, but that you're returning it." Cherokee's almost black eyes had turned light, almost the color of the nuthatch.

The elegant boy from school who rode the bus with him, and who was better than him and knew it, opened the door. Jesse Earl was tearful and miserable but did what he was told to do, because he loved Cherokee more than the shame of the moment, and this was the badge he would wear to attest that to him.

The elegant boy shrugged, said thanks, and took the toy and closed the door. The boy never heard another word from him about it.

When they returned to the house the boy assumed his submission was complete. Instead, the happy stranger took him to his room.

"I have to tell you what happens to delinquent boys in boys' school, in juvenile detention. I don't want to do this, but I have to make certain that you won't end up in a place like that." His voice instantly changed and he became hard and mean. "Get down on your hands and knees. NOW! Now give me push-ups until I say stop, do you hear me?" He forced the boy to execute push-ups as he called him names and jeered, and he put his boot on the child's hand. "If you stop, I'm gonna crush your fingers," he growled. "Get back up there, Pussy, and keep giving me those push-ups!"

The boy cried but continued to do the few push-ups his thin arms could manage. He quickly collapsed in a shaking and crying heap because he was ten and couldn't do push-ups, but Cherokee pulled him up and made him try again, and again, and then finally he didn't crush the boy's fingers. Instead, he picked him up and put him in his lap and hugged the boy so tightly and tenderly, and the boy continued to cry for failing him, and the happy stranger cried against the child's gaunt shoulders too.

"Jess, I never want to see you go to a place like that where they actually do crush your fingers," he said. And he asked the boy to promise that he'd never do anything like that again.

The boy nodded with all of his strength into his chest but couldn't get words out over all of the emotion he had for somebody caring about him and his fingers like that.

They sat like that for a while in his room and the rest of the house was dead silent. They knew everybody heard, but it was okay because the boy didn't mind them knowing that Cherokee cared about him. The boy wondered how many times he'd had to do pushups when he was a kid in a place like that. Afterward, Cherokee laid the boy on the bed and covered his exhausted body with the thin white sheet, tucking in the edges around the boy's frame, and touched his hair and told him he loved the boy more than he ever thought he could have love for a kid, and Jesse Earl drifted off into a complete sleep full of remorse and love for the man who cared enough about the boy to make sure he learned his lesson about that.

This life, Jeannie and her children, the poverty, this way of living was all just fine with Cherokee. It was enough because he had never wanted any material thing. Her children liked that. It felt easy. And there was her leaving her impossibly thick, blonde, wavy, perfectly parted down the middle hair, with a touch of VO5 for shine but also to calm the unruly nature of it that she had inherited from her mother, unrestrained and covering her face sometimes, and sometimes pulled behind an ear while she bent over to unpack, and her tee shirt pulled over with the casualness that they had for each other, and her cutoff and worn-out shorts, and those distinctive brown suede moccasins that hid some of her height but also broadcast her affected hippie stature and defiance to the normal respectable families that looked out the window at them, or stood at the curb to see what was going on, all preparing her for the big day, that moving day. That changing day that had occurred to all of them.

Jean and Cherokee spent a lot of alone time together, going to places neither had seen before. Mostly they traveled by hitchhiking, but sometimes in a run-down car they purchased off of some lot when work was good and they had extra money in their pocket. The funny thing about those two was the fact that, unlike in that first start, money was never an issue between them. If they had money or didn't, they seemed equally happy and that took a lot of pressure off of the collective her new family had become. He even loved the grumpiness of Marvin but refused to call him Charlie, opting for POP instead. He always said it like it was in all capital letters too, but that may have been because Marvin was hard of hearing.

They were on solid ground together and moving slowed down. Cherokee took up a factory job at a hard candy plant and brought home extras for his kids. The trials and the tests proved that the happy stranger wouldn't be leaving. So they moved out of the town of Paducah and into the little ramshackle house on a country road on that day that could almost be a mirage. Her Pinto was filled up and busting out with all of the before-Cherokee stuff that had dwindled down to a few ratty and useless keepsakes, like the photograph albums with the vinyl covers in greens and yellows and the adhesive pages to keep the memories from slipping away. There were also cardboard boxes and the large tin-topped shipping cylinders that smelled like butterscotch, which Cherokee had gotten for free, and which stood in for dressers and sometimes acted as end tables with a sheet draped over them, and they also took some hand-me-down furniture that she'd gotten from yard sales or donations or somewhere that she couldn't remember.

That stuff came with this once-again-family, and the best part was that he didn't mind what it looked like at all. Stuff like furniture and fancy brass and glass end tables weren't important to him, so it didn't become important to any of them any longer in those moments of forgetting that he gifted to them, to her children and to her. They didn't have to be embarrassed by lack and want with him, and it was no longer a shame they had to turn down friends who wanted to come over from school so they wouldn't see how they lived, with the sheets nailed up over the windows and over the doorway so that the one used window box air conditioner could cool the living room where they all stayed, or the box fan they'd put in front of the kitchen screen door to pull in the evening air over the pallets the children would make on the linoleum floor, with a sheet tied to the handle of the box fan that they'd sleep under to keep that night air streaming over them, wicking away the sweat of the night heat.

They had to start over again, once more finally, because of that firstborn boy, as so frequently happened to that once-again-family, but this time it was due to a practical joke gone awry.

The social worker had come again with disheveled gray hair stringing over her shoulders, with smudgy glasses and legal pads scribed over in big black ink, crumpled paper layers matching her hair curling over each other in her bag, and this time it was the boy's fault. It was a Wednesday night at the West End Baptist Church and the three children had arrived before services started. The three joined in with the other children upstairs where the Bible school normally took place. There was a piano and Play-Doh and toys and books, so the children of church attendees would gather there until it was time for service. The firstborn boy had been sitting at a small table and decided to pretend he was asleep, and the children all giggled as the adults came for the children to bring them downstairs. The firstborn boy maintained his limp state, slumped onto the table as the lady who normally took all of the children down to the service entered the room. The children were all in on it together. She called to the firstborn boy and he continued his pretense of sleeping as the other kids looked on, long after the game ceased to be funny.

She shook the firstborn boy by the shoulder and again he didn't respond. She left and the children again giggled, but again he didn't move as she reentered the room. This time, the aging church bus driver who collected the poor and susceptible children from the streets to bring them here to this place of salvation lifted the firstborn boy up completely unexpected and put the boy over his shoulder like a felled deer. Realizing the game had transgressed, terrified of getting into trouble, Jesse Earl didn't resist. The boy was admitted into the hospital as anemic and malnourished. The nurse saw through the ruse when she snapped a smelling salt under his nose and he immediately opened his eyes. As she smiled and winked, telling everyone the boy was just fine, he was thinking it was over, thinking that he had gotten away with the game and could just go home finally.

But suddenly the mother was there with Cherokee and the doctor was asking questions about what the firstborn boy had eaten that day. The boy was earnest with answers, but the doctor wasn't convinced that everything was okay because the mother honestly hadn't known what her boy ate because she had been working her ass off making beds and scrubbing toilets and bathroom floors in motel rooms and then scrubbing kitchen floors deep into the night at the Denny's afterward and, therefore, didn't have time to make regular dinners or lunches or to monitor such things, but the house had food and the kids knew how to cook and so did Marvin.

But the aftermath of that game was that she was assigned the social worker who had come into their house, and what did not matter to that once-again-family mattered greatly to the social worker. The fact remained that the boy had fainted, that he was underweight for his age, and that the doctor had to address these issues convincingly to the county, by law. The social worker's visit was announced, so the mother and her children spent the weekend cleaning the house like they normally did, by scrubbing baseboards and dusting the surfaces, making sure all of the dishes were washed and put away. Since the broom was broken, the boy used a hairbrush to raise the shag up out of its matted state from an endless stream and trampling of too many animals and too many kids with too much energy. The social worker did not seem to notice the diligence to detail.

When the woman arrived, the family all sat around looking solemn and none of the kids made a sound as this stranger negotiated their lives with the mother. Jeannie offered the string-haired social worker a cold drink, to which she acquiesced. Feeling guilty for having caused these new problems, Jesse Earl thankfully excused himself and furtively dashed into the kitchen to open the one cold Pepsi-Cola in the refrigerator, taking out the ice tray and breaking the cubes into the glass with a pull of the latch on the pale blue aluminum tray, sending slivers and shards into the worn glass and across the table, picking up the glint of the sun as they slid to rest on the Formica.

He carefully balanced it into the living room where this stranger sat on the edge of the furniture and put the icy drink onto the clean, un-ringed glass of the shabby coffee table, and he didn't take his eyes off of the moisture condensing and trailing down the pattern of the amber-colored glass as it sat in the sparkle of the window, illuminating the effervescence of the drink that exploded like stars onto the glass table it sat on, untouched by her, as his mouth watered. It would go flat and lifeless while they sat and watched, as she took for granted and possibly wouldn't risk drinking from the one glass of soda that would appear in the house that month. It had been purchased, poured into the best glass the family owned, and presented, just for her. She left the offering untouched as she scribbled onto the legality of her pad. After she left, the boy took it to the kitchen and drank it down in a few covetous gulps, rewarding himself for the chaos he had caused.

Shortly after the meeting, Jeannie moved them from the district where this incident mattered, was a cause of concern, to a different school district in a different county with different authorities, and they were no longer the problem of the doctor or social worker and therefore forgotten. Jeannie Mae had learned that she, too, could use the system to its disadvantage.

So they left that house with its butterscotch canister furniture and the brilliance of light that had illuminated the dust that had followed them somehow, that had illuminated their faces like Cherokee had done. It became just another moving day for that family, but their collective was now only four. Bumpaw Marvin had moved to Oklahoma to live with his eldest daughter and her family, complete with a husband and a full-time job reserved for men.

It was sometime in the transition between the shotgun house and the log cabin that Cherokee died.

The distance between his love and her reluctance to be loved was what had frayed the bond that separated them. In that distance, Cherokee moved away from all of the love he had for those children and for his Jean that could not be returned in equal measure. She and her children had been unable to do it, to not fuck it up, finally. In what were his final days, Cherokee broke away from the beautiful friendships his presence had formed between Jeannie's sisters: Linda, her favorite, and her husband, Cherokee's best friend, David, who was an Adonis seldom seen in a shirt; and Melody, who now lived in the third house on Jeannie's same strip with her husband, Anthony, one more beautiful than the other and profoundly in love with each other, and sometimes her brother Donnie, who had married Cherokee's sister, Judy. This whole-again family had been inseparable, and being apart from Jeannie meant being apart from this fabric that he could not live in proximity to and not be a part of. His departure and then the quickness of his death devastated the now-reduced family.

Judy informed them that Cherokee had died. He'd been riding his motorcycle, one of a pair. Jeannie had the other one. She kept it because it connected her to him after he was gone. Judy told her that Cherokee was coasting to a stop on the side of the road when the motorcycle hit gravel and tossed the front end in the ditch, which caused the back end to flip forward and fling Cherokee into the stop sign, which broke his neck. Her brother had only a little scar, just like the one Judy had. Amazed, she pointed it out to the once-wife. That's how you knew that he was dead; that little scar that was just like hers right under the point of her chin. It was like Cherokee's scar joined him to Judy, together in a way that life couldn't achieve, and Judy's lament was written in the stars.

Upon his departure, the collective had no comparison for the fissure gouged out of each of them in that instant. Pain was an anomaly, incongruous in the fierce, pulsating and vacuous emptiness. For his Jean, where there were no words before, now there was no consolation and no conclusion. His death had been treasonous, a lie, a plot against her mental health. It was simultaneous, too, that the mother died really, with him.

In Cherokee this family had been happy, had been one. In him, they had been joyful. The mother errantly expected Her and His facetious breach to heal itself in time; their intimacy, understanding of one another had to be too great to remain chasmed, but time was not something the two of them had and neither one knew it. Their separation was meant to be temporary, and now he had been taken away, away, away. Her children witnessed her loss, which was most terrible in the late evening hours when Jeannie felt most alone, most connected to him, most unhinged. The diminished family sat down to gorge on those last vestiges of feeling, the defeat and its acuity, and it perforated the core of each of them, simultaneously as a collective, and yet remained deeply intimate. Each child in turn or in pairs or all three would discover his Jean sitting on the matched motorcycle, where she would have been for hours, lost in some replay of an exquisite commodity of time She and He had had, and it was not a bitter moment, but one in which she was overawed.

Each child looked sad for her but didn't speak about their own loss, because it could not meet hers and the unit could not grieve because not one of them knew how to lose him and get through it. So her children kept it in and kept their chins up and got over it like they were told to, but it didn't really work that way. Each one of that diminished family had been endlessly changed, enveloped in a constancy of metamorphosis edging the bounds of incalculable loss. That was the instant when the change began, when Jeannie Mae began losing her life. Her death began when she lost him.

After Cherokee died, her family moved again, running from all of that limitless happiness. With the awful sadness, that

Cunningham girl became a friend, Jeannie's confidant once again, and bridged the overwhelming need to extoll her loss. His natural children were too young to understand, to know, and were excluded.

The log cabin she chose was a remnant, a Kentucky oddity on the brink of extinction, a relic of a hard living with living trees hacked into lengths of wattle and daub walls, hacked notches linking that rustic place together. It sat on a concrete slab with two big rooms and a galley kitchen and a bathroom and a bedroom carved out of one side of the second big room made up of split logs and plaster that was heated with a fireplace the size of a dining room table. There were various sheds and defunct outbuildings that had long ago been reclaimed by the forest, somehow lost, somehow still standing. It was emblematic of the coarse leftovers of her, and of her family now. These vanished spaces became his natural children's playground in those after-Cherokee years. The firstborn boy relocated to the glassed-in side porch because it had been added on later and had an electric baseboard heater, but it also gave the boy privacy that he had not needed before. It was the mother's idea that a boy of twelve needed his own space and could no longer sleep on the couch. She and her children were together then, once more a duller collective. Her circumstances had not changed much, had only rearranged themselves in this new space.

It was there that Jesse Earl quarried out of the abandoned shed behind the log cabin a forgotten, oversized black cloth and chrome baby carriage with white wall-spoked wheels. It was part of his plan to give back his youngest sister's childhood, to force the happiness that had eluded those children, to force it beyond their years.

Jesse scavenged a cast-off cotton bedspread the color of Pepto Bismol, decorated with tufts of flower garlands, and he nailed a milk crate upside down to wooden planks and secured it to the baby carriage chassis. With the bedspread, he draped swags of bedspread garland over that contraption with all of that pink bedspread, and paraded his sister around the outside of that house and down the gravel road like she was Miss America. She'd wave and he would, at times, be the horse with the bright yellow plastic rope in his teeth and around his chest, galloping and prancing before transforming into the footman to help her descend the carriage draped in the rest of the bedspread tied up with yellow plastic rope.

Other times, Jennie Kaye was Laura Ingalls Wilder and the horse had to help her get to town to save her Pa, so they'd race until the contrivance flipped over or until the boy was out of breath. Other times too, she'd be a princess going to the ball and the milk crate and the baby carriage turned into a charmed royal carriage, and the horse boy would accompany her as her handsome prince. These flashes returned a modicum of childhood and were mostly transitory, but they coddled the stirrings of sweeping away the loss, to begin again the foundations of joy.

His natural children had grown accustomed to being alone, leaving them together. Their world again, imperceptibly, had shrunk up around the two of them but had expanded with the imagination of fairytales and stories. Perpetually on the move, family was friend and friends were fickle, so the two relied on each other as both friend and foe. Money was scarce, so entertainment was as imaginary as friendships were passing. Jesse Earl and Jennie Kaye would lie outside in loungers made from brightly colored plastic tubing stitched to tin frames with the white plastic head and footrest, even as the dew fell and the air chilled, and they'd look up at the stars and pretend to see the heavens turn and pretend to transport to anywhere in the world and describe the fantastic sights each imagined would be there.

On summer days, the boy would sneak away from his sister to gather together minuscule items like wooden thread spools and Ball mason jar seals tacked onto remnants of twigs, or tiny hammocks cut from macramé, and arrange them under toadstools to create fairy lands for his sister to discover, and she'd pretend that real fairies had assembled the minute living spaces under a spreading chestnut tree, and both pretended that it was really true even though Jennie Kay really didn't believe it but pretended to for her brother's sake, having gone through the trouble. The firstborn boy would make treasure maps and soak them in cold coffee and hamburger grease, baking them with the sugar cookies until the paper was brittle and brown so they looked ancient, and he buried them in a wooden box he picked out of the dump or from the Goodwill. He added in odd bottles of medicine from the last century that he dug up from the mounded trash heap at the end of the lot and the two would wander off, looking for treasure that they never found but talking for hours about what they would do with all of that gold and money.

Jesse Earl collected Coke bottles from the backs of porches, or would ask for them, and in his state of worn-down jeans or twenty-year-old corduroys or plaid wool pants in the middle of summer with an odd assortment of too-adult shirts, would often be rewarded, and he would cash them in and take his little sister to the movies, just the two of them, walking the two miles to the dazzling white-and-cobalt-blue movie theater on Broadway, in downtown Paducah. He took her to see *Escape to Witch Mountain*, and the two earnestly wished to have the kinds of powers the kids in the movie had, to compel others to do their bidding, to control their surroundings, to escape. Brother and sister created their own spaces at the edge of the woods and transformed blue tarpaulin with brass ringlets from the dump into a makeshift school by tying it off to trunks of trees, with a high chair and a kitchen chair without its back to make desks for the students. The two made certain to ask for extra handouts at the end of school and spent summer days completing them out in their edge-of-the-woods school way out behind the house, behind the chicken coop, behind the vegetable garden, where nobody bothered to venture. The children went there and solidified the *us* and let *them* slip away, which by this time the *them* also wanted, too, although nobody said it out loud.

The separation became easier as the *we* fell away and again became *us* and *them*. The Cunningham girl was becoming a woman and had boyfriends and adult-ish friends and was learning to be a badass, so she stayed with the adults and didn't bother to play with kids any longer. Once, while his natural children were rummaging through the piles at the landfill, they found a two-volume Columbia-Viking Desk Encyclopedia in white leather with gold foil lettering on the cover and nothing wrong with it except its having been cast off like they had been. The two children each carried one heavy volume home, down that long, dusty gravel mile, full of isolation, to one of the three houses that remained before being torn down by the state to make room for the I-24 bypass. The two spent hours on the quiet of the couch looking through the volumes, reading about all they had never heard of, filling in all of those blank places they had never been to, and learning about mysteries like black kites and kestrels and places they never thought existed, and about ancient unions of mothers with children, like Isis and Horus, that were more revered, much older than the Madonna and Child, which seemed impossible, and they marveled at plants and insects stranger and more exotic than oaks and cicadas.

They were still brother and sister, however. Once, playing cowboy and Indians, Jesse Earl tied up his young sister and then became distracted, leaving her as he wandered off to swim in the pond in the woods and play with the mussels in the mud and lie on the hot clay dried by the sun. Jeannie Mae had the groceries halfway out of the car before she found the youngest still tied to the tree and crying, and the firstborn boy had to cut his own switch for the mother to wear out on his legs and back and ass. The boy apologized, and meant it sincerely and was ashamed, for having momentarily forgotten the secret bond they shared, unlike when he had to apologize to that Cunningham girl. In their bond, he didn't need to tell her all of the other stuff, other than the sorry part, because their diminished family didn't talk about the *us* and the *them*. There were two times that really required him to apologize, to be sorry for Jennie Kaye. The second happened later, in the other little blue house also on the side of what would become the overpass to I-24. It too was destroyed by the state, obliterating their family's history, its existence.

The final instance needing apology occurred as Jesse and Jennie Kaye reached the age of understanding differences in the other; the age of her knowing the boy better than he did, watching him so closely as to know this secret that had been welling up in her brother since Brown Street, but she didn't say. The boy sensed that she accepted, that it was acceptable; in her he could trust as he had confided so much more in her. It was kept in a dark place, a hidden place, unspoken. Unspoken by all of them, but they knew too. They knew the power of uttering it, of giving it a voice. Therefore, it had remained hidden until that time he needed to apologize to Jennie Kaye once more. Before that instance of utterance, it was a non-subject, unvoiced until it came out of her. Jennie Kaye said it and it was spiteful and she said it to be hurtful and she spit it out and she said it in front of the Cunningham girl, who giggled. It was one word: *faggot*. So the boy hurt her back and leapt on his sister and choked her like he wanted to choke the word back into her throat. Bumpaw tried to pull the boy off of her, and the Cunningham girl's boyfriend Tucker tried to pull him off of her, but he wouldn't let go until he realized that he had suddenly found the lesson he had learned so well from the Riverboat Man without meaning to, and he was terrified that he had found it at the throat of his sister and let go of his own accord, and the stricken boy walked away and stayed away for a long time.

Vengeance: Jennie Kaye had been brutal and he brutalized her in retaliation. It was that moment that he began to go away from her. Jennie Kaye knew what she had done and she was sorry about it, too, but mostly for bringing to the surface that which had been unspoken his whole life, and also for bringing to the surface the lesson that her brother should not have learned, but she never said it. The boy never asked her to take it back because it could not be unsaid; the hurt could not be undone. It began the time when *us* became singular.

Descent from the Ruins, 1979

The final destruction of that diminished family ensued shortly afterward, that backsliding Jeannie Mae did. She was a woman heading into her 30s, and she had three kids and three losses. That was a lot of baggage for a man to carry or even to get interested in. So the long working days gave way to longer working nights and exhaustion and repeating and subsisting, and managing loss and negotiating responsibilities. And those nights led to other nights of going out and pretending she didn't have kids, not even the other one that reminded her less of loss and more of love, but even that had faded to the color of a sun-bleached Polaroid forgotten in the back dashboard of the black Comet with no traction that she once drove. There were few places to go for a woman of her mettle in the late '70s. She had outgrown tradition and traditional men would not express interest in her, which in that rinky-dink town left only outcast bars and clubs where a divorced woman with baggage could go to and be left alone, or greeted on her own terms and party away the sadness of the great loss she had discovered too late she needed, of that love she had taken for granted, as if it could not end.

One of them was a gay bar where her lifelong friend, who was sometimes a biker's old lady, sometimes a stripper, and sometimes bi, was dating the butch owner named Tinker, who let Jeannie in and got her free drinks because it was nice for a change to have a pretty woman come in there, and they'd have a few laughs together, but there were no men there who were interested in her and the reality was that Jeannie was lonely. Perhaps relevance was what she really needed to boost her poorly shored esteem and to live with a capital L, if only for an instant in those rare nights when this loneliness for Cherokee still had the power to overcome her. It wasn't often that she was compelled to go—months would sometimes fill the interlude—but it was a powerful necessity, to be desirable, to feel relevant, and to be exceptional again. That gay bar was right next to the black side of town, next to the drive-through liquor store, next to the subsidized housing, which meant housing for blacks and those who had been reduced to that level of poverty. This bar was also close to the bars relegated to the blacks of that side of town, and so it was only a little detour to clubs like the Black Cat Lounge, where black people would go and dance like they fucked, and it was the '70s so nobody stopped her from driving there instead.

She kept her secret. Jim Crow wasn't dead there, but he was maimed and therefore more dangerous, so even though that area wasn't officially called Niggertown anymore, it was still separated by mutual agreement between the whites and the blacks, but mostly by the whites. And whites were neither welcome nor unwelcome in that area and in this bar, because the question hadn't been asked before her.

So Jeannie goes. She goes and she remembers all of those first times, those early times of love and romance and being a child-woman, and it greedily feels like home to her, like going all the way back to the beginning. It feels like fixing things. Jeannie Mae lingers in the lust of black men and in the envy of black women, which makes her a beautiful and desirable girl again, and all of those hard winter adult years melt away, and the kids and the tragedies and the unfairness of that little town and those hardnosed neighbors melt away and, for a few hours, she's free, absolutely free there, lost in the limbo of a black bar made of the same cinderblock that the county jail is made from, although it had been painted another color.

And a white woman with impossibly thick blonde hair that naturally hung in abundant curls with a precise part in the middle, that sometimes was draped over her face and sometimes was pulled behind one ear when she wasn't thinking about it, and who was tall and thin and fair and freckled, was a curiosity to all of those black men because, by her being there, she was within reach. At first she taunts; then she is curious.

Jeannie Mae soon finds that such a woman is a natural-born enemy to the particular kind of also-woman - thick and sweaty-thighed - pushing out too much tit and too many kids to be able to compete in a place like this, the kind of woman who goes to a bar like that anyway, that a certain type of woman of any color was the kind to go there, to try to find a fuck for the night or to hang on to that particular slippery kind of man who cheat on the side of everything, because they aren't tied down by a history of propriety and knows one thing and one thing well, and that is how to fuck and make babies but not really take care of them as she recalls from her first conversations about race with David. And Jeannie thinks that it can only happen to black men and black women, because she has sidestepped the same kind of places where a particular kind of divorced white woman with few options go to find white men who aren't really looking for anything past that one night, or maybe a few months free board, with a woman like that. Maybe it is time she is that kind of woman, she thinks.

From Jeannie Mae's perspective, that was all right for those women who managed to hang on to one as her man, but she was not aware that such women fought for that privilege if somebody got between them. But this wasn't something a white woman really knows about, growing up segregated in a separated but not really town, where each group self-edited places they went and who they hung out with, except here was this white woman fucking with the system, and nobody really liked it except her and a few curious black men.

It was in this context that she met Gerome. And Jeannie Mae liked him because he looked like Lionel Richie, but that is where the similarity ended because, in reality, he was a petty thug in an unimportant town. But for someone like her with lowered morale and confidence, she had someone paying attention to her, taking her to dinner, taking her out, spending cash on her. And it went like that, where they spent a lot of time together, and her three kids spent a lot of time making Kraft Macaroni and Cheese or Kraft Italian Style

Spaghetti, heating up cans of cream-style corn and peeling and frying potatoes to go along with it, and sometimes getting chicken but mostly bits of ham from the ham hock cooked in the crock pot with white beans that one of the kids sorted in front of the TV, then put on to slow cook while they all went to school the next day.

Jeannie was cautious in those first months of that first time with a black man. The experience was languorous and filthy and exciting and novel. Gerome did not come to the house, and if he did it was in a poorly thought-up code of slow-driving his long, metallic-green and chrome Cadillac by the house to park a block away. That was his signal to Jeannie to hastily put away what she was doing, mid-doing it, and hustle outside. Her three children nosily watched as she'd quick-comb her long blonde hair and smooth her t-shirt down over her jeans and ease up to the car window, and they'd chat or they'd go for a drive, but he never came in and her kids never met him.

Once, in a complete break with decorum, Jeannie Mae drove with her children to his house for something that must have been incredibly important for her collective to venture there, but she parked a block away too, and they had to stay in the car and not make any noise. His mother came to the door, a black inversion of Etta, and she noticed that white family for a long time while she was standing on the porch but pretended like she was looking at something else, which was fine because Jeannie Mae's children had never been to that side of town even though they'd heard rumors about Southside and the gang-style violence that occurred there almost on a daily basis, which was probably just another way for the town to keep everything segregated. But the stories didn't work on Jeannie Mae, and she kept going and she kept seeking out that living with a capital L, but it kept eluding her and this was no different.

She had quenched her thirst for Gerome unceremoniously. She and Gerome had stopped by Southside Drive-Thru Liquor on the Strip, on a Saturday night, when black people would hang out in the big parking lot and get drunk before they went home to their shotgun houses and all the kids and the poverty. And that is where they were hanging out, leaning against the hood of his metallic-green and chrome Cadillac. A man like Gerome was pretty well known, mostly for his trade but also for his looks and the kind of successful lifestyle some black women would like to have, but now a tall, skinny white woman with blond hair was enjoying it, and she was where she didn't belong so someone was bound to put her in her place. And that was what happened that night while they were both drinking from a half-pint and leaning up against that sparkling Cadillac as Gerome entertained his clients.

A black woman came up to them and started making a scene, claiming to be fucking Gerome and demanding to know why this White Woman was there, hollering that Jeannie was not one of them and to stop pretending that she was because she was not wanted there, not accepted. This was not the kind of confrontation Jeannie Mae had been accustomed to. She stared at the interloper, not with disdain but with speechlessness at the confrontation, at the hostilities that would be waged against her, should she act on the confrontation. Realizing that she is the intruder suddenly, her position on the unmarked line of demarcation, she saw no escape route and stood defenseless as the accusations escalated. The interloper began throwing out the vile names that had likely been used on her, as they came so easily. The name-calling had no effect. The white woman must have realized that there was no way she could emerge unscathed, so she remained silent, searching instead for supporters. She found none. Her silence was taken as weakness, as encouragement for the woman to resort to punches and hair-grabbing. Jeannie had some experience fighting for what she wanted, so she gave it right back to the interloper, grabbing her hair and dragging her around the parking lot while everybody looked on. The strength and agility of the silent white woman, who had worked manual labor and fought her second husband, surprised and overpowered the confronting black woman. The punches flailed on both sides.

This was a part of town where black people had once retreated and then regrouped, where everyone now abided by the unspoken truce—the line drawn with white people to maintain the segregation implanted by those same white people. This escalated argument over a black man didn't set too well with those standing on the sidelines, who felt no empathy for the white woman misplaced here, inappropriate among them. Bystanders started deriding the intruder for getting her fat ass kicked by a white bitch as the woman rushed at Jeannie again, and they tangled while Gerome continued to lean against the warm hood of that Cadillac, smirking at the commotion he had caused, but also uninterested in alienating his clients among the bystanders by choosing sides. It ended as abruptly as it began. The intruder was heaved to the ground, shunted sprawling into the asphalt, where she came to a panting stop there among jeers. The white woman was relieved that it was over and began walking back to what she hoped would be the getaway vehicle. It was not to happen in that way. There had to be a stronger climax than simply walking away. The intruder found within her reach a discarded dark-green liquor bottle next to where she had landed on the Southside Drive-Thru Liquor parking lot and smashed it into a weapon on the chipped brick of the drive-thru window.

Wielding it, she lunged at the walking-away white woman as if she were spooning her, coupling the white woman from the back, wrapping her glistening and jiggling arms around her, engulfing her in her folds and large breasts hefted onto her slim back, slashing at her gut, cutting a neat demi-lune deep into the soft tissue of the white woman's right side, slicing into the fat, displacing the thick covering, exposing the crimson blood that began to well up and then out of the newly imprinted huntress moon on her white flesh.

As Jeannie fell, people rushed not to assist her but to reach their cars and get the hell out of there, including Gerome and the fat-assed black woman who had gotten her ass kicked by a skinny white bitch, but who had vindicated herself in her final act.

Nobody helped the white woman as she packed her starlight blue-colored Aerosmith tee shirt into the cut and held tight as she walked herself twelve blocks to the hospital, alone in her quest for salvation. Jeannie collapsed just inside Western Baptist, reaching not heavenward but toward the artificial light of the nurses' station, and they filled her with blood transfusions and stitches, but it would be another day before she came home, before her children discovered why their mother had forsaken them. Jeannie was simply not there as morning came, as it had always come. It ended with Gerome, but the incident did nothing to slow Jeannie's astral descent.

For her reality had changed too. The message Jeannie had received from the scar she sported had been twisted somewhat. She saw that now she had exited from the experience stronger, more capable of being this woman who could stand against, fortify herself, and take what she wanted from those who would deny her. Jeannie went back to the Black Cat Lounge after a little while, glaring and defiant. The newspaper had printed the spectacular scandal of a white woman stabbed in Niggertown, prompting all those proper white people around her to peg her a nigger lover and keep her in her place on that ever-thinning margin of society into which she was left to fit.

This was easy to do. Jeannie had become accustomed to poverty, was poor, with poor kids and a poor life, segregated but not segregated, until suitable folks discovered through the rumor mill where she had gone and what she had done or was about to do again. She didn't care. A woman uncontrolled would be ostracized in the basest way. Jeannie became unaccepted by either race, because of her unnatural desires, which were unforgivable even in the late '70s and wouldn't be accepted in a small unimportant town like that one, ever. She was no longer fit for white men or company kept white.

Another change had occurred with that incident. Jeannie became old. Physically, the taut, white skin with the flecking of freckles had grown just a bit sallow; the steely gray, sometimes blue eyes had wilted under the brow; and the interesting aspects of her features had grown heavy with their interest, making them uninteresting. A white fleck had appeared on her eye tooth. The swell of children had left creping flesh around her mid-waist. It was a small mercy that she had no gray in her hair, in her still radiant blonde hair, now worn in tight ringlets around her shoulders and back. But this was not the reason for her having grown old. Collectively, she still retained her beauty, in a different light, but still beautiful. It was the loss of her youth that she mourned and that mourning brought on her old age. She was not the same. She was no longer a young woman. That is what aged her, what left her vulnerable.

In those days, Etta had stopped speaking to her, was on the very thin precipice of death. Jesse had been dead for some time now, for which Etta was thankful and made clear the point to those around her. Jeannie's sisters had married and moved away or stayed and were friendly, but not accepting, and would banter around the words used to keep her in her place, in her subordinate place, now that she had fallen so low. She had not been completely forgiven for dismantling the golden age in which she lived with Cherokee and, in some ways, her kids felt the same. It was acceptable to be poor, but it wasn't acceptable to be a nigger lover and it wasn't acceptable to go to bars, and certainly not black ones, and it wasn't acceptable to have degenerate low-life friends like she was making. It was much worse because she was doing it to herself and she had kids she was dragging through that mud too.

The tools a family has to discipline such a woman are seldom enough, and the ostracism and words and treatment only steeled her purpose to love outside of them. She was a woman in her 30s living a marginalized life, with three kids who demonstrated premature proficiency in raising themselves and learning the lessons that Jeannie Mae taught them, just as she had learned (although perhaps in a different way), now trying to relive her moments of pretense, to experience being lovely again without the compromise of consternation, and it was easy making debilitating choices without guidance about such things. Jeannie, blinded in her constant search to show them, lost or confused the search for the higher path and was sightless to those who prey on blinded women.

It is there that he meets her. Since the night he saw her in the Black Cat Lounge, he has pursued relentlessly, purloining her number from friends and leaving long cassette-recorded home phone messages on the thick black slab of an answering machine—how he feels and how much he wants to be with her—stalking out where she lives and leaving token gifts, like a plastic-wrapped red rose from the 7-Eleven or a Hallmark card with base poetry scrawling eternal love, and always, always declaring devotion to her. He owns a childish charm like that. And without that guidance from her family, without guidance from society on picking the right one, it is easy to settle for this kind of attention, to overlook the flitting tatters of revulsion he has for white people forcing him to work at manual labor in tobacco fields or on a tractor all day without a break, for paying him less than the boss gives his white son to do the same job, or for making him work at shittier jobs, like cutting the balls off pigs or cleaning troughs that his white son refuses. These are the kinds of opinions that emerge once the sheen goes flat, when days are constant instead of special, when he stops pretending.

It is easy ignoring a desire: to possess what Jeannie symbolizes, to own white privilege in an unimportant town where respect and equality couldn't be bought, even if he had money. He yearns to display her as a great big fuck-you to the white men who demean him and make him less than. The White Woman is power and that is what he wants most of all. Power over. To defeat. He is short and squat, balding. Crooked teeth crowd his thick mouth and he drinks too much, so much that his breath is the second thing you notice about his orifice. His fight-scarred face lets you in on the fact that he is uneducated. He repeats sayings like "Old enough to bleed, old enough to breed" and revels in jokes like offering a job planting tulips and saying "Your two lips right here" as he grabs his cock and shakes it at you, laughing. It doesn't matter if you are a fourteen-year-old girl. Animalistic in his behaviors, farting and scratching his nuts or digging in his ass and then rubbing his fingers together to get rid of the stickiness he finds there is a pastime, and he pisses anywhere in public and digs food out of his teeth with those same dirty fingers. Skintight jeans show off his swollen dick that is also his worth as a man, a totem of strength he is happy to discuss with anyone who notices the sex he pulls on or perpetually adjusts through jean fabric until he wets himself there. He shows it to Jeannie too and he tells her all sorts of filthy things that he could do to her with it and how much she'd like it to be fucked like that. It thrills her like her first time, this next step, this next decline.

Jeannie has it all mixed up. He is good at being an animal, and all the other tastelessness disappears when they fuck. He treats her like an animal and she learns to respond like an animal, and that carries over into everything else they do together, is now more important than all the rest, even her kids she fought so hard to take care of, because that validates her and all of those decisions she made before he came. This man makes her whole. This is mistaken for living with a capital L.

Billie-Wayne doesn't show it to her all at once. In this way, Jeannie learns to acclimate to the lie, this lust that stands in for love and respect. And in short order, he moves out of his mother's house in La Center and into her house, and she takes up supporting him, more or less, because he really doesn't have that need to work except for when he wants to drink, and when he drinks he makes himself scarce, and so do her children. And it is in that house that the family learns to detest the smell of Whittaker pig shit from their farm, the pens too close to their house to escape it, the reek of wet pig shit that clings to you, clings to wet August, that cooked chitlin' smell that lock-steps with your pores. And the woman and the Usurper entertain themselves a great deal outside of the house, as her children busy themselves with getting through school or getting out of there or both. But Jeannie quickly finds that living with animals exacts a price and she must expect to pay it. Just as he is a fucking animal, he rages like one too, with no civil damper. The undying love and attention turn to something else.

The Usurper controls the mother and dominates her now. He breaks her and he batters her. Her children watch helplessly as he shoves his property through glass windows in the little house he isolates her family in, way out in the country on old man Whittaker's property, and close to the pig shit and pens so the Usurper could be closer to the work he does not do. He interchanges vulgarities with normal speech, uses them normally, lascivious and lewd language replacing everyday words, where bodies are objects for actionable lecherous commentary. Her children fade to invisible while Jeannie and the Usurper careen into terrible rages. They hide under furniture as he drives by, shooting his .38 into the house to let her know she better get that restraining order taken off of him because he'll kill her before the cops get there and he means it.

The mother breaks it off again with him now, and for good this time around, and she lays low, but the Usurper waits until she isn't home and breaks in and kills her dog right there in the house to let her know he means business, and then he disappears into the labyrinth of his people in La Center or skips state for a while so that the law can't find him and nobody who knows him knows where he went. It is a criminal's code, even on so ignoble and petty a level. The white cops of La Center, who used to come, now only half-assed respond because Jeannie Mae is poor, she is a nigger lover, a less than, and she got what she deserves and she probably likes it. She asked for it anyhow. And then, finally, they no longer respond when she calls anymore.

Eventually, the sympathetic sisters stop being sympathetic and distance themselves from this dysfunction. Etta, too, moves away to Oklahoma in her last years. Jeannie's oldest sister takes what she wants from the estate, that old white farmhouse at the hard bend in Oaks Road in Symsonia, and sells the rest at auction, without mentioning it to any of her remaining sisters, and Jeannie particularly because she no longer deserves anything from this family. That is how the mother discovers the difference between fucking and getting fucked. But it is too late.

Jeannie is fucked.

The Usurper transitions from declarations of love to demonstrating that she is property, that he possesses her, that the mother is his and that validation of his power over white men will not flee him. Now, the Usurper disappears for days, drawing out trepidation for the woman and relief for her children in that sometimes family. He returns again, reproving Jeannie's whoring behind his back and she pays for that, so he repeats his heavy blows upon her while she strikes him right back. And there is that one time when he drags the woman into the street because she refuses to comply, and he slams a tire iron into her face and she goes to the hospital for that concussion, and he is now missing again for several days and the kids stop wondering why. But he returns. Desperate and heaving, Jeannie takes him back because they are now intertwined in that dark dance together. This is the time when she finally loses herself to the Usurper and his compunction in possessing her, his need to make her his that demonstrates her belonging.

The mother comes to think it is need and adoration and nobody tells her differently, or she becomes too tired to fight those cold, slick walls that are somehow erected around her, and so she stops calling out for someone to help her. Either way, it is too late. She and her children live in a halted motion, forced to comply by reaction and not from forethought any longer, suspicious of the next moment or sparking flares. Daily living now entails strings of hard-pressed maneuvers, intending escape to maintain self-preservation. After a while of this, after the Usurper establishes himself in her home, owning the mother is no longer enough—as it can never be for that kind of hunger. Unbeknownst to either of them, the Usurper's need is not contained with just the singular ownership. Possession must be complete.

"I just don't believe it, Jennie Kaye," the mother tells her flatly.

The Usurper tries to touch her, tries to convince the girl, telling her not to tell or there'll be consequences. It is an open secret that the younger daughter hates the man, has despised him from the moment he enters the house; she refuses to speak to him. She stares at him with disgust, with contempt, with bile in her mouth. It is for that reason the Usurper tries to break the girl first, and in the only ways he knows to break women—with his sex or with his fist—and the latter he is unable to deny. It is easy not to believe, to call her a troublemaker, a liar, and for him it is easier to cast the blame than to terminate the quest for showing all of them. Besides, since the Riverboat Man walked away, the girl has been devoid of emotion, except for that contemptuous one she holds for all men in general and the Riverboat Man in particular, or for anybody else who acts in the role of patriarch, including this one. It is a singular emotion coursing in her blood until she draws her last breath, prohibiting the thawing of a frigidity she has for that Riverboat Man, or now this Usurper, or any man forcing her hand. All that the girl relented to Cherokee in that brief interlude is now rescinded by this Usurper. Actively separating yourself is a dangerous thing in a cobbled-together family of disassociates. Defiant, telling, Jennie Kaye deeply marginalizes herself in a family like theirs, where affection is cheap, sold for a compliment or a little attention.

Lisa Jo has ways to butter her bread, knowing how to preen and charm to be accepted, to wheedle in, to get on the good side. She sidles up to the Usurper, basks in his attention, flirts once more like she had with Cherokee. Her ministrations are received very differently by the Usurper, with different designs for fourteen-year-old children. Jesse Earl and Jennie

Kay resent this ability that they are unable to master, unable to muster up, or even to comprehend its workings. Lisa has a way of convincing, of contriving, of lying so that there is so much truth to it that you believe the lie. It is her lifelong pursuit. She uses it against the Riverboat Man's natural-born children and against Jeannie, and she turns mother against daughter and brother against sister and uses that singular skill to get boys who aren't interested to take her places and to give her money. And after the Cunningham girl's own string of bastard children come, she will pit them against each other too, proving momentarily that somebody really does it for her, because that means somebody loves her.

Lisa's distorted personality overtakes her mental frailty shortly after Jeannie and that Cunningham boy's sham marriage begins its unwinding. Lisa takes the story of her birth in through some mechanization that is skewed, pulled off plumb, with pieces scrapped together about her past. The Cunningham girl's perception of herself is founded on the premise that she is less than, unable to achieve a whole state, and so convinced, she never does.

The girl makes the acquaintance of that Cunningham boy, her father, twice in his lifetime. In that meeting, the girl slips, becomes the end product of a wonderland, borderline functionally deranged, and it is instituted primarily in Jeannie's silence, which is intended to keep pure, leaving the structure of Lisa's very existence a void, voiceless, that leads the child to believe that the truth is more terrible than she can imagine. At first, Lisa attempts to fill the vacuum with animals, then lovers, then runaways, then her own dispossessed children—true bastards—to recount her life through painful mimeograph, the end result of a perverse conjecture, the mischance of having been born a bastard. Believing the lie, Lisa does not seek out the more convoluted truth of her true father, now drunken and bloated by their first meeting, does not excise truth from him or from Jeannie. While this untruth keeps the child close to Jeannie Mae, Lisa cannot recover from the spellbound half-truth that she is a bastard, corrupt by the consequence of sin.

Grown, the Cunningham girl sells herself cheaply. Lisa keeps her dark secret about the Usurper and is therefore unable to negotiate, maneuvers with so little experience when experience is critical. The men who follow outsmart this Cunningham bastard. She is unable to make a fair trade. Lisa does not know the worth of a woman's body with a girl's mind. They, like the Usurper, take and pay for her cheaply. There are no dinners out, choosing instead to show their ardor by a quick trip to McDonald's. They get it to go. She eats up their feigned affection until they spit her out, used up, faded, less than. Lisa learns too late how much they extricate. Her innocence is incidental and she spends her life trying to find it again. Her body is betrayed and she is complicit in its violation. Her smoothness, her skin, a little girl's face, her preening and her hope of being wanted are squandered first on the Usurper and then on those others who took. In her mystery, she twists her prism of little glimmers, that pure light found even in the worst of people, but now it muddies, sullies, makes filthy, and her innocence vents from a darker plane, trickles out contaminated. And then it is over. Her youth, her untrained childhood, and her goodness, such as it is, are gone. She believes she is a bastard, but in reality, the cruel truth is that she is the daughter of the man Jeannie marries, made sacrosanct by the fact that it is a marriage based in love, that perhaps it is the sole union of Jeannie Mae and that Cunningham boy that matters, a purity in which Lisa is conceived made purer by the innocence in which Jeannie gives herself to that Cunningham boy.

It is not enough because Lisa does not know. Artifices come cheaply. You are not cheated by Lisa at first. She does not learn how, at first, before the Usurper. That comes but not now. It is easy to persuade her. Sometimes it is a ride in a real nice car, or maybe a Pizza Hut pizza or a two-liter of soda brought over to her house, because that is how you measure interest in poor people, and her siblings do not have these things. She'll give you a slice to do her dishes. That is what gets Lisa in trouble. Just pretty enough to pay attention to, and she sells out for a trip to the movies and she goes all the way because that is what she wants more than anything, to be loved like a daddy should, but she confuses love with fucking too, because that is all she takes away from this long trip of being her mother's best friend.

Only Jeannie understands the beauty behind Lisa's conception and the conception of her secreted-away elder sister, but she is unable to vocalize it to her child. Jeannie demonstrates favors instead, hoping for understanding instead of the words that cannot come, brutal words still gouging at her chest, clawing to force the voided space left behind in her. Lisa confuses the void with permission, with acceptance of the permissible. Truth doesn't come to light until years after Jeannie's death: that Lisa had been wanted, and consummated in want. In her darkness, in her ignorance of her birth, Lisa coils back, taking, manipulating. She gives it to that Usurper. Whatever Lisa has left after, by the time she discovers her new talent for lechery, she siphons from unsuspecting ones around her, leaving mortal husks littering a terrible path toward her own ruin. Men, brothers, and children: none are immune. Soon she is a predictable ask-want-take, looking for someone to take, someone on the take.

After the Usurper's attentions, that Cunningham girl uses forced affection, fake affection that the Usurper has skewed; she drives semblance and pantomime like a razorblade, cutting deep into her victim, who discovers this only later when the resentment of being used by her crusts, opens up, and all of the deadness and emotional infection left to fester bursts and the black emotions empty out before her quarries heal.

Later, but beginning in those fatal flirtations with that Usurper, hers is a character driven by neediness, by compulsion for sheer survival, guile, and deprivation. Lisa is a queer, lilting inequity and has a careless affinity for animals that don't know better than to love her back, despite the starvation and days of forgetting and the inattention the creatures sometime endure with her, but not always, not in the furtive, attentive moments of her loneliness, just in the darker periods when Lisa draws deeper into herself and lets everything else go, including herself, and her habit of saving people, a trait left over from Jeannie, devolved into something macabre by those first short intervals alone with that Usurper.

Lisa now resigns herself to poverty, helpless to help herself, unable and unwilling to find another way, revising and rewriting her victim card for another run. Once her prey's resources are used up, Lisa barters away to her detriment, trades down, and loses. What that Cunningham girl can't get deviously, she gets by other means. She searches blindly for relevance and rages against a society that finds her irrelevant. It happens before all of the cruelty, but Lisa's hard and withered attitude traces to that night of attentions from the Usurper. Lisa's actions, and the actions of her mother, vindicate Etta in her puritanical vigilance for those three generations: Marjorie, Jeannie Mae, and Lisa.

With this Usurper, Lisa too becomes wrapped up in his convictions, in his need for owning. From him, Lisa learns to lope, not crawl; to form misshapen moons, pulling into her minor orbit the lost people she can score a little bit from; and how to get used up too, and scarred. Formed by misinformation about who Lisa is, defined in a silent void left by Jeannie and that Cunningham boy, and mauled in her innocence by that Usurper, consumed by him, Lisa learns to mutilate her own children and their children also, left to her ward, binding the Clytemnestran hands of those she had created.

After, Lisa regales with candid stories all the selfless acts she has performed and is bewildered by her children's misery, why they turn misshapen, given all the love they got, that Lisa thought she had given them, and the mystification is genuine. Lisa is lost. Her children are unable to save her. The world is unable to care that Lisa is unsaved.

The end result of those perilous moments when a child flirts with disaster, when she thinks the Usurper loves her like a father and not like a possession, defines for her that men use women at any age, and the Cunningham girl is again reduced by one of her bargaining men. At fifteen, she becomes a mother by a guy who does not love her, is incapable of it and tells her to her face that he is too young and that she has attempted to trap him, and the Morris boy flees until she vacates the child from her body and hands it off to Jeannie Mae, and then the Cunningham girl rejoins the Morris boy and another child forms, so she hands that one off to the boy's mother, which is like Jeannie Mae's story too, but tarnished by a filthier filter. When he leaves, the string of inconsequential guys arrive with a little something of benefit for Lisa but then slip into the void until the Cunningham girl is a rendering of her own creation, full of unrealized affection and regret and brutalized emotions.

From the periphery, Jesse Earl and Jennie Kay are outsiders really, second best; they remain the Riverboat Man's children and are already sidelined, on the out. That accusation first hurled by the younger girl and directed at the Usurper only reduces their ranking, and the gulf swells between Jeannie Mae, the Cunningham girl, now full of flattery, full of vice, and full of good times at that tender age, and Jennie Kaye. The firstborn boy holds no power to intercede.

And the day arrives that Jennie Kaye goes away, and the family knows, just as the girl does, that it is because she has been too much trouble, that she speaks when the punishment for speaking, for telling, is ostracism. It comes too easily before this moment not to be the solution staring that compartmentalized family of individuals in the face. It is in this way that the Cunningham girl learns not to speak of it, not to tell, not to transgress. The mother, the woman, is blind to see, in the last of her own young years, unable to believe. Jennie Kaye now lives with the Riverboat Man and his fifth wife, the stranger with a new son from the lot of various wives picked up out of bars, and he is forced to take Jennie Kaye in for just a little while, because his natural daughter is making life miserable for the mother and the Usurper. It is clear that Edward Earl needs to do something for his kid, even if he doesn't come and see them. The Riverboat Man reluctantly acquiesces, but more to get her away from that nigger and lover than for any genuine concern for the child. The Riverboat Man adds the troublesome child to the pile of misery he has accumulated since disassembling his first family, puts her up where his other boy lives, the hunting and car-loving and manly one, refuse from another failed marriage, but somehow equally inconsequential.

Jennie Kaye speaks little of her new stratagem for survival, her new predicament, telling her brother about living on the margin, somewhere between the bedroom assigned to her and shuffling out to Starr Hill and the house of cast-offs, but there is no room in her father's heart for her or anybody else for that matter. His natural child lives perfunctorily, anticipating her exit, planning her exodus. For the Riverboat Man, in the end, his daughter living there or not is of no consequence. He keeps the same hours and absences as before, protracting them past the lines of the setting sun reaching far past Kentucky. His disappointment is too great in all of them. His children are expendable, as are the wives he acquires and casts off, perpetually searching for his Madonna.

With loosened bonds, the girl is part of that collective of individuals somehow tethered to each other as family one day, and then isn't any longer, excised like a bad molar. One day, briefly, momentarily, perhaps to retrieve a random set of items left behind in her abrupt exodus, Jennie Kaye returns, joyful but insufficient compensation since the evacuation, to fortify the subset, a strength of bond between them afforded through circumstance: protector and protected, shield bearer and shielded. She slips away and the tethering is loosened. Jesse Earl is adrift.

The girl dissolves into her particular void, leaving just two of Jeannie's children within the voracious grasp of the Usurper. In his subdivision that then amounts to one without the youngest girl, the firstborn boy learns that he must prepare for his own flight.

Since the beginning, their family has emulated modesty. Until this Usurper, this dirty one, the boy hadn't seen his mother disrobed, had not heard her perform any of the bodily functions all of those houses resound, hadn't seen his father naked. Jeannie keeps her family modest through their seamless descending slide. Jesse Earl is silent and vigilant as this new stranger eats his steak in his underwear in front of the TV that he buys with his money from his sometimes jobs, while her children eat Hamburger Helper without the meat (which he also consumes) and he drinks his twelve pack of beer that he buys with his money, or his bottle of Seagram's, while her children swallow water. In their new dynamic, this peculiar new definition of a cohabitating unit, an antithesis of family, an entity that fractures and not a family, they let him release his intestinal gasses whenever and wherever he feels like it, although appalled by the behavior, and let him joke about shitting himself with that one, laughing at his own joke, even though nobody else is laughing with him, which does not matter to the Usurper, because it is a way of letting them all know that this is really his house now.

As his comfort level grows, her children fall silent and sidestep the both of them as he drinks and fights with Jeannie Mae, with his words and his profanity and then with his animal fists and his feral slaps and his dragging her around by whatever his rude hands land on, and with the shoving and the pushing, her children shrink farther into the background as best they can to avoid him, because it is the only way to be nothing like him. And the Usurper systematically cancels the mother's friendships, poisons familial bonds, and works at dismantling her union with her children through his coarseness and vulgarity, and the diminished family soon ends with only dangerously circling and scurrilous, makeshift, derelict friends, dubious and criminal ones. They are nothing like the mother or her children, not yet at least. The boy is mortified by this intrusion of base behavior and calls no one friend, lest they visit, and so now school, like home, is a wasteland, and Jesse Earl pulls from the strength within, closing the noose tighter without knowing it.

So circumstances are like this in the twelfth year for Jesse, with that big stretch of woods behind their house, only one of two houses now standing, habitable, as the I-24 bypass inches toward claiming them too, with the gravel road leading to the city dump where people leave all kinds of trash, even if it might have value to someone. The dump sits just beside the now abandoned lot and collapsed log cabin, where the diminished family first lived, in the halcyon Cherokee years. There are no cardinal sightings here. The landfill and the abandoned places around it are also the dumping ground for too many animals, left-behind pets or the unwanted union of pet and other pet, that through the years of desertion metamorphose into a pack of feral, survival-of-the-fittest dogs that rummage the mountains of stink and trash and rove through woods devouring other kinds of game, weaker and isolated, freshly abandoned animals.

The diminished family witnesses firsthand the results of what the unwanted are capable of. Left unattended too long, the family dog is ripped into flesh and strips of meat, gobbled, cannibalized by savage dogs, leaving as testament to the living clots of blood, matted flesh, and freshly washed wisps of curly golden blond fur caught in the wind and on tips of overgrown weeds in the abandoned lot between this little blue house and the gravel road that leads to the landfill.

Before Jesse and Jennie Kaye are separated, before the youngest is sent away, they live in a forgotten little house sitting alongside the new I-24 bypass. From there, Jesse purloins fresh roosting hay that the county workers throw over new seed on the hard, sloping embankment, originally laid to shore up the steep, red clay gravel inclines that the big picture window in the tiny house stares down on: immovable, overshadowing the facade of the doomed little house, another road leading somewhere, but on higher ground. Jesse keeps chickens—Maybelline, May Belle, and Charlie—in the backyard. He constructs little houses for them from the refuse of abandoned buildings, placing them on stilts, keeping out wild animals hell-bent on killing them off like they did little Jesse, his bantam rooster, tucking the surviving brood into their boxes at the end of each day and closing off the chicken-wire fence with bent sixteen-penny nails. They provide no eggs but are eager to clean insects from the little kitchen garden the boy tends from spring until fall. That hand-me-down family inadvertently inherits their grandmother's Kenmore Water Witch gyrator wringer washer with the gravity drain hose that somehow still works, and it is the boy's chore to haul the relic onto the back patio from the laundry room where he sleeps because it has a locking door. As the mother washes clothes, her children collectively stomp out the soap in the rigid plastic, cerulean blue pool with the Chinese interpretation of what fish look like embossed into the mold. The boy perfunctorily pantomimes Jeannie Mae, what she teaches him in those good years, taking up chores discarded by the Cunningham girl, his lost sister, his lost mother. These are final moments of solidarity between mother and child, last of the times where memories still flow.

After washing, the boy carries the flattened clothes out to the zinc clothesline that runs all the way to the back of the yard and dead ends there, just where the kitchen plot begins, where a peach tree acts as exclamation point to his garden. He hurriedly tends vegetables that mostly recur each year now of their own reseeding and rushes off past the worn-down patch where he and his sister once played school under the holly tree, where yard's edge meets lonely stretch of woods, eating watermelon on newspaper, catching seeds and juice and rind, afterward rolling up the paper for the incinerator barrel and garden-hosing sticky sweetness from hands and faces and legs and bare feet. He lives mostly past all of that, in those wilder areas now, mostly over by the pond that seemingly only he knows about anymore.

Confined to that little blue house at times when the boy cannot get away, shortly after school lets out, a singular unit among the other units that now prominently include the

Usurper, the dirty one, it is inevitable that on one of those not-away days, the Usurper invites Jesse, that first son to Jeannie, to learn to drive his metallic green Pontiac. The car has whitewall tires and a white vinyl top, dappled like snake skin. It is a late spring afternoon that lets you remember what summer feels like, that day the Usurper teaches the boy a lesson about himself, defines for the boy who he is, and how new strangers can be when you really get to know them. It happens when the mother and that Cunningham girl take one of their increasing and exclusive *us* outings and cannot warn the boy of hazards, now that the first son is alone with the Usurper on that forgotten slip of gravel.

It is a moment both exciting and confusing for Jesse Earl, because the Usurper hasn't paid any attention to him in any capacity, both coexisting in a vigilant neutral zone. Jesse believes he has hidden his revulsion well, now ruminating on this newfound interest and what a truce might look like as he scoots across the sticky plastic bench seat and begins pumping at the manual crank window. They start out slow on that dead-end gravel road leading back to the landfill, and the dusty gritted lane soon bursts with dirt roiling behind the vehicle as the Usurper picks up speed through the brambles and scrub trees that grow squat and thick just off the rutting gravel, thick and velvet-coated with layer after layer of powdered silk that settles and then resettles on them, changing the color to the baser brown of gravel, with oaks and sycamore and beech rearing tall and verdantly thick behind, real trees and a makeshift forest that filter the dump smell and noise some stretch after it.

It is a Thursday, a little after four. They eat a white bread sandwich and Ruffles potato chips at the house, so it is also a little bit of a lazy day, with the heat and the thirsty crackling air whipping into the window of the car and over the boy's skinny arms, sticking to the veneer of sweat coating translucent hairs as he mocks plane motions through the blurring murky tunnel of sunlight, jostling by, half listening to the Usurper's small talk as he drives toward his destination, avoiding the potholes furrowed deeply into the lane by the numberless refuse trucks. The sun catches on the ruffling down of his freckled arms, and he squints through the trees at the lopsided glare of the sun. School is out and the trucks make the garbage haul on Saturday and free dump day is at the end of the month, so the road is vacant except for that grimy Pontiac with the shiny tires working their way over the gravel. It is also a great day because the boy is somehow a man as they initiate stuff men do together. The boy is enjoying that and the attention of an adult, even if it is the Usurper, and he feels like an adult as they continue to the Usurper's end.

The boy momentarily puts aside that the Usurper is crude and forgives all that repulses him as they inch along. This is imperative, a rite of passage. The mystery of driving is gifted to no one he knows except himself. The boy has become exceptional. The two drive about halfway to the dump when the Usurper asks.

"You think you ready to take over this here wheel, boy?" He smiles at the boy broadly, knowing something Jesse does not.

The boy nods and forces an excited "yes!" giddy thinking of it. The Usurper pulls the car to the side of the road and exits the sparkling vehicle.

"Get on over here and switch places with me then, Jesse. This is gonna be real special for ya. Hell, I still remember my first time. Was about your age, I suppose...."

The boy notes that the two of them wear almost the exact same pair of cut-off shorts, which adds solidarity, but the man's thick frame make his look like he is being squeezed into two as stomach muscles and fat from his back protrude over the waist and thick legs burst out of the cut-off legs, forcing them to roll up frayed edges into a piping, wounding his dark brown skin with red ringlets, exposing the balled-up leg and stomach hairs that black men sometimes have. The boy hasn't noted that his own wiry, undeveloped frame is now somewhat filled out from his pedestrian means of escape, and by his running, since taking up track. Running is a lonely sport, so it is a good fit for a lonely twelve-year-old kid. The union is symbiotic. In contrast, the boy's wiry legs are taut and muscular, with a high backside in loose shorts. The boy steps outside of the car and walk around to the chrome grill, where the Usurper still stands.

As the boy moves to the front of the vehicle, the Usurper stops him at the chromed point that intersects the hood and the Pontiac symbol like high noon of a sun dial. The boy feels the heat of the hood, from the sun and from the big block engine, rippling up his back as he listens for instructions on how to drive the car. With that broad, crooked, and chipped grin, the Usurper asks again, looking the boy directly in the face. "You sure you ready to drive, boy?" The Usurper's voice raises and tightens.

Jesse eagerly but weakly nods *yes* to the huge leap he is about to take.

Then the Usurper lets on, lays it on the line. "You wanna drive my car, you gotta drop those drawers. Bend that ass over the hood of this car for me, boy."

It is a ridiculous thought. Absurd. It has to be a joke. Jesse even let out a snicker at the idea. The heat from the sun and the heat from the engine make the hood too hot to lean over for anything, the boy ponders. 'Why? Why would I do that. What for?' he thinks.

He must have looked dumbstruck because the dirty one, still grinning, continues. "You gotta pay with something and you ain't got no money! I say it's time to give up that ass for me! Now drop those shorts, like I told you!" He stares hard at the mute boy, but makes no move toward him, instead, adjusting himself, stepping back on one leg so that its state is apparent. The boy stares back, uncomprehendingly.

Then, the realization of what the dirty one means sinks in, as the man with the crooked grin that exposes the broken front teeth glowers the boy down. He wants to fuck the boy. And if the boy allows him to fuck him, he will in turn be allowed to drive this vehicle. The boy looks down at the swell of the Usurper's permanently exposed manhood lumping to the right side of his cutoff jeans as it pushes up impossibly far into the right pocket on his hip. The Usurper has taken his time to plan something like this. It is all about the ask. It is about the carrot before the ask. The boy does not understand that this is about power, but the dirty one may have—probably has—done it countless times before. It is about lust, but it is also about fucking the white man, and to do that it should be a white man who won't fight back. Thankfully, that somehow registers with the boy, and he finds the deadly black ace that he has but does not know he possesses.

"My dad. Will kill. You." He mutters with all of the marshalled conviction he has in him.

The boy believes it would happen. He needs to believe that it would happen. The Riverboat Man is a redneck with an equal propensity for fighting, a man who hates all black people, but black men fucking his ex-wife particularly, and the boy sees that Riverboat Man standing there over the body of the Usurper, dead and bleeding, a corpse with the shotgun blast jagged and gaping, and the boy lets that knowledge transfer through his sure gaze. The boy has the dirty one deadlocked in it. The boy raises his lowered head defiantly and has the Usurper cold cocked in it. The boy doesn't flinch.

So many years the Riverboat Man had been gone, vacant, worthless and out of the picture, but even though he had vanished, Jesse fully pictures him with his shotgun, hunting down this man who fucked his white son over the hot hood of a shining green-metallic Pontiac and killing him for having done it. The flicker of doubt that this is a possibility dances across this dirty one's face with his crooked grin as he stares at the child, and the boy stares back just as levelly. The boy doesn't utter another sound. The boy never flinches. His face must never have changed, and his conviction must never have wavered, because the dirty one buys it. He sees it in the boy's eyes. His nerve dissolves. He reverts back to that little boy that had God knows what done to him to make him into this creature standing before the boy, and the Usurper crumbles and shrinks back from what he is about to do, what he had come to do, what he had planned all along. He laughs like it is all a joke, a misunderstanding, but the laugh isn't one the boy has heard before. It is the laugh of a terrified child, an innocent.

"Shit boy. Fuck this. You never was gonna drive my car."

The Usurper gets in and spins the car around in a sputtering U-turn in that gravel and flees past the boy, pelting him with gravel and leaving him standing there alone, shaking, let down, light-headed, giddy, dumbfounded, with the dust settling into the cold sweat on the arm and leg hairs, in his hair, onto the wet nape of his neck, on his buckling knees, coloring him the even, velvet shade of dust.

Some time passes, the boy has no idea how long it is, how many minutes tick away in his stupor before he becomes aware of time reconnecting with his circumstances, and it is then that the boy realizes the dirty one isn't the only one excited by what almost transpired. Maybe it is the escape of an unforeseen and certain peril that he is unable to comprehend, or that the child has finally beaten this grown Usurper at a game he knows better than the boy does, or maybe it is eroticized in the thrill of escape, or a little of all three, but there it is and the boy notices and understands a little more about power and control, about how men work and how men like that work to work you over. Jesse knows the Usurper would never be alone with him again, and he isn't afraid of him any longer, either. Jesse realizes now. Jess sees the Usurper in that moment for what he is, sees that the Usurper lost face, that he is weak. It isn't something the Usurper can allow. The boy had seen the once-fragile child within him, and he detests the boy for seeing it. The Usurper despises that the white man has seen him frail once more, made him weak, broken his resolve, and has taken from him. He and the boy do not have to speak of it. They both know now.

The incident instills a modicum of bravery in the boy, but he doesn't identify it. That millisecond of comprehension changes how the boy demarcates his position, finds it on the map, that little kid who takes on the abuses doled out to the kind of people that family is now, the kind of people they'd become, wanting nothing but the desire to change this definition of reality they'd all been misstepping themselves downward and into. It is soft voice without any capital letters, a minute voice, a realization, and he had not recognized it welling up and changing, until brutal desire grew much larger than his fear, but then it inundates him after it is all over, standing in the dust on the gravel road heading to the landfill where people leave their trash, even if some of it is still good, has value. That is the perverse lesson the dirty one unknowingly gives to the boy.

The Usurper doesn't come home that night. He spends the rest of that week and the coming weekend drinking purple drank with codeine, chasing it with cheap Seagram's gin, and then he drives off to La Center, leaving those leftover units alone. There is a worried hush over the house, but though the boy knows why he does not tell. Jesse culls a clear understanding from the fate of Jennie Kaye for telling, and he knows they couldn't believe. And he then patches together a lot about adults and unwatched children, but he still doesn't know enough. That comprehension would come, and he would come to understand that too. And besides, where would the boy go? The dirty one is scared, wounded. He leaves. The boy stays. The child has won. The boy is unaware that it is only a battle in which he triumphs, not the war, but he momentarily revels in victory, quietly, gloating to himself.

Sunday night arrives, and around seven o'clock in the evening, the Usurper returns—loud, belligerent, drunk. Fear penetrates the house, singing with the tension. His mewling deafens the TV and dinner is suddenly abandoned, like those untouched plates found after the eruption of Vesuvius. The boy finds himself suddenly crouching behind the door of his bedroom, tensed up through the feet and legs and back and arms and fists, smaller now, smaller still behind the door, as the dirty one swings and hits and breaks objects, and Jeannie meets volley with volley as she lobs back his viciousness and is smashed into things. The moment of fear rewires in the boy and he stops crouching but instead finds himself coiled, now lying in wait for the dirty one and, within the milliseconds of synapses firing, finds he has formed a plan, even though he doesn't know where it comes from. But it is at this precise moment that these two flashes collide, as the Usurper crashes through his bedroom doorframe.

He isn't rushing at the boy or the older sister; He and She simply brawl themselves into the hallway that leads to collective bedrooms and, in happenstance, there is the boy behind the door as the dirty one shoves through it. The boy is blank and white as paper, transfixed, and he has the plan, but it is the furies or the fates who have shoved that beast down that narrow channel and into the awaiting plan the boy has been inspired by, where he waits coiled for him. The dirty one doesn't have his shirt on and Jesse can see his broad, short back with the fat hanging over the same cut-offs he still wears, and he remembers that day and remembers all of the hideous things this Usurper unforgivably transgressed upon the mother and the younger sister that nobody believed, and he remembers what happens to the far-away family because of this one, and suddenly the boy is wielding light-blue, plastic-handled scissors collected from his dresser for this exact instant, somehow still in his scattering hand, and he plunges them with all of his might into that beastly back.

Skin. Muscle. Sinew. Bodies are not like in the movies, so the scissors do not plummet to the depths of the Usurper's heart. The man does not die an instant death. The dirty one does not bleed out on the cream-colored carpet of the bedroom, writhing out his last moments of life like the boy had imagined, and the child is still a thin and terrified twelve-year-old, so they only perforate and then glance off the shoulder blade just beneath and cut into the flesh, but only in a flimsy millimeter-measured slit into the shoulder. The dirty one turns, completely shocked at what has happened, and stares at the boy and the bloody scissors in boy's hand with his blood on them, stares unbelieving through the daze of alcohol and reefer and pills and codeine cough syrup, and he must have wondered in that instant just how deadly the burning infliction is. Jesse takes his moment of inaction and steps backward into his darkened bedroom, scrambles across his own bed, throwing himself through the screen of the raised window and letting the night air in, lands in the bushes, and runs the distance between that little blue house to the only other inhabitants on this sliver left of civilization, caught up between the new highway and the dump, which is also the house Jeannie Mae's sister lives in, set farther back from the highway but closer to the creek the overpass covers.

As the boy runs, those minutes stop again and the hormones increase the speed and force of his contracting heart, adrenal glands surging, but in a calm and focused sort of way, and Jesse slips once more outside of this running boy. The child elatedly feels the luscious dew of the tall grass lap at his legs, and the calm in the mist that settles into the hollowed-out depression where they live on the bottom side of the raised bypass and seeps out of the woods as it clings to and cools his naked chest and whirling arms. The boy coolly observes fireflies that flit and bounce alongside him on his way to his aunt's house. Jesse is filled with the little joys that evening brings as he bolts, unbothered by the man he has attempted to murder. And he recollects that there has been no sound to his sojourn. It does not occur to the boy that the Usurper is not in direct pursuit, so he does not cease running until he bursts unannounced into Melody's kitchen, where senses flood back to the boy and urgency again overtakes him and, greedily panting, yells riotously for her to call the cops.

She sees the bloody scissors still in the boy's hand and she does as he orders, stricken and without question. The boy begins to tremble all over, wracking over double with them suddenly. He stays the night there.

"We took him out of the house, son, but you should know your momma won't be pressing charges. She won't file a restraining order… says it won't do no good. In my book, you did the right thing. Him a grown man. Ma'am, you should be with your sister. He messed her up pretty bad, son. He's cooling off but he'll be back, just so's you know. Watch your back, kid."

The cop winks at the boy as he leaves. The sister looks on without comment, lost in thought, in the cycle, but the boy can tell his aunt is terrified, and also pleased that the dirty one got a taste of his own medicine, because she has seen him in action but gave up on Jeannie too and now turns a blind eye.

'Will I do it again this time?' she must be wondering.

When the boy returns to the house, the mother sits him down and thanks him for protecting her but says that he shouldn't have done that and he shouldn't have called the cops, because it only makes him worse and the cops won't do anything anyway, which the boy knows is true. She kisses the boy and holds him and, for one of the few times in his life, he feels dear to her because she takes the extraordinary step to express it, not in the demonstrated way by taking care of the family, by providing for them, not even in taking the blows while letting the Usurper know that children are a boundary that will not be crossed, but in a loving and gentle way, in a motherly way, a way that removes all trouble from the world so that a boy finally feels safe.

The mother escapes the dirty one briefly. The boy escapes his wrath somehow. They all do. She throws the Usurper out and throws out all of his clothes and calls his mother and explains that she wants nothing more to do with him, that he is of no account, and she better make sure he doesn't come back or the next time will be his last. It has happened before, but this feels final.

The Usurper increases the stakes and consequences for leaving. It hasn't been on his terms and therefore is void. He does come back, forcing his way back in. Jeannie takes the blows for the boy's actions and for her own. That is inevitable. Nobody notices from the interstate what goes on down that embankment, in that little light-blue house with the picture window staring out at red mud and gravel. It is that little blue house that he drives past after she leaves him, shooting into its rooms without reservation, emptying the rounds of her stolen .38 through the walls and windows without anybody caring, without rescue, as the family huddles behind, in back of, cowering at this new level of insanity. He shoots her dog in the head, just like that, in front of her, dropping the beast into a pooling dark stain on the mottled brown carpet. They are all possessions to be kept or disposed of, their choice. Jeannie shoulders it, owns it. But she will kill him if he lays one hand on her kids, she reminds him in her own wrath. And darkness engulfs them in that truce, acquiescing to being owned in exchange for accepting that which is off limits. He returns. And she surrenders to the fact that escape is no longer possible, would never be possible for her. It is in that moment the family loses her.

The boy puts behind all that he has seen. He is inaccessible, removed, a recluse within that little blue house. The boy spends waking hours distant, locked in the little laundry room that is all his, books piling on his bed, drawing, escaping, a fugitive in the outer corners of their encampment, away from the microcosm consisting only of them in the Usurper's return. At school's end, or weekends, the exiled boy bolts the inescapably close proximity of their presence: the fox, the game, a departure route. He scurries over treetops, skipping easy lures of sandwich lunches and Coke and sometimes Fritos offered at the house, and instead gathers together mulberries or cherries growing in the orchard, lost in bramble fields and overgrown thickets until the boy rediscovers it, that someone had planted long before their family arrived. He takes solace in being alone. There is a great pear tree growing thirty feet straight up, hard to climb but he does it anyway, and a Granny Smith apple tree too, but he braves the bees to get to the apples. The boy invites himself and the creatures allow the communion. He steals away in his shorts pockets young cucumbers or tomatoes from the vine that he grows in the garden, privately taking pride like his papaw does, and remembers sunny days with him who called him Junebug, forgetting the other, darker times with which those times coexist. Memory makes for such allowances if you bend it hard enough. And the incident fades like the still livid chokecherry-red gash on the Usurper's otherwise brown back, resembling the mark left by a whip, the boy's lingering admonishment for misdeeds, punishment for his and the boy's missteps. Like all endings, the days do not plunge deep into darkness and stay there. The individual units join with good days, when the boy brings home what he gathers up and Jeannie Mae makes pies like old times, like she remembered. But the terrible times come too and disassemble those times, and the boy attempts to regain control by tying thread to the haunches of frogs, dragging them to the bottom of the creek and watching as they thrust upward, futile, struggling for the surface of the water, only to be dragged down again. When they stop kicking and go limp, the boy massages their white bellies until they revive, releasing them from his misery, relieved when they overcome the trauma, only to catch another, repeating the grim task. Some survive; some do not.

The boy is not the only changed one with the return of the Usurper. It is in those last days too, when the Usurper awakes from a drunken and drugged stupor, too lax to react and muscles too starved to thrash effectively, waking to find his eyes bulging, choking on his tongue, with the mother straddling his chest, braced around him with her long leg bones clenching his sides so that he cannot buck her, long slim white fingers dedicated to severing his throat, cutting off his oxygen, cutting off words.

"See here? I'm not the only one who can die in my sleep, you motherfucker," she cobra-hisses through her slight underbite. "You remember this next time you think about hittin' me," she grits as she digs fingernails into flesh to remind him. Jeannie releases him just as he loses consciousness. She has put him on notice.

It isn't long after the scissor incident that the boy finds that his favorite hens do not run to him, expectant of his afternoon corn grist, as he walks the dirt drive. It has been the pause only, finally, before the war is won, he thinks, knowing without being told what it must mean. That is the bellwether, the measuring stick, the meter reading out the shortness of his time left there. Summarily, they have been disposed of, given away to the mother of the Usurper, carried off without consent. He needn't think that he owns any property there that it can be disposed of so readily as this. Jesse does not protest because there is nothing else said about it; knowing it underlines the fact that the child has no power about what is to be done with him in the fashion of eliminating impediments.

The transaction occurs on a Saturday just before summer, a matter of weeks after the scissor slice that decides the boy has to go as well. The Usurper chooses by force and she by acquiescence after a wearing down of sorts. It isn't put like that to the boy in so many words exactly but the end result is the same. Jesse doesn't protest, object, with nothing to barter in this new adversity, reactionless to the news.

Instead, makeshift boxes and grocery bags fill with a few

effects: three pair of jeans, four t-shirts, a sweater, a pullover from his friend Eric, a coat; three photographs in frames—images of the people he had known paralyzed in motion, memories lingering affixed to a Polaroid-still—and a few more kept in a wooden recipe box, collected together to brace against forgetting, not knowing that he would want to forget; three pair of shoes consisting of one pair of Army-issue black shiny patent leather dress shoes one size too big for him that he got from some boy the older sister once dated, a pair of sports shoes he uses to run against the clock of being cast aside, and a pair of Docksiders that he paid for from a summer of earnings for stripping tobacco, because they connect him in some small measure to the normal ones in his school; a brass turtle paperweight from a yard sale; a chance plastic giraffe he finds in the street; a low-lidded Japanese bowl that he takes away as the only vestige of the private room he created from the laundry room with a locking door in that little blue house alongside the new highway. It was his refuge, a budding exodus, where he could pretend that he lived in Japan, cutting four by fours with a handsaw and nailing them into a four-posted twin bed paneled with pale-green privacy sheers, laid low and pooling on the uneven concrete floor, and a tea table made with his own hands from cast-off lumber and nails from abandoned sheds and outbuildings of that once functional farm left to rot in the woods behind them, all painted red to emulate the room in *The Japanese Girl*, a book he once read about a woman who is reduced to prostitution for want. The boy especially cherishes the wool pullover, dark blue with a horizontal green and rust-colored stripe, because he had refused to return it to the only friend he had. Eric dared reveal his own deep secret to him as he, in turn, revealed his in a torrential confessional during the gasping last minutes of a midnight walk through the empty wet streets of Broadway to the Waterfront. It is a friendship born of attraction to each other, not in a sexual sense, but in a brotherly one, defined by recognition of oneself in the other, that climaxed in confession. The revelation occurs just before Eric's father sweeps him away to Chicago to unlearn the behaviors he acquired there in Paducah with his mother, he'd said. Eric, on the night he is carried away, stops by that little blue house on that sliver left of civilization after the bypass is put in, just before the landfill, to retrieve the loaned sweater, but the boy cannot relinquish it. That boy fades, the sweater disintegrates in time but remains tangible, and remnant memories of a sweater linger thirty years after. Jesse wonders if his own lost brother would have been like that, if they would have carried each other through, wonders if others like Eric exist beyond this little blue house. Somehow, Jesse had found him, temporarily had, in turn, been found. It is in that revelation that the boy steals a sweater despite the protestations of Cherokee, of his friend. He cannot let him go.

All of these trivialities of a sometimes unloved life that doesn't have enough to go around are crammed into a hurried obliteration of makeshift paper valises, and he is severed from a punitive and despised world (the only one he knows) and discharged to a kindly, plump stranger's house out by Barkley airport. She is an acquaintance, a woman whose main qualification is that she lives in the same school district where the boy currently resides, a mystery woman who works with Jeannie Mae in a hotel, in whom the mother confides her perpetual problem of too many men, shares her family—and to whom she is willing to relinquish her son. Jesse is ushered into a small back room with lively prattle about how well they will get along and how lovely his mother is and what a wonderful person and good friend she is. Jeannie hadn't mentioned her.

Jeannie escorts her boy into this new existence with assurances of visits each week and telephone calls any time he needs, which isn't the case but she needs to believe it even if Jesse doesn't. He witnessed Jennie Kaye's disposal. He gets the gist. A cleaving in two like this must be brutal, executed with force and conviction. Her mealy-mouthed approach sickens him. Disposal has to be a complete severing of limb from body for the body to heal. The boy is aware that it is he who is the defective limb.

With this new woman, Jesse commands intrinsically good behavior: becomes less than, disappears, removes any negative perception. He gets good at it. He learns his lesson well. He amplifies all that once made his mother happy. He smooths out his bed with no prompting, mostly sleeping in his clothes on top of a tightly tucked twin bed so that levelling any creases is all that is required to eradicate his presence. Jesse is mute and spends hours scouring the kitchen after meals as a means to pass the silence and fastidiously eliminates any trace of having been at the table or at the stove or of having used the sink. The boy makes himself even smaller, more invisible, in this stranger's house.

He pockets away thoughts of the little insignificant room he had pieced together as a bastion against those little adversities that became normal; he had forgotten the supplies he hoarded

under the bed in case world disaster from the remnants of a
Cold War or other tragedy engulfed them all, hoarded in the
hope that he would be prepared, so that he alone could save
them. He quells lingering images of the little speakers and the
small stereo that herded Jeannie Mae and that Cunningham
girl and the Usurper out of his head, singularly pressing down
against so much remembering. He received it from Judy,
the heavy and bleating aunt who lost her brother Cherokee.
There, the boy disremembers nailing each separate piece to the
interior rail of the bedframe, trapping in the music, ensconced
in pale green sheers, learning to croon in the wretched voice
of Billie Holiday and beat down the blues with Ella Fitzgerald
and Sarah Vaughan and the lively Andrews Sisters, attempting
to distinguish himself from his family, from the low-life they
came to embrace, what they are becoming, a pointless attempt
at regaining all that is lost, dwindled down to the size of
the interior of a twin bed, made of repurposed materials in
a laundry room with a cement floor, in that house by the
landfill. In his new silent bed, he obliterates them all there,
lying on top of her bed cover; space and small solace he finds
there, sanctity, and refuge of space. It is a game of just how
perfect he can make himself now and it etches into his fibers:
sinking down, carving their vicissitudes into his bones, this
having been left behind, eliminated. It takes practice.

He is polite and thoughtful toward her because he is
focused on the fact that the strange gossamer binding the two
temporarily can be disengaged as abruptly as the move was
decided, and he reiterates this fact to himself whenever he is
too tired or desires something else other than these things,
these mute offerings of persuasion to her happiness with

his presence; where and if the door next opens, a swinging pendulum brushes against the hairs on the child's neck. There is no other door. Jesse focuses attention on schoolwork and quiet hours of reading and invisible practices in a little back room of a stranger's house, and he seldom uses his voice: not to strangers, not to teachers or classmates.

There too he disappears. The now unburdened family moves away to La Center and forgets to visit or call this new place. Jesse is not lost but purged, eradicated like his sister, but they are no longer aware of each other's fate, disassembled. Later, the boy finds that Jennie Kaye is lost too, in this same way, in this incongruous way. And it is a loss that nobody notices because the two are inconspicuous in their fear and trepidation of the big question mark, so they remain quiet about being cast away too, even to each other. It becomes unimportant when it isn't spoken of, and one finds in that solitude that individuals aren't so much against you as they are for themselves. The boy combs through the recesses of his mind, looking for flaws, for redirection, mapping out new as completely separate from what has been, perfecting ways to be perfect, modeling actions and studying reactions. Jesse keeps within him Cherokee's remembered words and he practices like a mantra and he builds new models upon them, obsessing to emulate perfectly how to perfect honesty, rigidity, studying downfalls of Medici and Borgia, Roman emperors and the Greeks; owning his mistakes and misgivings, living by an internal moral code, without relying on beliefs of the acceptable or passable, answering only to himself as to the veracity of deeds. It is an antithesis to his humble foundation. He scribbles out on interior walls of his head ways to be courteous, interested in manners, and reads endlessly to aspire to the higher stations of noble pasts. Jesse emulates and accumulates those manners until they are ingrained, self-taught. He experiments on strangers in new ways to be a model guest.

Jesse Earl finishes a year and a half of school in purgatory, introversion seating itself within him like a tumor, cautious, guarded, but always, always watchful. And one day this perfectly polite stranger in whose house he cohabits announces that she is moving and that he must move. The announcement elicits no emotion, he having anticipated the moment from his arrival, and he silently repacks his few things into the same boxes that he hadn't fully unpacked and tidies the room as it was before his arrival, arranging as if he had never been there, no mark of him, no trace of this nobody. He is in the car in 18 minutes.

And the plump, pleasant lady prattles on, as she is prone to do, as she politely drives the boy back to them, and it is in this way that Jesse discovers they had moved yet again in that time and are living in the same school district as he and the stranger. It elicits no emotion. The reception is the same—as if he were moving into that stranger's house again, into the back room, without it belonging to him, and as if his time there were also borrowed. He is no prodigal son and dismay wells up at stepping backward.

But waves are not something that he is interested in making any longer, this new change. They are not required to take him in, he realizes, except by law. Jesse is expendable and had been expended and it will surely come again in short order. He has diminished affection for Jeannie and the Cunningham girl and complete apathy for the dirty one, knowing now he is better than, a cut above, and can cast them off as he had been cast off, linked but by a slimmest margin. A revelation comes.

The boy discovers that this time which is borrowed is time in which to map his own departure, on his terms, from these circumstances, these limitations, from these small hard lives that poke and jab and hurt toward each other in perpetual and small and petty wars in which wounding but not killing your opponent is considered the victory, and in which those same victories are claimed by the opponent in the next volley as the substitute for love for them. Theirs, he observes, has been a futile and wasted life. This dance they learn without him and he, once removed, is sidelined and from that vantage witnesses: neither as part of, nor with a part in, these strange entreaties of petty domination, retaliation and retribution in the effort to be seen, to matter. Jesse Earl fades to the little unused screened-in porch without glass at the back of the house, like long ago where the better dishes of Etta's house once resided, and he walks away from those inside the house who are jostling for position in a game nobody else is playing. Excluded here, especially here, without the creature comforts of mooring, he reminds himself of transformation, of concluding. The last year of junior high is also the last of his thirteenth year.

"When you graduate, I don't know where you'll go, but you can't stay here, hon. You know that." Or, "I just can't keep supporting you. Maybe a job, go to school, but move after. You know that, don't you?" Jeannie Mae clicks the countdown clock.

The messages are underscored smaller ways in the house

on the south side of town, with overgrown and untended grass, with dirty windows now, with the general smallness and hardness that steels *for* and *against* without perhaps really meaning to. Conversations interrupted and then unwelcoming looks from the Cunningham girl, the Usurper (whom Jeannie relented to marry and now has become her third husband, which thankfully occurred during the boy's absence); dislike and wariness over Jesse's distance, his books and books and endless absence, his disappearing, his better than and disdain, not accepting his place. His newfound better-than-them attitude grates on each of them in different ways. Jeannie is silently complicit, grating on her third husband. The woman is less than she was. Her working potential, arduously lifting them out of the morass, is extinguished and she settles into mire. Jesse is repulsed. The labor Jeannie applied to finishing business school casually takes a back seat to getting away from all of this by other means, easier means. She sings with apathy, vibrates with sloth now. It hadn't worked for her and she is beaten. The Usurper claims her completely. And it is also evident in the broken-toothed grin of complete conquest that her third husband sports on his face each time he looks the boy over, staring him down as if he is a dominating Big Dog among the rabble living off the landfill once more. He fucked him, fucked all of them, without so much as touching the boy.

Picking the Bones, 1979

Just as Jesse transforms, he finds them changed too. The boy notices that, in his absence, this Third Husband, this Usurper, has grown bored with Jeannie, bored with conquest and drinking and unfailing servitude to his lust which is power. The beatings subside with his owning her, - his sexual conquest expands to endless others - friends, strangers, and children of friends. The Usurper reminds her and himself of how much of a man he is in his conquests, flaunting them to her, gloating on them. She hates to love this Big Dog and the excrement he leaves. And because she hates, the Cunningham girl also learns to hate but maintains allegiance in a neutral way: still relevant, chosen, the better one. The result is predictable.

Allegiance and order of love and hate and love again fluctuate as Jeannie and Third Husband parry and dodge emotional lances, using one against the other and then abandoning that alliance to wage war on the ally in the next moment, which is entertainment and consumption of their endless cannibalistic attentions. The dance becomes so intricate, so ingrained in each of them, that all of their energies are used up first against and then in support of each other, ending in a meaningless ongoing feudal sparring that concludes each night, having accomplished nothing. Except Jeannie and the Cunningham girl and Third Husband do not acknowledge, have no recognition of the hours wasted in exercising hate and love and hate again or diversions and redoubts of alliance and allegiance. It is how they dance.

There is little left for the first boy. Jesse refuses to launch, maintaining instead a new self—inconspicuous and silent, listening: a watchman. He flourishes academically but does not mention it because the Usurper and the Cunningham girl ridicule achievement. Jeannie sees the near end in his seventeenth year. The staged play is finishing. This is the moment, a focused vista.

Before transformation, before his discharge, left unspoken but on those internal fissures, Jesse scrawls down nauseating illustrations hidden from the eye, from family, naked scrutiny, perverse intrigue, and for some time, from himself – blocked – locked away. These morose suppressions, horrific instances, take place not in the same moments in time, but throughout the last vestiges of the together time this family has, those last years as a cobbled-together unit, in its final deterioration, and decimation begins innocuously as a legitimate treatment for ills Jeannie Mae suffers with her Marfan Syndrome, but expands and engulfs her in its consuming, needful darkness, engulfs the girl and the Usurper, engulfs the boy by association. This house collapses.

Ruin begins with a series of heinous and dark events brought about by dependency and the disease of dependency that infects blackening affections and the bonding of mother and son, mother and daughter, mother and self. It exhausts those bindings with self-implosions, spewing out emotional and physical shrapnel that gouges out flesh and tears out love, tears at the remnant tethered bonds and roots of those in her tow. It destroys love. It flittingly obliterates any context of them that is left. These annihilating chemical cravings that develop after the doctor's prescriptions, Jeannie Mae partially confesses to, atones for, some but not all.

She does not confess the greatest of these transgressions when she so early on identifies the peculiarities of a child, her son, perhaps knowing that they remain their open secret and that, when he is the small age of fourteen, her greedy actions compel a reality for her first boy, makes notion concrete, unmercifully leaves her greatest sin unatoned.

Jeannie does not confess to it, perhaps could not, not to the boy, not to anyone, not to herself. These are also squelched—not shared, not illuminated, not exhumed—amid all of the turmoil of a descent into dependency; but, if they had been exposed, should have been remunerated carefully for the grace of a fallen woman to spare her dignity, her essence, which remains pure in memory, and sorted gingerly through such earthly cinders, as if expunging a phoenix that cannot rebirth. But the first boy observes well when it begins, this odious thing, this engulfing thing, without his understanding that perhaps, in her prism, controlled by her dependency, Jeannie Mae possibly considers she is deciding for the boy, forcing a reckoning, that this is her end-equation of acquiescing to his anomaly.

As simple as a transaction, the act forever alters the first boy, becomes indelible as if carved into his flesh. It changes the mother too, and it converts the boy's vision from Madonna, from giver of life, absolver of sin, to that of a woman flawed: as simple as that, a shift from unadulterated to defective, from saint to malefactor. All that came before does not transcend motherhood. It is this action alone, this lack of telling, and the refusal of forgiveness that shifts a paradigm.

The aortic dissection crippling her body befalls her after she moves back into the duplex on Second Street, when the landlord forgives the back rent she is unable to pay, allowing her diminished family to take up residence there once more, like second chances. That is when her pain begins. She is 32, nine years younger than her mother when it had happened to Marjorie. Jesse, thirteen, is beginning high school. All of his middle school years are spent running, finding one place of small respite, stitching together friendships, with abrupt terminations of that respite when the bills are overwhelming, too much for her, moving with them to the next do-over. Cherokee has recently died and left them in the void that follows him.

The mother completes her GED. Her children manage their own lives and she is now finishing her associate's degree in business and discussing all of the possibilities resulting from such efforts. In this small respite, Jeannie regains some of her old self, so this aortic tear is unwelcome, an inconvenience. Her life halts in an instant. The dissection paralyzes her momentum. The aortic tear also allows the Usurper to regain the upper hand, validate his own exodus, and he takes liberties to drift in and out of her life, taking up with a woman, coming back for a while, then gone again, until the mother prefers the gone times over any validation he provides on his return. She alienates herself, had isolated from him some time ago, even after their living room marriage. As the luster leaves her hair, as time weighs on her once perfect skin, so does his interest and her interest in his being interested.

The Usurper uses her newfound frailty to temporarily take up with her friend Nora, fucking her. He briefly takes up with her friend Carol after his boss, Old Man Whittaker, finishes with her, but that too dissipates, loses his interest, because he was exercising power over the mother only to demonstrate his vitality, but she shows no interest in his exploits. It is the hard use the Usurper wants, not the caretaking, not the aftermath of use. The mother soon grows accustomed to this too. Briefly, Jeannie refocuses, making him insignificant. Mostly, the history of her family is that each of them gets that second shot of seeing how deconstructed their lives are before they die. It is like that for Jeannie Mae too. Hers is one of those long and aching pains that comes on strong and incapacitates her that she then acclimates to. She comprehends its significance, knows what is to become of her, having seen it happen to Marjorie and lately to her brother Donnie and sister Linda, all dead now. Jeannie knows what it is even before she finally relents to doctors, before getting the certification, the seal, and their kiss-off.

There is nothing they can do about it just yet, they explain. Nothing has changed since her mother's death, since her brother and sister. Her aorta is enlarged but not large enough to operate, because any procedure is a temporary fix, an interlude before final death. But the side issues of the disease cause more pain than her heart. Her cartilage is gone, so Jeannie's bones drag across bone in her joints, paralyze her with blinding hot pain, leave her unable to get out of bed with arthritis in its last stages. It is every joint, every juncture, every day. The disease tortures her back, knee, hip, anywhere joints collide. And then her aorta splits and doctors split her open and temporarily fix her aorta but not the joints, prescribing masses of opioids instead. And when Jeannie develops a tolerance, they increase the dosage of the Demerol or Percocet or Vicodin. These temporary fixes to the deeper issue carry her through shorter periods of time, shorter intervals than the timeframes of the dosages, making her anxious, desperate.

With the pain and the certainty of succumbing to that which befell her mother and her siblings, Jeannie grows fearful and dependent again and all of that possibility she worked toward goes into the pill bottle. Her rocking slows, her moving forward ceases. Jeannie talks to the Usurper about not wanting to be alone when she dies; she forgives him these last trespasses too, and he thrills in his renewed power over her once more, in owning her, in her owing him. He and she share prescriptions for pain medications now until hers are used up and then they buy more on the street, compensating for time differences in pain and high, and forgetting, and the next self-prescribed dosage.

The funny thing with doctors is this: those same medications handed out are quickly rescinded if the doctors suspect the patient is a liability, suspect the inevitable has happened, dependency of their own making. Once this reliance is uncovered, the prescriptions wane but not the need and not the pain and not the forgetting. So her source of pain management becomes Peggy, a leviathan of an ugly woman who covers her faded looks and girth with too much jewelry and cologne, hoping no one notices the alteration. She drives a new Cadillac and dresses upscale and is therefore somehow more respectable, with more access, calls more shots. Peggy has better insurance and better connections to several doctors, but not much of a need to medicate her verified back problem, so she shares her pills for a price. The shift down for the mother, the fall, comes as easily as this, a handshake. This is where it begins. That price entails selling some pills for her and Peggy pays Jeannie and him in prescription medication from profits, for their own use. And this is what they become.

When Jesse and the Cunningham girl learn this, in a strange act of solidarity, they corner the woman named Peggy after a monthly transaction, explain that she is killing their mother and creating a drug addict, and order Peggy to leave her alone or they will take matters into their own hands. And this woman does leave them alone; Jeannie's children never see the woman again. When Jeannie finds out about this intervention, this intercession into her destruction, she is furious in such a way that has no comparison. She screams and curses at the two for interfering, calls them names and smashes their useless trinkets and the dishes, until she is spent and sobbing. And then Jeannie goes silent and all is seemingly right for a while. But her children are too late in their pleading. There are many sources for destruction, and she seeks them out. Her children know her anger is at her own dependency and not at them, not really, but anger must crash on some shore. It is in this way, in his attempt to stop these illicit transactions that everything changes, that the boy participates in his own demise, in his own near obliteration, in both her and his own annihilation alike.

It takes place in the duplex on Second Street, that risky slip, that shadowy turn. Her new supplier is in his mid-forties. His name is anonymous, lost in the shadows of black transactions, a distant accessory to Jeannie's low life. He is rough, a blue-collar type with a legitimate back injury that isn't as great as his need for extra cash to pay for an ex-wife and kid but that warrants a host of doctors with ready prescription pads. He exploits Union Insurance and permissive doctors for sources to supplement his blue-collar living.

Jeannie, the Usurper, and the Supplier are now fast friends. It comes with the territory of dealing, of using, and of the perfunctory trust in illicit trades. At no cost, the Supplier fills prescriptions with their cash. He has enough to go around. That bodes well for a few scripts without the rest of her family knowing anything about it. It isn't unusual that a new derelict penetrates their small cell of units, as her family exists on the outskirts of society and like attracts like. "Normal" for her boy entails preparing for school, waking the Cunningham girl, and finding the living quarters perfectly quiet as he slips out, striding over the puny pinging, submarine-like sounds of humans exhaling in unison, unconsciously syncing their breathing as they sleep. One more new derelict, this Supplier doesn't make a difference.

But this pusher, this seemingly quiet and duplicitous man, loiters and gallingly attempts conversation with her children, testing alliances for himself, not just with Jeannie and her Usurper, but seeking out collective friendships, to be one of them. He leaves traces of peculiarity her children can't quite place. Jesse Earl recoils from his mother's new life, slips secretly into drawing and reading and studying, exempting himself from her associates. The boy extricates himself from her mediocrity, sliding into a world that is more fantastic than their living arrangements. Her son anticipates the next falling shoe, its descent quicker if his presence is conspicuous. He is not conspicuous. These are immediate concerns of a calculating mind—clemency and refuge—not the presence of another stranger in the house.

Only by observing from a distance is it evident how the mother medicates her pain, all of the pain. In this observation, the boy develops his rudimentary understanding of the sacrifices his mother makes to self-medicate, of the ruined person Jeannie is becoming, her poor state of health and lost youth and the mental pain, the disgrace in which she finds herself living with Third Husband, this Usurper, and her compromise surpassing shame. He understands the euphoric discharge from her shattered remains that the illicit medications afford, the salve to her condition. The need inundates her will, vanquishing those survival skills generations before her put into place to ensure her success. Jeannie, deluged by need, sightlessly treads into the abyss. This is something her boy comes to know after his transformation. But it isn't how the boy discovers that he is complicit in her murder, in her suicide, in her death, as her death is true in all of these things. Jesse can't discover for some time how he has done it, how he contributes to her demise. And to his.

The end begins like many afternoons, with Jesse Earl returning home from school in his freshman year, a boy, fourteen years old. As a December child, Jeannie's son is perpetually a year behind everyone else in age and in understanding. He lands a summer school program that pays him $20 a weekend and then, beginning in his fifteenth year, is selected for a work project at the library, which is there in town so he can walk to work. Life is looking up. Escape is near. The boy changes clothes after school and takes long, heavy fabric shears to cut down the obviously overgrown grass in the yard, particularly incriminating around the edges of the house. The lawn is about ten feet by six feet and easy to cut that way, since the family doesn't own a lawn mower. The dogs and the woman with her three children from upstairs have rutted the grass into dusty spots, but where the grass grows it is as high as the knee. A makeshift brick patio had once been added to the backyard but is now decaying and in disrepair, so the boy reassembles the bricks into a low checkerboard wall, hiding the brown stretch of dirt where the grass has been beaten down by the runoff from the porch roof since the gutters fell off, long before the diminished family moved in. The wall stretches along the entire length of the porch of the house, and the dirt and gravel splash up onto the bricks of the porch, leaving it marred, highlighting the peeling paint. The neighbors do not flagrantly look down on them when the yard is clean, and that is now important for the boy, keeping those little appearances.

The boy finishes the chore and is wiping off the blades of the scissors, entering the long corridor that runs the length of the house. It sequesters his walk-in closet, now bedroom, making use of the unused space under the stairs that lead up to the second-floor apartment. The corridor isolates the boy's room from the other entrances in the house—a succession of four doorways on the left wall. This gallery of doorways connects first to the living room, then one bedroom, then through the galley kitchen, and finally dead-ends at the add-on larger bedroom in the rear where Jeannie padlocks the only working door in the house. The boy quickly steps through the cigarette and pot smoke wafting from the living room, where voices emanate into the hall. For most purposes, Jeannie's boy lives stoically on his side of the house and them, on theirs.

For privacy, Jesse raises high his twin bed's metal rack and nails it to the thick wood clothing bars that run the length of the stairs and, for access, he adds lengths of two-by-four to the wall for a ladder. The tight crawl space retains body heat, insulates from the drafty house, and provides a safe haven from his family. Jesse lives a speechless, monk-like existence there, slipping meekly in and out without fuss. The naked bulb serving the closet now lights the loft crawl space. Underneath the mattress and coil spring, the boy adds a yard sale dresser and armchair and a chain-hanging, green-glass swag lamp nailed off the slant of the boards that cover the underside of the stairs. The closet has a built-in wooden shoe rack toward the back that serves as a bookshelf for the small sack of belongings the boy unpacks, for the few 25-cent Paducah Public Library book sale finds on ancient Greece and Rome. In removing himself to this private sanctuary, this invisible space, he is no trouble. This too contributes to his downfall: being alone and vulnerable in his singleness within the unit. He is consumed by solitary confinement.

The boy is fifteen when the demise begins, runty still in that somewhere-age between child and man, when the price is exacted for his rights of passage, his isolation, and his difference. In reality, it begins when this Supplier, this mystery, this anomaly who comes to his little room, observes the boy lying on the floor, doing his homework under the green light of the swag lamp. The Supplier approaches. He needs a babysitter.

"My weekend to keep the kid," he mumbles. "Your momma said I should ask … and I gotta step out, made other plans and my ex is just a real bitch about it. I just plain forgot so it'd be a big help if you could do this one thing for me. It's a favor, really," he says gruffly. The Supplier glints off a shifting smile at the boy. It twitches a bit, the boy observes. Jesse knows the Supplier's kid. He sometimes tags along, a boy of about three, quiet, who plays by himself most of the time.

"It'll be good for you to get out of this house too, out of your room, Jesse, always locked up in here."

'What good luck,' Jesse thinks. He and a few art class winners are going to Murray State University, and the boy needs money to pay for the trip. His weekend job had already ended because he is fifteen and had maxed out his hours in the poor kid's summer work project. The two hundred dollars he earned already went for a Sears three-piece tan suit that Jesse hopes to wear to his first real job, for white paint for the front porch columns splitting into flaking squares from the heat of the sun, and the rest he gave to Jeannie Mae in exchange for staying there. The charge for food and transportation to and from the university is more than twenty dollars, and the boy is busted.

As arranged, the Supplier picks Jesse up around six, driving him out to his house, well past the desolation of country surrounding Paducah on all sides, an hour along small winding roads leading farther than nowhere. It is a forlorn and sinewy building with no other houses for miles like most of Kentucky. When they arrive it is seemingly abandoned. No lights show in the windows. The debris casually advertises that the main house hasn't been occupied for a while. The Supplier's apartment is leveraged over a garage covered from roof to siding in faded, hunter green asphalt shingles, and stripped-out beige trim, with mountains of undisturbed leaves, wet newspapers, and bleached-out bags of aluminum cans piling together around the staircase to the door above. They both hold the weak handrail, cautiously trying the spongy wooden stairs stripped of color and safety by the elements, leading to the small apartment above it. It is the kind of overlooked place best forgotten.

As the two make their way up the creaking stairs, the Supplier nervously chatters, little small talk, baffling the boy.

"Yeah, so I lost pretty much everything in the divorce and rent this little outta-the-way place for the time being, but it's good enough for me. I just work down the road about ten mile from here. I hope you like it."

It's a strange thing to say, Jesse concludes.

The Supplier grins with little facial jerks, a tick that is a transitory smile, nonstop toothy smirks ending as quickly as they appear, as he lets them both into a harshly lit, squat place with shabby, dated furniture and a singular 1950s German Alps print on the wall. The corner is busted and Scotch-taped together, but the tape has yellowed like the print. The place seems seldom used, almost abandoned, like the house below it. The boy is accustomed to such furnishings and isn't ill-at-ease. The large room has a makeshift kitchen with yellow-

and-white-speckled Formica countertops trimmed in rusting chrome, and little pale green metal hospital cabinets, a brown square couch the color of gravel road dust grouped with a couple of unmatched recliners, a kitchenette dining room set with two chairs, a small dorm-sized fridge on the counter, and a hot plate but no stove. In a small hallway, two doors to the bathroom and small bedroom are ajar.

"That all came with the apartment," he says, looking around like it is the first time and he is apologizing. "None of it's mine." The apartment traps the indistinct scent of unwashed bodies, the stale odors of decaying leaves and mold.

The boy nods, appreciating the place, looking around trying to look impressed, and shakes his head absentmindedly in agreement to whatever the Supplier is saying, trying to be personable to a man he doesn't know, practicing his best guest skills, a requisite politeness. The dealer's nervous chat and distracted straightening up of the tiny apartment runs its course and slows. Watching the boy, he finishes picking up the piles of work shirts and blue Dickies trousers and moving them from the couch and chair, folding worn-then-slipped-off jeans and hanging flannel shirts on wire hangers on a yellow rope nailed to the wall, tossing crumpled underwear and tube socks from the floor into the open door of the bedroom, picking up empty cans from the coffee table and putting them in the paper sack that stands in for a trash can on the kitchen counter, while the boy absentmindedly waits for instructions.

Finally, just after the quiet that finally sets in between them becomes too pressing, and because it becomes obvious to the boy, Jesse asks about the Supplier's kid. The nervous clamor resumes.

"Oh. He ain't here yet. His momma'll deliver him in a minute." The man explains that he is going to use that little free time to grab a shower, if the boy don't mind, and it won't be long and he'd pay for the boy's time. "Just wait right here and answer the door if my ex-wife comes."

The boy looks around while the Supplier showers but there is little to look at, so he waits on the cleared-off side arm of the couch, the Supplier forgetting the other half of it. Nobody comes. The Supplier re-enters the scene in a towel, continuing with the small talk, asking for a beer out of the fridge

"… And you want one too? I don't mind and I won't say nothin' to your old lady if you don't." That jerking smile again. Jesse fetches the beer.

"I better not if I'm watching your kid. Any other time, sure!" The boy makes nice and maybe more money down the road. The boy hands him his beer.

The Supplier collects the beer but also takes advantage of the boy being so close by grabbing his arm, and holding the boy there, suspended, the dealer looking at him in a strange new way. His lids lower and his mouth slacks almost imperceptibly while he stares at the face of the boy for what seems like a long time, looking for recognition, permission. The boy can't tell if the dealer thinks he stole something while he was in the shower but doesn't know how to put it into words. 'What could I steal? There's nothing here,' the boy thinks, as his mind races. As the dealer inhales, the boy remembers that look. He has seen it before but couldn't remember where. The dealer moves his beer hand behind the boy.

"So I gotta say, you ain't really here to watch Robby," the dealer says, pulling the boy in until his bony chest is pressed against the bulge of his protruding, distended stomach. He drags the boy up so close to his chest that he sees the graying bits of hair at eye level, smells the beer going stale in his mouth, and tries pulling away from the realization of what is going on as the Supplier rasps about other plans he has for all of this time the two of them now have without his kid, about how they are going to do this real slow.

Jesse realizes that the nervous laughter is coming out of his own throat.

This dealer, this user, sets his beer down, his other hand still clamped onto the boy's thin freckled arm, and slowly starts touching the chestnut hair hanging over the boy's eyes and massaging the back of his neck with the wetness of his cold beer hand. The boy tenses, goes rigid, trying unsuccessfully to pull away from the sinewy clutch as he stares at this hand on his arm. The boy's mind numbs, knowing any threat from a father unseen for six years isn't carrying any weight with this Supplier. No thoughts materialize about what to do next or what these mysterious things he mentions might be or why he thinks the boy should perform them. The boy releases himself for an instant and discovers that it is just a skinny kid squirming to get away, trying to get out, trying to stop the unstoppable.

The user drops his towel and pushes the boy's hand down into the fat of his pubic mound and the coarse hair around it, onto his genitals, rubbing the boy's knotted fist against him as Jesse twists. He realizes he is crying now.

The boy hasn't seen anyone with pubic hair, hasn't seen his father naked, and hasn't seen his mother in her brassiere and panties, only in a slip once. This disjointed thought is in his mind, and simultaneously the boy is mesmerized and appalled by what is happening to this disconnected kid, as he cannot help him get away. The Supplier is able to do it easily as the boy's resistance is feeble, effortlessly countered by his own strength made from manual labor coursing through his heavyset muscles, and he likes that the boy is mute, that he is crying, terrified, and struggling timidly in his confusion.

Jesse, conscious again that he is in the grips of this Supplier, this dealer, can tell in that instant that struggle excites the man, that a child excites him, and the boy is now made nauseous by the man's excitement, by the hot stale beer breath on his face and in his hair and on his neck, and the coarse fur scraping his flesh. In that confusion, the boy utters no word, forgets yelling out; he is accustomed to a noiseless existence, inaudible, making no waves, not even here, not here, not even with this. The sorry struggle rallies the dealer's efforts and his breath is now shallow and gruff, hands traveling down the boy's thin ribs where bone and muscle meet spine. He pushes verbs of his appetite into the boy through a slack mouth now wet and salacious on the child's neck, in his ears, drenching gaunt shoulders, hands sliding between powerless legs, lifting the boy off his feet and into his dank, sticky skin. The tenement blurs. The boy wonders about escape, envisions it so often in the abstract, wonders how to stop, but the two are in the middle of nowhere and nobody is home below them. What if anything is the appropriate reaction to this unwelcome attention from this user, this dealer to his mother and the Usurper but not him, this adult, this Man? The boy's consternation, the fact that the advance is unwanted, are lost on the dealer. Jesse races to find the source of some capitulation that he somehow asked for this. Steeled to his objective, furtive leathery hands press into flesh, the boy's mind hazes, freezes up, circuitry overloaded. His loveless life is reduced to this sweating, grappling old man, vile with lust, stinking spittle slathered over his bony neck and shoulder. Is this love? *Is it repellant and disgusting and against your will* flashes through the child's mind. There is no time to answer. Without another wasted second, the Supplier lifts the boy up by his haunches, legs dangling and limply kicking at him, still inoperable, and paralyzed to kicking, squirming arms pinned between the user's chest and the crushing arm that drives the boy's breath out of him, lugging the whimpering boy into the cramped bedroom. It is too much to endure. The boy's mind now wanders away from this helpless child, unable to assist and dismayed at refusing to help himself, the Supplier pressing his limp kid face down onto the bed, the boy instinctively balling up there, clothed, arms clamped under knees, locked there, unable to speak, unable to extricate himself physically from this mess he allowed himself to get into, unable to figure out how to protect himself from he knew not what, to return himself to his little angle of protected space under the stairs of that red brick duplex.

The user lies down naked on the boy's clothed body, pushing himself and his excitement into the boy's frame, forcing the boy flat on his stomach, yanking spindly legs straight, pressing himself into the threadbare and slick fabric of boy jeans, dripping sweat into thin pant legs soaked by his excitement, pinioning boy arms to his sides with his knees, hands on the boy's shoulders and upper arms, grinding the child into the bed as he relishes his prize. He pins him to the bed as the boy's grandmother did with the wayward chickens needing wings clipped, assured that they would not get away under the heel of her bare foot. He is massive on top of the boy's thin, malnourished frame and he wriggles himself in between thighs and works his hands into the boy's belly, undoing his pants as Jesse futilely squirms against his success. The user pushes those down just far enough to begin his work as the boy stifles screams of terror now into the mattress and dirty pillow, not knowing what to do or why he invited this somehow. The Supplier takes his time. He masks his eagerness to consume his prize with jerky movements meant to be tender and croons soothing words as if he were making love to an adult with reassurances and how beautiful this or that is, but the boy is arrested with fear and shock. He enters the boy first with coarse sandpapered fingers and then with the hardened adult male parts that the boy too owns and so secretly handled himself, in the privacy of a dirty bathroom when nobody was looking, thinking thoughts that are nothing compared to this: the sliding in and out, spitting on fingers, shoving them into the boy as he thrashed in alternating red and white pain, fighting and flailing now to get out from under the hand now pressing the boy's ribcage into the mattress, then pulling them out, holding the boy down the entire time by his heavy hand on his spine at the base of his neck, cutting off the boy's screams and breathing, his alternating shrieks and sobs, pushing in again with his prick, cutting off bleeding pain by pushing the boy's face deeper into the pillow with his hand over the entire side of the boy's face now, fingers sometimes over, sometimes in the boy's mouth, until his nose feels like it will come out of joint, then pulling out and putting more fingers in again.

Simultaneously, the dealer husks words of how thrilling this must be for the boy, his first time, isn't it, isn't he enjoying it, you want it there I can tell, and what a nice time he is having and how much the Supplier likes him: the words of a lunatic who cannot be having the same experience as the boy who is there but not there, present but now in some other reality. His sadism is apparent as the user becomes more fervent, the boy violently resisting his efforts. The firstborn boy squirms away from the rawness, protecting himself from the searing pain as the user stretches into him, but his legs lock the boy's thin legs in place as he finds his rhythm. The user repeats, telling the boy that he knows it hurts but that he will make him feel good, oh so good, if he just lets him, and the boy wants it to quit hurting so badly he tries with all of his might to make it stop hurting, but the user is a liar.

After, the boy just lies there, pants and underwear crushed down, cutting into thighs, and no sound comes out now, making no movement of any kind as the Supplier lies on top of him, still inside him. The boy closes another corridor, making himself small, insignificant, something not to be bothered with. The silent cries he does not know he is making suddenly enter his ears too, but then somehow stop of their own accord, and he rests there with nothing but whiteness in his brain as the user croons and strokes his hair like they are lovers. Jesse returns to the boy after it is over, wanting to run, but he does not know how at this point and is too exhausted and shaken from his struggle to manage or even care to run. The physical damage seems insurmountable. The user undresses the boy slowly, carefully, and the boy lets him because he is broken already. The rest does not matter. The boy has failed. The Supplier tidily puts the child's shoes together, then the socks, then the pants folded across the chair, then his little underwear laid out on top, like the boy is going to school, like he is an adolescent again, and the boy allows all of this, allows himself to be undressed. He is bleeding and the user says, "You're bleeding," like he is completely surprised by this, and he leaves the boy and the boy does not bother to move. Jesse slips away again, leaving this child to his own devices, escapes to another place where he cannot hear him cry like a little wimp, see his baby tears, somewhere where he won't be sickened by this child unable to man up. He leaves that little youth lying on the bed and he turns away from him.

The User runs a hot bath in that gray ring-stained tub with scratches from who knows what in the bottom, haphazard black lines cut into the porcelain, putting salts in the water, and he carries that child in and places him in the hot water, and the kid shakes all over as if his cold clammy skin were still connecting at all of those indecent points. The entire time, the little boy says nothing as the water washes away blood and semen and the stale smell of spit and beer and his sweat, and the salts sting raw and bleeding parts of his ass that he never knew could be used in that way. The User croons to the child that they can do this again if he wants, but it won't do any good to tell his momma about their secret because she wouldn't believe it about him, a family friend, a dealer, as he runs the washcloth over tender skin, fondling his genitals and caressing his ass and legs and thighs. It dawns on the boy then, through his state of shock that she'd somehow know!

Jeannie Mae would figure out what happened, because the User hadn't brought the boy there to babysit, and Jesse can't make up any story about watching a kid because he has no idea how to make that kind of stuff up while hiding such a tremendous assault and pass it off. The User had brought the boy there to fuck him and the boy isn't going to get paid to babysit, and Jeannie will figure it all out. That is something that his mind can actually process, so he fixates on that instead.

"I cain't…go back. Without babysitting money. She's gonna know and I cain't lie about this. I'll tell her. I need to show my momma the babysitting money or you're in real trouble," the boy blurts out.

"Tell your momma and she'll put you in the street, kid. That's just fact. She talks about gettin' you kids out of the house all the time. Maybe you'll end up livin' with me. Think she'll let a little whore stay in her house?" The user is now mad that the boy reduces this special thing they have together to getting paid and quips back that he isn't going to pay a little whore for what they did so he should just shut up about that, and the anger is murderous, but somehow the man seems hurt by the turn of conversation, and the shock is new and fresh and somehow more humiliating, which shuts the kid up again.

"This makes me a whore," the boy thinks astonishingly.

In a whole new terror, the boy just wants to be home, in his bed under the stairs, and hopes the mother won't ask, won't want to see the money he made. And when they arrive, the Supplier slips in and jovially chats with Jeannie Mae and the Usurper in a low voice, like nothing transpired, and there are low chuckles and politeness and this goes on for an eternity as the boy stands on the edge, mute with shock. And Jeannie does not ask and the boy is dumbfounded, paralyzed. The boy engages, the shock purges, and he bolts for his room, climbing as far as possible under the covers in the far end of the bed where it meets the diagonal timbers of the ceiling covering the stairs above, and curls up there, staring stupidly at the perfect darkness created by that constricted space under those stretched out stairs, and with the blankets pulled tightly across his head and back, still feeling the Supplier's hands pressing there, pretending to sleep so tears can flow out of clenched eyelids. But he is not racked with sobs, for which he is thankful, because he is not a child any longer. And nobody comes. Nobody asks how it went. It is as if it had not happened. But it did happen. And it would happen again.

The next day is Saturday, and the Supplier arrives unexpectedly for the boy again. He pulls up and the boy hears him arrive and panics, struck once more by white terror. The boy devours every word, pouncing on them like a cat, searching for clues in his small talk as he presses himself into the extremity, the darkest region, of the twin bed with his back against the wall that meets the diagonal of the stairs. The boy counts to himself each footstep on the hallway boards, scraping loudly from the living room to the only door on the right side of the hall, and ceases breathing as the Supplier calls him, "Hey, Jesse Earl! Wake up, boy! Come on down here now, Jesse." and "It's okay, come over again. Your momma don't mind...." When ignoring him is no longer effective, the boy feigns sleep. Unsuccessfully cajoling the boy out of his nest, all goes silent and the boy breathes again. Then Jeannie Mae enters his makeshift room. She commands the tone only mothers have, demanding why her boy is so rude and what in the world is wrong with him, acting like that, saying he asked for this and to get down here *now* and go with the Supplier again. "No," whispers out. Then the boy finds his voice and pleads weakly that he isn't feeling well and does not want to go, is not going, but the mother insists that he stop acting like a little brat and to get down here and I mean *now*!

Incredulous, Jesse refuses to believe that his mother does not know, hasn't figured it out, that the horror had been too great for a mother's intuition to ignore and that she is oblivious. Jesse chokes on blurting out that she didn't protect him like she was supposed to, like she once had, that he still needed her like so many times before, and that *this* is the time for that kind of battle for his sanctity, for his defiled innocence, and yet he knows that what has been done to him has stripped him of all of that and there is no going back, that he must have done something, something to make all of this happen, but what? Deep within the boy, he embraces his responsibility for his own inaction, believing that on some level it was what he must have wanted, calling out for it to happen, participated in his own humiliation, such brutal undoing, that the User found the cues, the message, the go ahead. It must have come from the boy. The boy is the root cause. Otherwise, otherwise, Jesse would have protected that child, sheltered him, would have resisted that he was, at that moment, feebly wishing someone else would do it for him, calling futilely to the mother to excise him from his obligation as sentry for the assaulted child.

Jesse resigns himself to his fate, finally, because the discovery that it is his fault is too much to talk about, what he allowed to happen to that child and what a pussy he was to not stand up, fight back, to handle it like a man. That kid got what he deserved. And it also occurs to Jesse that it does not make *sense* that this is going to happen again and again and again, and what has he done, bringing this down upon himself, and who could he tell, friendless as he is, living among singular units of his family, those who do not talk about sex and rape and deviants and Users? And so he shuts up, does not cry out, not telling Jeannie Mae that all of this is true in what transpires, his own undoing, the perversions he welcomed onto his frail body, the destruction he elicits, and he refuses to share his shame, so he shuts up. Besides, his sister who told was sent away. Mute, Jesse climbs down from his sanctuary, resigned to his fate. He'd devise a plan but must find time to *think*. So the boy goes with the User and sits in the passenger seat like he is told, and the User drives away, taking the boy's hand and placing it on his leg like they are lovers and asking if he'd like to lay his head in his lap as he wrenches the mute boy by the arm, prone now into his crotch.

Jesse does not devise a plan finally. He lies there in a cold nauseous sweat as the User strokes his hair affectionately, sickened by the User but also by his own inaction. The boy lies there rigid and staring through the steering wheel up into the windshield with his hand mashed onto the User's leg where the User had placed it, crushing it there like they are lovers. He fucks the child again like the last time but this time in the back of his car, forced over the front seat unlatched and leaned forward, with the boy's knees jammed into the floorboard and his feet trapped onto the ledge of the back seat, the user's weight pinning the child into place and the crook of his arm strangling off the cries of pain as he takes him again.

And when the User takes the boy home, the child has grown.

"That motherfucker didn't pay me either time, Momma," he tells the mother flatly. "I'm not going to go again so don't bother asking."

And there must have been some resolve in the now man-boy's face. Some change. Jeannie does not insist that her son go again. The Supplier returns again and again, sometimes trying to talk to the man-boy from the underside of his bed with no response, without the bother of an answer, or sometimes with a "get the fuck outta here." In the end, an astute teacher foots the bill, covering travel costs to the art fair, and the man-boy takes that rendition of Napoleon on his charger crossing the Himalayas, and another drawing of a crowned Seagram's 7 from the Usurper's empty bottle, sitting next to a young girl on a grand piano, to State and is awarded first place, and he goes hungry and forgets all about getting fucked twice by some drug dealer who the mother and her third husband know, but not him. He burns the book he had foolishly taken along, his clothes and shoes from that first night, incinerates anything touched by that moment, wanting no lingering memory.

The Separation, 1979

It is only a few days after, countable in the number of hours that pass, before the pain extricates itself from the child-boy-man, the physical pain of the intrusion, of having been used, when the connection is made. It falls after Jesse arrives as usual, directly to his room, without a word to anyone. Quietly, as he does everything, he changes clothes and slips into the kitchen. It is only when he passes the threshold that he discovers the two of them there, sees the complexity of it all, the gossamer thread that binds the incidents, knotted there inextricably. It is then he discovers the secret. Time has become inconsequential to the mother and the Usurper in their haze. There they sit slumped back from the kitchen table with a yellow Bic butane lighter, heating water and soaking a cotton ball in the mixture in the bowl of a spoon Jesse often uses on his cereal, the remains of a crushed oxycodone tablet the boy recognizes as the same kind provided by the user who had fucked him twice, once in the moldy apartment and once over the front seat of his car, for a cost. Two bottles of pills, thirty count each, sit on the table between them, street value six hundred dollars, hypodermic needle between them.

She raises heavy lids and licks a set of dry lips, scolding her son: "Go to your room."

They do not mention it again, but he knows in that instant that she has ceased to see the boy, to see her children, to see herself, that she is lost to her medication, to her medicating. And it is years later that he realizes that perhaps she too was complicit in his murderous undoing, the undoing of her fourteen-year-old son, who was old enough to bleed. Perhaps he paid in ass for a six-hundred-dollar haul, so that a twenty must have seemed like a pretty big tip for whatever drugs the user had already traded for a virgin ass that he hits twice— three hundred dollars a go. But poor boys and poor girls are bought and sold all the time from the families of nobodies, and nobody notices. Except him. Jesse took notice.

No matter how normative one makes one's actions, others will see through you. Some secrets can't be hidden, not completely, and these small changes, these chinks in the armor, are revealed. Those his same age somehow discover, not the secret, but the abnormality that Jeannie knew about and exploited for her own gain. The boy rages because of its unfairness but does not know he is raging. He is an easy target because of his size, because of his caste, because his mother is married to a black man, because he is less than. The catcalls and the shoving and the threats and the gym-cum-English teacher who calls him Jessica now and whistles as he repeatedly sends the boy to the chalkboard each day, the onslaught is relentless until control overshadows his fear, a change that comes over his face when he realizes how much his ass is worth, the face that Jeannie understands when Jesse resolves to take it no longer.

Boy to man: the violent forcing—the betrayal—brings about early transformation. In those pleasant halfway years, sudden fear mixes with rage and strengthens that boy. In that crossroad, in this new understanding of the failures of a mother, without feeling, without protest or sting or privation, Jesse enters a public school bus carrying him home with his tremendous weight. Jesse does not know this recent crucible anodizes, burnishing the skin.

The older Freeman kid couldn't know it either, this boy's burden, strutting down the aisle, his target three seats in, on the right-hand side, slapping Jesse in the head, uttering "fag" loud enough for his friends trailing behind him. The boy crystalizes, congealing all that had transgressed, possessing him and turning on his oppressor, mouthing "FUCK. YOU. FREEMAN." Pandemonium of bored hoods urging any excitement ensues. "Your ass is getting kicked at your stop, bitch." The Freeman kid flattens out his words to a statement.

He could not know that Jesse has already had his ass taken, that it is not his to kick, wouldn't be kicked again as he exits at the boy's designated stop. The Freeman kid is larger than Jesse, confident in his physical skills, but Jesse does not see, holds no regard for it. He swings once, twice. Jesse watches from the sidelines as anger turns molten, making him quicker, easily dodging swings. The Freeman kid kicks at the boy. Fascinated, Jesse latches onto the Freeman kid's foot, wrenching hard, bringing the dazed tormenter face down onto the pavement, breaking out two front teeth on impact. Stunned and humiliated, the Freeman kid picks himself up, backing off from his *easy target*, begins walking away. Jesse makes up his mind. 'Never, never, never again, not you, not nobody will fuck me again,' he says quietly to himself, running ahead of the persecutor to his own house, running indoors. The Freeman kid must walk past the house, Jesse calculates. He has a plan now. Storming his mother's bedroom, busting the padlock, he erupts with her .38 pistol, the one the Usurper used to kill her dog to show her what he was capable of. Jesse marvels at its weight and the thrill of its surging power as he hauls it out in his frail hands to the front porch. The Freeman kid can't expect it, not this. Not at first. By the time he does lock eyes with the pistol, un-cocked but leveled directly at his face from the upper vantage point of the front porch, Jesse is tracking his every step. Terrified, the Freeman kid simultaneously ducks and runs a zig zag waddle across the street and into the abandoned lot with brush cover, screaming at his friends to run too. As fate has it, Jeannie Mae witnesses his ability to not get fucked again, sees what he is now capable of. She drives up in the instant her son is tracking, watches him calmly stalking the torturer there, triggering his flight with her pistol.

"Jess, put that down, just put it down right now and I mean it, it just ain't *worth* it!"

The boy is calm and glances her way, locking eyes with his mother, but completes the Freeman trace until the bully is out of sight. He then lowers the weapon. "I won't have it happen to me again, momma, never again, by God."

Her son levels the facts as collectedly as he can, no tears this time, no folding, steeled to his resolve still. Jeannie listens like old times, white knuckled, nervously agreeing to the murder in the child's eyes. She defends him to the authorities, but word gets out that Jesse both knocked out the Freeman kid's front teeth and tried to shoot him and would have if it hadn't been for his momma. With the news, harassment comes to a standstill. In that heady instance of power, of now thorough disassociation, Jesse is liberated from his mother's confession and the lack thereof that had made him, but won't be made again. Fucking him won't be easy. Not again.

Being a new man at fifteen is easier after that, for a while at least, until it is normal, accepted. That look men like the User has lingers, seeps deeply into his clothes and pores, sullies him. The boy now knows what it looks like when men look at him, men who have it. With that kind of knowledge, it is easy to find, and finding it became part of the combat, part of the prize, part of his own version of Confessions. Each time now, he controls circumstances, controls the variables, and the elements that make it transpire empower him, who he picks, what he allows them to do, what he says no fucking way to. He understands the Usurper, what it feels like to use up. He picks them up while perpetually walking, walking, walking in the deserted downtown to the Greyhound bus station or to the riverfront where the most licentious acts take place, actions of those filaments dreamt up in the secreted places of minds, out of the way of acceptable society, behind the protection of those high flood walls along the riverbanks designed to keep the wild muddy waters at bay. It happens in furtive passenger seats with overeager married drivers with a wife and kids at home, after he drinks a half pint of schnapps he makes them buy for him.

Sometimes it is an alleyway between buildings built for seamen who worked the river a century ago, slanted with the weight of its own history grinding against and pushing it down into its faulty foundation. At the age of fifteen, this new man picks up the couple that live over the Mr. Tuxedo and fucks them in their bed, together, because he is in control. The rage subsides when he is in control. The community college professor with the Mazda 626 is a particular prize, because he is handsome and flirts outrageously with the boy of fifteen, secretly grazing fingertips over hairless arms along with technical explanations, lingering on the boy during class outings for some hands-on experimentation with lighting and sound equipment and videotaping. The concert pianist fucks the boy on the pristine white carpet of his living room, after the kid bikes all the way to the house with a two-storied foyer on the west side of town. Overstaying his curfew, Jesse defiantly sleeps in his mother's truck because she won't let him in at such a late hour. His behavior side skirts conversation.

Jesse Earl supposes that Jeannie saw his modification that fucking day and silence is her acquiescence, an admission of guilt, a consensus between them. That kind of fire consumes or it cleanses.

Jeannie has her own price to pay for his pound of flesh, if she notices through her sometimes daze. It isn't every time, but it grows more frequent. Either way, her guilt is no longer an item of interest to him because she refuses confession. He hugs her as she washes the dishes from the supper he hasn't bothered to show up for and tells her what a great mom she is, still drunk with the sweet smell of cinnamon on his breath as he says it, still stinking of rutting. She pretends not to notice, but her lack of response speaks of her noticing. And the secret trade of his ass for knowledge and pleasure and revenge and rage, never money, continues unabated. Some men guess and some ignore and some pretend not to know that he is fifteen or sixteen or seventeen, and still they do it with him. And he allows it to be done to him, but soon rage turns into something else, into a way to both rage and keep his eye on the prize. With each conquest he discovers what he is looking for. He covets. He admires. He learns how others conduct their lives within the lie. His rutting evolves into hands-on experience that, if not perfect, allows him to see past the walk-in closet on Sixth Street.

Without his sex these are not homes and cars and businesses where his kind are welcome, so he takes it all in and proximity drives him to finish what he starts, what he intends to do, to emulate, to pantomime the normality he finds in his tricks. He grills them with questions, he compliments, soaks up their small talk. After, he is sixteen, taking a job at the gay bar owned by the ex of the friend of the mother, who is a stripper sometimes, sometimes the old lady of a biker, sometimes in jail for bad checks, and Jesse cleans up after bar nights on Saturdays and Sundays. He meets drag queens who invite him to house parties that last all day or all weekend, and he no longer shows up at home, and he drinks and forgets the hideous pain, and abandons and slips so far away, and executes himself with others with precision: forgetting, leaving behind, removing himself, and calling the shots and calling the shots and calling the shots, but most ardently forgetting. And this defines his last two years as a sum of the unit, as he is now a party of one, until he finally slips away to college, where such behaviors are expected and normalized. That is his legacy, how he became what he becomes before he remakes himself with all of this knowledge into someone respectable, someone with worth. Someone who is not a whore. It is a vicious learning curve.

Luck is with him. He is lucky finally, a repayment of sorts. Jesse, at the last instant, finds some small salvations that illuminate this obscured transition, this change he has had to take with no direction and little support. The guidance counselor arrives at his puny school exit meeting, and he leaves her office dejected, returning to class. It should end there, his story. It should end badly for him. Perhaps it should end with him becoming a food chain manager and renting a trailer at the Saddle and Spur Trailer Court, somewhere on the outskirts of that broken downtown, subsisting with 32,000 other miserable units until he breaks down like those around him. In eating his anger raw, washing it down with drink and sex, he burns up some of that fear and rage. He escapes with an accomplice, an observant teacher who presses him, prepares, presents him with the opportunity to sever, to list himself as financially independent. Using the little money he makes at the gay bar and a scholarship allows him to slough off, lighten the load for the next level, to revel in that first step, that first departure. From there, he sees his own light for the first time: limp, leaden, thudding like a dull headache. Jesse extracts himself unceremoniously, bound for the little university and with little remorse for what is left behind.

Exodus, 1983

In the long-distance line, there is a kind of confessional built between the two. Jesse is a young man in transformation, school to college. It is easier not to be the prodigal son when the aftermath can be avoided, without consequence of past, without the ramifications and costliness of forgiveness. Jesse calls her after his metamorphosis, shedding past and immoralities, feeding the public machine quarter after quarter to buy the precious minutes he has for them only, uninterrupted. Confessions begin with a genuine heartache and a recollection that the mother once gave clemency, permission to confess. It starts with the departure of the Carbondale boy studying biological sciences. The loss occurs in the same fashion in which she lost Cherokee, too much one-sided love. That seemingly trivial loss, feeling like a great one, is acute because of the first actual, real intimacies afforded Jesse by another, outside of *us*. Although he has not entrusted the Carbondale boy to his own secreted-away histories, histories that are too great to begin, the Carbondale boy lavishes the young man with confidences of his own loss, which form the bond. It endears Jesse, even though he cannot express the cumulated emotions and release of impurities associated with endearment and trust. The callus is still too thick and too enduring. It is immovable, and he pushes the Carbondale boy away, out, his grievances against intimacy too great to confess.

In the hope of confiding, and the possibility of a confession, Jesse, the young man, is the son once more. It is a possibility that stems from this loss that the son mourns with Jeannie Mae, having reached out to her over the long distance of a phone line, in a telephone booth the approximate size of a confessional, closed away from all others that are not their own. The distance keeps the cold out, should the cold come, should the professed acceptance of the mother for the son be a sham. It is a gamble the son takes, acknowledging to her. Perhaps, too, it is that distance that opens the possibility for her to accept the son's penitence for those shortcomings a son has to a mother, and she responds as a mother to her child— not the trinity but something more intimate, something with love and compassion and acceptance that begins a turning point, a glossing over, and the bygones that only transpire between a mother and child once her child moves toward the understanding that adults have, forgiving fully and without judgment. Neither compromise the seal of the confessional they together forge. The firstborn boy maintains a sacred confidence for those college years in the same pattern of reaching out, on his instigation, compelled by his need, from the solitude of a phone booth.

But Jeannie Mae not only accepts the son's penitent privilege, she is also penitent to her son, as well. Compelled by the intimacy, compelled by her need, Jeannie opens a full heart and lets the contents spill out into a blank, black receiver, confesses her pain to the son in that same way, not all, but some, enough to bridge the abyss, the chasm.

"Don't you think I know he's awful for me, to me and all of you too? I knew from the day we met what a bastard he is, Jess. I didn't have it left in me for anybody else. Who'd have me by the way? I knew that and I think he knew too, was lookin' for it in me. That's why we ended up together; a couple of the low, bein' low together made it natural. It was like that but I never meant for it to get out of hand like it did, sorta spilled outta control and I never figured out how to get it all back in again. And God knows I tried to get rid of him, I really tried—for y'alls kids' sakes and for me too, I wanted him outta our lives."

She whispers out about the Usurper, the dirty one, and how it came that he is her third husband, about why she didn't leave. She speaks out about his endless infidelities and how that ceased to matter to her because she did not love him and perhaps had never loved him. "Everybody is against me. Y'all was against me too, and that made me hard-headed to prove everybody wrong. I been like that since I was a little girl and I got that from my momma, I suppose. I can't lie." Jeannie speaks about entering into the relationship out of defiance and spite, out of feeling young again, wanted, that there was some of that too, but then defying the consternation of those around her by staying with him. She tells the young man about how much she hated her family's unsolicited advice and the neighbors' tongue-wagging, and about the concussions and the fractures. She summons up for her son ruthless illustrations: Billy Wayne dragging her through the street by the hair of her head, bashed her face with a tire iron. She maps out the details of the Usurper's systematic degrading of her person until she confirms that she is less than, accepts her imposed isolation, ceases to struggle against her dependency.

She also unburdens about her raw first love with that Cunningham boy and about her Abundant Ripe Love for Cherokee, about all of the regret that she holds for both, and how this all could have turned out differently for her if the world hadn't been against them. The mother looses Marjorie from her memories, shaking out the truth and its putrefying shabbiness, how her mother's desperate lust for freedom turned her thinking and made all that was to come possible for her, changed her perspective on the imaginable. And then she confesses to having had a first child, a daughter whom she does not speak of aloud—Marjorie—gone, gone. She moans out the name still, haunting the boy over the receiver, slipping from the small, black holes of black plastic like a séance. Jesse waits too late to seek the girl out, too late for the opportunity to tell Jeannie that he has found this first girl and that she looks just like Jeannie's mother Marjorie or that she loves horseback riding more than anything else, that she loves living on her Iowa farm like Jeannie Mae, because of all of the animals. He cannot tell her because he waits too long and the discovery happens after his mother's death, and after the death of her first daughter too.

"I want you to know how bad I feel about my medicine and you kids. It isn't my fault really, but it's not right. Still isn't. I hate what I turned into because of it. It's this Marfan's, you know. But I need 'em now more than ever. Our whole side of the family die out before 50 and I expect the same'll come to me. Besides, who cares if I quit or don't, by now. You turned out okay but I just don't know about your sisters."

She confides in him her escape, that it was once necessary because of chronic and overwhelming health issues, and then how easy it became to be dependent, to escape the bitterness that engulfed what she had become with him, reduced, less than, like the old times with all the false starts. Unwittingly, she is unable to link the two, staying with the Usurper and the escape she designs for herself, which incidentally ensnares her simultaneously, ironically linking the two of them together in their dependency. Over the next four years she confesses all of this and more, but the calls and the letters begin to be less frequent, slip away with the months because the son is now distant by necessity, cannot bear the burden.

The extreme and overpowering violence consuming the boy dulls once validation is complete, once he understands her fragility and his worth; it lessens after exorcism and grows less noxious. The compassion welling from her confessions weighs more now, a vulnerable burden illuminating her humanity, which Jesse does not want to see. Lifting Madonna's veil from his eyes, he studies the cracks, the imperfections, and fingerprints in the all-too-human clay.

Jesse cannot save her, so he saves himself instead. His calls slow and then stop. And the line is broken. In this last eddy, Jeannie too becomes broken and lost. She is unable to do it herself. The boy is unable to help her to do it. It is insurmountable. In this way, in no longer trying to save her, she dies. That is how he plays his part in her death.

In those intermittent lulls of intimacy between them, in the distance he places between himself and everyone else, the harvester of souls comes with rancorous swiftness and in breathtaking succession pulls apart Etta and then Marvin, devours her sisters and her brother Donnie, and reaps the souls of Papaw Ed and Mamaw Jessie and Starr Renee into his great maw where the dead reside. And in his insolence and silence, no unit thinks to send notification, no beacon nor funeral pyre. Jesse has missed too many Sunday dinners and there is nobody left when his ostracism is complete, if it ever would be. It is just desserts for who Jesse has become, the boy who leaves them all behind in his recreating of himself. He left. They stay. It is an unspoken retaliation for leaving, for no longer being a part of. The tethering is more tenuous, threadbare. Jeannie is in the hospital three weeks with her aortic dissection before they tell him.

He returns to Paducah and visits her there, in the hospital, where old times and memories overtake the two, urgency of signing final papers overshadowing them, patching the relationship with the pathetic little knowing's and reminiscing's a mother and son have, but it is not enough to sustain his interest in her cries for help that still come after him, over the pay phone of the student union building, so that each receiver he cradles hangs up on her calls for the kind of absolution that only a son can give his mother. He cannot wash away the sins of her life, and he could not take them upon himself. He is not strong enough to do it while attempting to save himself, so he sacrifices her instead.

Jesse visits, acknowledging silently the consequences of his inaction, the decay and the rot of someone stagnant, of someone resigned to death. The final visits transpire first in a subsidized housing apartment she sequesters herself into, with peeling paint and piling garbage, rife with cockroaches, and then finally the one-room cinderblock house in La Center, common with the heaviness of someone waiting for death, who abandons the contest with nothing remaining for the victor, ceasing to struggle against the onslaught of death that is within her. He sees her shrouds of filament curtains filthy with waste and heavy with unchecked vermin taking their sacrament on the piles of squalid dishes burdening the counters, stove, and table. It is those minute beasts that reproduce so rapidly on such decay as this, gorging on the untended, overflowing stacks of garbage and unwashed clothes accumulating in the corners of her purgatory. No one assists her in her confined bed. The people who are left behind with her—the eldest daughter and her children, the Third Husband who is sometimes there—wait for the other shoe to drop; they learn those lessons instead, forgetting what came before, the great woman she had been. This last vacuous-vestige-woman they emulate, carry forward on her sacred bier this last, lesser trace and portion of the mother instead of the more radiant purer one, venerating this oxidizing cast and not the resplendent idol she had been in her youth.

Jesse looks on, unfeeling, as she and her Usurper fill their needles and strap off their arms and amble to that place where none of her diseased life matters, where death does not wait for her, and he knows in that witnessing that he should stay and save her. Curtly, the boy severs remaining bonds and shrinks away and does not look back, cursing himself for failing to resist this last need to see this lesser mother, for having made concrete an abstract that is now etched viscerally into his pictorial reality, his witnessing that which he brought about with his ass and those pills in the days that could have possibly changed this, and by his separation and his saving himself instead. It is a memorial that cannot be erased, making cloudy the pureness of the woman who raised her son up, shielded him, and then let him go.

It is Saint Valentine's Day that Jeannie dies in the tenement occupied by that Cunningham girl and her children, reared by Jeannie in the absence of a mother that Lisa refuses to become. It is they who accept this fallen woman, this flawed vestige, and become part of the relic, participating in what she falls into, they who actively forget who Jeannie had been. These are her vestal attendants, striding tolerantly alongside Death with her after Jeannie reconciles herself to death; they are there for her moment. Jeannie Mae is high. She is laughing with them.

The woman stands as if hearing her name called out, alerted to the fact that she had been called, and then she dies on the filth-stained sofa, covered with a blanket to hide the tears in the fabric, in a subsidized little house made of the same materials as the cinderblock prison that comes to hold the Usurper after, followed in a procession by that Cunningham girl, her son, then older daughter, and then younger daughter. Jeannie's three grandchildren are incarcerated in that same jail. One after the other, each one pageants into that cinderblock city jail within view of that little house on Second Street on the black side of town, in a successive line of living failure, of living without her, of living in the vacuum left behind her. It is the Cunningham girl, the other portion of *they*, who first emulates, copies, pantomimes her last rituals of self-sedation, self-seduction, living in the lesser caste of who Jeannie Mae had become in her final days. That Cunningham girl takes up the gauntlet, the challenge, the baton, and she carries it forth, like the mother, until it too snuffs out the flame, until it leaves her broken too, an unscabbarded sheath, an empty vessel. Lisa Jo teaches the moral to her three children much more quickly than Jeannie learned the lesson.

Jesse finishes college. The young man, with 200 dollars and a satchel of clothes, takes the Greyhound bus to Washington, DC. There, he finishes the last of his three jobs for the evening and walks to his little shared apartment on the hill in Rosslyn, overlooking the Marine Memorial and, farther on, the white outlines of monuments in the District of Columbia below. That brittle February evening, on the cusp of the end of Saint Valentine's Day, Jesse arrives home a little after eleven o'clock in the evening. He disrobes quickly, simultaneously tidying his things away in the orderly fashion he does everything, mentally preparing the list for the deep scrubbing he'd give the apartment, and thinking about asking his boyfriend, Larry Fish, to see Kubrick's *Lolita* sometime that weekend if it doesn't interfere with his new play. The boy is an actor. Amidst his mental cacophony, Jesse pushes the blinking red play button on the black cassette tape recorder and answering machine plugged to the taupe-colored Princess corded telephone. The first message is an unknown voice with the unmistakable cadence of a Kentuckian, rushing the 32,000 voices of Paducah back to him, telling him that his mother is at the hospital and he should come quick, that her aorta ruptured again, that it doesn't look good, that they will call when they know more news. Then, incongruous to the urgency of the situation and his desperation to know, a pre-recorded telemarketing message follows, stretches on forever, a disguised solicitation aimed at him being lucky, that he has won the prize, that he is going to paradise, free tickets to Hawaii, that it is a dream, that he should answer the call.

The other shoe falls. The third message informs him in that same unknown voice, with that affected vibrato reserved for sad news, that she is gone and that it is too late. He is too late for goodbyes. It tells him that she died with her aorta pumping four of the five quarts of her blood into her chest cavity, staining her face, her neck, and her chest crimson with her blood—death by exsanguination, usually reserved for slaughtered livestock—and the first boy remembers instead all of those men chaining up the white cow and cutting her throat and bleeding her out, cutting her up into more manageable pieces, except this time the livestock had led herself to slaughter.

Jeannie Mae chose the time and the place and did not wait for Death to come to her, instead greeting him with defiance. In his devastation, the boy remembers her mother Marjorie and the terms she set for herself, for her own self-annihilation, and despite his callous back turned against her, he weeps without consolation at the loss, but mainly weeps for his own shortcomings to his mother. Jeannie Mae administers her own sedation prior to the act, stunning herself, anesthetizing her body, and she dies without resuscitation, willfully going. Jeannie had been anticipating her moment for a long time before that instant, had written her salutations for Death in her own hand. She prepared as best she could with the drugs and the forgetting and the want of trying any longer. She could not have been surprised as the maw opened finally for her, too.

A Song of Requiem, 1992

The son is fixated on the fact that it has been exactly one month and three days after her birthday, on Saint Valentine's Day, the day of hearts that hers gave out. The Valentine's flowers he sent are still fresh on display as a token of his love when he arrives in that little town once more, for his final farewell. The check and the card he sent are still in her purse, opened, appreciated, and itemized with everything of value in that one little bag. The quick and inept funeral completes her final slow and drugged anticlimax. Time hurries on, forgetting her once-fine life and the snuffed-out dreams she set aside to finish later, then suspended, ultimately finding she could not resurrect history.

The reduced family can't afford a burial, so they cremate the woman. The units are emotionally and financially destitute. The little La Center funeral home accepts only cash in exchange for death. Her penniless family can't purchase a respectable urn to hide away her remains, the son arriving too late to make the exchange, to shroud her properly.

In their haste, their inability to plan, her coffin is instead a simple cardboard box, the size in which she stored letters from Cherokee, from her sisters, from her son, until her death. And the box is hand-scrawled in slanting black marker with her number, lettering out SKINNER across the top by the undertaker. It sits humbly on a table that usually holds offering plates, draped in a pale blue sateen cloth with golden trim and a felt cut-out of the chalice for Christ's blood on one end and the Lamb of God on the other. Looking at the back of the room, Jesse sees Daryl, Jennie Kaye's first boyfriend. As the fates come first circle, he is the gravedigger, running the crematorium for the funeral home. The gravedigger had done to Jennie Kaye, what that Cunningham boy had done to Jeannie, and that Morris boy to Lisa Jo: the lesser parallel to Jeannie's own Cunningham boy, and now the undertaker cremating Jennie Kaye's mother. He walks over.

"You know how Jeannie was, Jesse Earl. She was jest too stubborn to burn," as if he is telling a joke. "It was the damnedest thing. When I opened the kiln, yer momma's right arm was still pokin' up toward the sky so I jest ran her through again," he says, smiling. He still wears his dark green work jumpsuit.

The son sits through that funeral wondering what she was reaching for, what she had missed. Or if maybe she finally found a way to get past that clothesline that runs all the way to the end of the yard and ends in a dead-end stop, like her mother. He hopes so. He expects she finally escaped the Usurper and all the earthly shortfalls she lamented.

Jeannie actively ground herself out, faltering on her own standing. The mother defies Death by cheating her own measure with the resources available to her, as her mother did before her. Her life is not one that people remember, the brief transients who did not stay, but a scrap of patchwork family and faded friends, finding themselves in a tiny cinderblock Baptist church built for blacks in La Center, filling an enclave of a bleached generation of black matrons no longer begrudging a white woman and a black man, understanding that a life needs to be honored in the tradition of a race of people who know loss, hardship, and the power of lament. They are forgiving of those trespasses that her children cannot forgive. They understand falling short of the Glory, and that these kinds of spirals lead to the fallout of collateral-damaged loved ones, who are unable to escape the whirlpool of descent, the failures that come and come and come again and are sometimes expected but have no bearing on the soul.

As the assorted lot files into the chapel on a crisp February morning, a mourner drops a scarlet shawl shuffling into the hard little benches of the cold church, which another, trailing behind, picks up and places squarely atop the SKINNER box, not knowing that Jeannie has been so basely handled, relegated to a cardboard box, her remains swept from the concrete kiln, some scratched up and into this box, pitched inside, while most are tossed aside with the numberless faces before her. The box takes on a more welcome apparition of the girl who shrouded herself in a scarlet sweater meant by her grandmother to protect her, and it seems no coincidence and somehow fitting that she is lastly draped in her burial garment of scarlet.

'She would have liked that,' thinks her son, with a wavering smile, but he does not know if he means Etta, Marjorie, or his mother.

During the funeral, lovingly, these women guard over the traditions of honoring the dead, lifting up the part of her life that is good, extending their expertise in caring for those left over. It begins in the homily, commences with a slow and low hum from somewhere behind her children, igniting them with unusual emotion, then sizzling and popping like a refuse fire from an oil drum, and expanding to fill the church. Old women with sorrow in their hearts, but not enough to snuff out the joy of praising the dead, lift Jeannie Mae up, exalt her, and chorus her soul to heaven. She is not laid out in refinement like those afforded a finer burial and she is not regaled with eloquence and words. Her children are mute, listening, stifled by their own regret, their shortcomings to her, their forgetting sacrifices she made to rear her children, the hard love she administered, she who demonstrated love through hard work and careful caring but not by being free with the word *love* or with the frivolities of love customarily reserved for family and loved ones. Her children are mired in thoughts of forsaking her in her time of need, greedily leaving her to her own expedients, impassively cutting her down before they are ready. There is no Catholic funeral and she is not held up to God with those traditions, having remarried and fallen so far as to be unrecognizable to those who perform such rites for those deemed worthy. The mother is not in the midst of the revered ones, not in that way.

Without the vestments and clutter of Catholics, a black preacher stands in for them. He is not a man known to Jeannie or her family, has not met any of them, the preacher of the mother of the Usurper, and he offers up his traditions to God of putting those who die too early into the ground as best he can and in a manner that is queer to the grieving family, which is finally more fitting. It isn't supposed to happen to her, to *we*. The preacher speaks to them about the immortal soul and heaven and God's wishes to fulfill a destiny on earth, and how when it is done and over with, when we exhaust usefulness here, it is time to depart, it is His wish, and to counter that with mourning is to go against those desires and is sinful. No matter how soon, no matter what is left undone, he continues, God has deemed her job here on earth complete and has called the mother home, and it is now the time to rejoice in her reunion with her Maker and all those who went before her.

Those weary voices, as if on cue, rise up again in refrain and praise as her children endure, voiceless in their suffering. It is a message they cannot comprehend, but they are unable to argue, for she is gone and they are left unmoored and she, this entire woman who stretches herself over her children in a shielding blanket like Egypt's Nut over the night sky, with the stars of heaven painted on her belly, she has been and then is not. Her children are left behind with each other, with these loving strangers in a black church with black hymns and black prayers and black hats, and with shouting and genuine sorrow that mourns their loss for them. And so it is too with her, just after the Saint Valentine's Day of her death. Wrapped against that hard winter, stumbling through those abhorrent emotions around that firstborn boy, selfishly gloating on what has been lost for each individual, with little left for what has been lost by her.

The firstborn son cannot determine which is baser: that he still retains such emotions, is still capable of them, or that he is ruled by them. But it is now time to scatter her ashes into the nothingness of that little clearing, placing yellow roses of friendship burrowed into the bits of bone and flesh, now cinders and grotesque, remembering as she asked to be remembered. The children consecrate the mother as she lived, a brief interlude of cause and effect, pulling but not dictating, not leading, not guiding. The Usurper, who cast her off, wails as the tragic and stricken husband, managing a slow strand of old black dresses and hats and brittle suits worn down with time but kept impeccably crisp, who come with cakes and pies, casseroles and chicken; he shakes their hands and accepts their checks and condolences. The Usurper pockets the cash they all give him and sells the car Jesse had bought for his mother. And the boy later finds that the Usurper forged her name across her uncashed birthday check but put nothing toward the funeral arrangements. The Usurper perhaps knows he will need cash later to make all of this go away. Her children are left behind to tidy up for the generations coming after.

Afterword: Dirge

In the darkness, he recalls the saving times.

"Jess," the mother's voice is with him again, clear once more and without death's pallor. Jeannie Mae touches her son's shoulder as he plays solitaire at the kitchen table with the worn set of Bicycle playing cards. "I want you to know that I think you're gay and that's okay with me, son. I'm going to the store, but if you want to talk about it, let me know when I get back," she affectedly chirps, masking the gravity of her statement. With that, Jeannie picks up her purse and strides away from her iced-up son.

Jesse remembers his mother's touch still, how the fingers tremble and the inconceivable daring she possesses, a single mother with a solitary, firstborn son. Jesse deduces how a singular moment reforms his self-view. He wonders if events have shaped him or if this is intrinsically patterned on his

DNA? In that kernel of reconciliation, two units are again drawn up, white flags of surrender open that overgrown path of love that stretches forever between a mother and a son, a path that rarely fades into oblivion, much like horse-worn circlets left in a meadow out past the hard bend in Oaks Road, or the indelible mark of a coffee cup on a discarded novel. It cannot be erased. In her death, her son evokes the role each plays and the easiness with which the two fulfill those roles and the understanding the understanding the fucking *understanding* that she has when her son abandons her to move and then separates from her feeble astral pull for his own, egoistic, higher plane.

Finally, her son binds up the lessons taught him in a positive light, in a purer light, refusing to warp her coaching by a murky prism. Through the pride of the mother, her defiance, through her rebellion, through her fall, Jesse also claws through each juncture in tandem, alongside this resilient mother. The boy reveals the losses, in the grim surrender of the mother, how not to sacrifice himself to his own destruction, a lesson more valuable than the rest for he also witnesses how easy that is to do, how it is easier to do it. In the years that stretch before him after Jeannie Mae's death, the firstborn boy, now the man, takes up the finer pieces of those who ransom themselves because it is felicitous to do so, including those sacrificed fragments of himself, scouring, cleaning the ruin for a higher purpose.

For the rest, her children cease to matter at the conclusion of a generation of anyone's remembering: exactly one generation before anyone tells her children that they possess any importance, individuals leaving vague indentations of a life upon those who follow. Blemishes, something barely visible, only the slenderest tinge remains of the presence that had been. There is no social commentary as the slate wipes clean, only a legacy of mistake and sin and regret and odium and self-sorrow and rage heaping onto the shoulders of children left behind too soon, without instruction or legacy, without foundations laid to support such a weight of unfulfilled promise.

The final quest of Jeannie's remains, an equation of a lifetime of memories is gathered up, agitations of letters and pictures now resting in a discarded box, abandoned to a sorting room at the Goodwill thrift store along with donated sheets, discount books, and oddly numbered dishes. The precious and sacred details of a life lived, tendered away, perhaps overlooked in a dilapidated rental attic, the wreckage of a preceding age, a speculation at a life led, extinguished and then forgotten in a taped and re-taped carton, insubstantially yellow and brittle, soiled from creaking rafters and a damp corner. These disjointed mementos, once coveted memories, now excess baggage of an individual unit in whose care these trivialities are entrusted, fails in the coveting. This has been that story, a woman's story: how she lived and died and bleached pale without anybody noticing. Her children are those severed images, selfishly mattering to her and to them, and then sometimes not, then not. These physical objects, these vessels no longer belong to her or her children but have instead been entrusted to the realm in which they subsisted, culled by the unimportance of the lives documented, cherished, then overlooked and discarded. These four generations make up the background noise, the chattel, the forgotten. This has been their story.